The Dragon

&

THE ROSE

David B. Schock

Published by penULTIMATE, Ltd.
545 Gidley Drive
Grand Haven, MI 49417
616.844.1061

ISBN 978-0-9894101-2-0

AUTHOR'S NOTE:

There are at least six other books of the same title as this work. The authors include: : David Scott Daniell (1957) , Roberta Gellis (1977), Diane Hundertmark (2000 and 2001; a two-volume set), Gini Rifkin (2009), Julie D'Arcy (2012), and Addison Moore (2014). There must be something about the combination of those words.

Cover illustration and design by Betty Beeby. Cover and book designed and typeset by Amee Schmidt with titles in Matura MT Script Capitals and Charlemagne Std, text in Book Antiqua.

Contents

Dedication and Thanks

This book was written with love for JungYi, Dan, and the one who first spoke the title—David. David has walked on, but he will be forever in our hearts.

This book also is dedicated to Bernice Dersnah, my ninth grade Latin teacher at Northeast Intermediate School in Midland, Michigan, and Miss Gaughan of Midland Senior High School. Mrs. Dersnah was an inspiring presence, and Miss Gaughan a teacher who remained convinced that the Holy Roman Empire would return any day and that it was a good idea to KNOW YOUR LATIN! Alas, I was not her brightest student and was sometimes dismissed as *Stultissimus* (male superlative for stupid or foolish). So I remain. And I wish either one of them were here to review my phrasebook Latin. Thank goodness Dr. Stephen Maiullo of Hope College was at hand to prevent any greater embarrassments. I give him my profound thanks, and encourage all students everywhere to study this essential language; it is no more dead than a dragon.

When it comes to Anishinabek culture and language my thanks go to my dear friend Kookoosh Roger Williams Kchinodin, who says there are stories of dragons in his people's history.

My thanks also are due to editor Amee Schmidt, who has helped me to craft this into a better book.

Chapter 1

OF VROLICH AND ROGER,
BRIAN AND KATIE

Katie cut the corner, running as fast as she could. She had to make it home before Brian, but she didn't dare spend the energy to turn around and see how far he trailed her. He might be older, but that didn't mean he was faster. She was swifter on a straight-away; the only way she could lose now was if he cut through the parking lot behind the bar next door—The Dragon and the Rose—and jumped the fence into their back yard.

She peeled up the driveway to the side door, winded with the exertion. And there he was: already inside, behind the screen. He stuck out his tongue at her as she dragged to a stop and looked in at him.

She panted for breath for a few seconds before she spoke. "Next time try a fair race," she said indignantly.

"It was fair...I won didn't I?" There was something about his attitude that made Katie's blood boil. He was twelve, just one year older, and a lot bigger. She thought that should be enough of an advantage. But no, even though Katie was faster...at least this year, he never would let her catch up. Katie sighed.

"So, where's Mom?" she asked, changing the subject and opening the screen door.

"Not home from work yet," he said, leading the way up from the side door landing to the three Linoleum-covered stairs and into the kitchen. "Remember? She's working extra hours this week...something to do with end-of-summer sales."

"Yeah, just four more weeks and school starts."

"Yech," said Brian, grimacing as he opened the refrigerator. "I think I could do without school for another year or two." He really disliked going to school because of how different he now felt from his classmates; it hadn't always been that way.

"Oh, come on," said Katie. "You get to go to the middle school. That'll be so neat...all those kids. And besides, there's a football team, too. I mean, practice starts, what? ...two or three weeks? Aren't you excited?"

Brian hunched his shoulders in a shrug as he bent over the open vegetable drawer. He liked carrots best and their mom always had some washed and peeled for him. Katie reached past him and pulled out some cheese to nibble. The snack was more a matter of form than anything. They had been fed a late afternoon snack at Mrs. Robinson's before they were sent on their way home to await their mother's arrival.

"So, what do you wanna do until dinner?" Brian asked.

"Well, we could go see if Reme is home. Maybe then we could go see Mr. Teagarden." Katie pondered the idea as she spoke. Reme was always good company; he was the one friend both Brian and Katie could share without competing. It had something to do with his laugh, she thought. He was always calm, but maybe that had something to do with being an only child.

Brian led the way out the door, leaving it to Katie to lock. They walked up the block to Reme's house, which was something a little bigger than their own and much fancier. Their house featured prominent white trim around eaves, windows and doors and faded blue aluminum siding. All that aluminum covered old wooden siding, a glimpse of which was visible through a seam in the metal on the back side of the house. Their father had time and again pledged to fix it, but he never had, and now he never would. Reme's house was built of burnt-orange brick with an attached two-stall garage. Tall, graceful trees shielded the house from the harsh afternoon sun. It was a really solid house, thought Katie, as she walked to the front porch. Solid and comfortable.

Katie rang the bell and Reme's mother — small, thin, and well dressed — opened the door to usher the two children in with a reserved welcome. Yes, Reme was there and, yes, he could come out and play for a bit...but not more than half an hour. After that came dinner.

Reme brushed past his mother and joined the other two children on the porch steps. Shorter than Brian, he was barely taller than Katie. His complexion was dark, unlike that of his blonde and fair-skinned mother, and his dark brown hair matched his dark brown—almost black—eyes. Katie had overheard her own mother say that he had come from Korea. But his mother came from Idaho, she knew, and his father came from Michigan. Adoption.

The three headed off at a rapid pace back the way Katie and Brian had come. The brisk walk turned into a fast-walking contest that turned into a slow trot that turned into another fast run. And there, Reme outran even Katie. He passed their house and reached the corner with ten paces to spare. Katie was a little out of breath, and Brian, bringing up the rear, was winded.

Standing and waiting for them Reme smiled, flashing his white, even teeth. Reme knew he was fast, but he was both fast and gracious about winning, something that came naturally for him; he both wanted to win and to have others enjoy his winning. Then he turned the corner with the other two and walked up the street and then the sidewalk to the bar...The Dragon and The Rose.

But it wasn't simply a bar. Oh, sure, adults could buy a beer or even stronger drink, but it was really a place people met each other. It was a pub...at least that's what Mr. Teagarden called it. And he should know: he came from right next to England and spoke with a kind of English accent. He had told them before all about his place of business.

"Oh, aye, there was just such a place as this in my home town, Hay on Wye," he'd said, looking up at the beamed ceiling. Mr. Teagarden was a smallish man, very trim...what he called "spare." He was in his late fifties and had white wispy hair that bushed out at the sides and was a little thinner at the top. His skin was pinkish and glowed through the thin spot at his crown. He looked delicate, almost fragile, but for all that, he was a very hard worker, always doing things around the pub and outside. And he sponsored local sports—most notably a women's softball team, The Dragoneers, and a Kids' League baseball team. He also supported a soccer team and he even went to the games on Fall and Spring Saturday mornings. Most of the time he brought treats for the team.

That was the difference, he said, between a pub and a bar. "Sad to say, but very often the bar owners just want to sell as much liquor and beer as they can pour out. That's the ruin of society. But a pub is more a part of a civilized life. You don't go there to get drunk. No, you go there to share the warmth of human kindness, a wee dram, and an early night. Maybe with a game of darts, a good sandwich, and always a good talk if you want it, and peace and quiet if you don't."

Katie had never heard of anyone going away from the pub any the worse for drink, a policy Mr. Teagarden strictly enforced. And it was for that reason that Katie and Brian's mom didn't mind living next to the pub. Almost all the cars were out of the parking lot by 11 p.m. and there never was more than an occasional raised voice outside the pub, nothing to disturb the sleep of the two youngsters or their exhausted mother.

And the pub itself was a work of art, at least that's what Reme's mother had said to their mother during a cookout a few weeks ago. The building might have started life as a gas station or some other common structure, but under Mr. Teagarden's patient hand, it had changed to a cottage, complete with climbing roses beside the door. The roses grew through a trellis on each side of the entrance, and their scent throughout the mid- to late summer was a bit of heaven, Mr. Teagarden assured the children. They noted that the smell of roses often combined with the waft of burning tobacco from his pipe.

The pub certainly seemed out of the ordinary. Even in the early evening, the time when bars were celebrating their very dismal "happy hours," Mr. Teagarden had time enough to welcome the three children. All of them frequently were entertained by Mr. Teagarden, even without their parents, and their parents had no qualms about their frequent visits. Mr. Teagarden studied them as they came in and served up three lemonades, a small, slightly bitter treat the children had come to enjoy.

"And how are all of you this fine evening?" Mr. Teagarden asked brightly.

Katie explained that they were out on a brief excursion before dinner. "Our mom isn't home yet, but when she is we'll have some dinner. Reme's mom has his almost ready, I guess."

Mr. Teagarden looked up at Katie and said, "If your mom is too tired to cook I put on a lovely pot roast this afternoon. I was planning to sell hot beef sandwiches, but this would make a very fine dinner, too. Just you tell her if she's too tired to cook that there's always something here."

Katie sniffed and detected the fragrance of roasting meat. Her mouth watered as she imagined what meat and potatoes would taste like right now. With gravy.

To take her mind off food, she considered her host, the goodly Mr. Teagarden. He moved away from the three young people to refill a glass down the counter. When he returned he was chuckling at something his customer had said. Over his shoulder he tossed: "Very true, Jackson, very true. But not always nice to talk about the dearly departed in such a manner. *'de mortuis nil nisi bonum....'"*

He caught a look of wonderment on Katie's face. "That's Latin, that is...and it means 'of the dead speak nothing but good.' Old "Horsefeathers" down the bar there was speaking ill of a late, great local politician...a royal old crook who shook off his mortal coil some dozen years ago. It's amazing the stories people leave behind them."

Katie saw a break: "And, what's yours, Mr. Teagarden? Why would you ever come from England if everyplace there was like here...like The Dragon and The Rose?" She gestured around the room inside the pub.

"Well, truthfully, there's only one other place like 'here,'" said Mr. Teagarden. "And it's not in England proper, but very close... Wales...right next door. That's where there's the *other* Dragon and the Rose. A very proper pub in my home town...been there for donkey's years...ages and ages. So when I came to the States — and I came here because I very much fell in love with the lady who is now Mrs. Teagarden, and she with me, I do believe — I left my homeland behind."

"But don't you miss it?" asked Reme. "I think I'd miss my home very much if I knew where it was."

"Oh, I miss it all right. But we go back every couple years — not to the old home town because I've only a few distant cousins left there — but we go to Scotland where my sister lives. That's in the far north. She married one of them. And she comes to visit every so often, too. It works out sort of like the best of both worlds. I like the States just fine, and things in Britain aren't always so rosy and comfy as you might think. A lot of unemployment. Here I'm my own master, at least when Mrs. Teagarden allows it." With a wink he added: "Besides, I had to come here to meet you three. Who else would listen to my stories?"

"Oh, you mean about The Dragon and The Rose?" asked Brian, finally getting into the conversation. He'd been standing off to the side, away from his sister and Reme.

"Well, chiefly that, but the other tales, too, about King Arthur and Sir Gawain and the Green Knight, and the other legends that fellow Shakespeare *tried* to tell. It's quite nice to have somebody to talk to about the old days before the word 'modern' was invented. Mind you, I like my doctors and all the stuff they know, but I've no use for the hurry, hurry, hurry, and the television and the radio. Man wasn't meant to live that way. Not by any measure."

Katie knew that Mr. Teagarden would talk on for a few minutes about the dangers of what he called "fast times," but that eventually he'd turn to the tales of the olden days, and might be enticed to talk about the legend of The Dragon and The Rose.

The tale, as he had told them often before, occurred some time in the 10th century. The Dragon and The Rose were the nicknames of people—brothers—who actually *did* live then. At least, Mr. Teagarden said they did.

The Dragon, whose real title was Vrolich the Second, was a prince of exceptional leadership and valor who came from a long line of very powerful military leaders, most directly from Vrolich the First, his father. As a very young child he had been single-minded in any pursuit and had earned the nickname of The Dragon. Early on he mastered his short sword and small shield, usually vanquishing his playmates but leaving them uninjured. He might be determined to win, but he was fair, even in the rare event that he was losing.

The Dragon came from straight Saxon stock, a people who had invaded England in the 5th century. The Dragon's father was pure Saxon as was his mother, but upon the event of her death, the king, Vrolich the First, married an outsider, a Norman gentlewoman of some connection in order to cement an alliance. After a few years she gave birth to a son who was only half Saxon. The other half was a mix of Scandinavian and French. This younger son was very fair with light blonde, almost white, hair. His skin was almost translucent but he was ruddy of hue...red. His mother named him just that in native French tongue: Rouge. That translated to "Rose" in the common Welsh language. And like a rose he had thorns and even from the cradle he seemed eager to bring down his older brother. At best the boys could barely tolerate each other. And then the younger boy's mother died as well. The Rouge — or Rose — was then thirteen, old enough to be on his own, and the king sent him away to France to learn more in the land of his mother's birth; it had been her dying request.

His leave-taking was uneventful and something of a relief; The bad blood between the boys would lead to worse, they knew, in the years to come if either one of them had anything to say about it. Vrolich the Second was content for the time to be rid of his brother. And, as the Rose sailed over the Channel he was determined to return and overpower his brother, the legitimate heir, by means fair or foul.

The Dragon and his father were of one mind when it came to the ruling of their land. And the Dragon learned the finer points of statecraft and warring at his father's elbow. The two also were very much like each other in physical appearance and temperament. Each was broad shouldered, tall, well muscled, and dark of skin and hair. Their slightly hawkish noses were identical, with the exception that the king had a jagged scar that ran from the bridge down the left side of his nose, through part of his cheek and ended just above his narrow upper lip. He had earned his war wound in a long-ago battle. Their agreement and mutual respect led to a period of equanimity in the kingdom. Peace, rare at any time, lasted for a space of almost ten years.

All the while the Rose spent year after year studying alchemy. Now, alchemy is the forerunner of chemistry and physics and has within its purview of discipline not only science — the science of the day — but also more than a dash of magic thrown in for good measure. An alchemist commanded great respect; and the Rose also became a magus — a magician — in the order of Merlinus.

The Dragon knew something of what his brother was about, but paid it little heed. He would rue the oversight.

Vrolich the First died and the Dragon — then in his 30th year — succeeded him. The Rose came across the channel as soon as he heard the news of his father's death. His subsequent return threw the royal court into turmoil. There was no issue in the minds of the Saxons of who was king: the first born—the Dragon, Vrolich the Second. But there always are malcontents who will create mischief and gossip. And they set about their business with a vengeance.

And, for as much as the two brothers hated one another, they shared a love in one respect...Vrolich the Second's young wife, Triosha. She had been a stunningly beautiful daughter of a king who ruled in the far north. Her dark brown hair was streaked with highlights of gold. Her wide-set eyes calmly considered all that came before her. She was more than beautiful, though: she was modest and cheerful. The Rose was enchanted from the moment he set eyes on her the first evening of his return. He blushed hot as he looked unblinking at her. That open stare fueled his brother's anger: such boldness served as a challenge.

To pick up that challenge would be unseemly, for brothers who fought might slay. Then, too, the kingdom was under pressure; the cherished peace had drifted into various border skirmishes with suddenly quarrelsome neighbors. A fight between the brothers would strengthen any intentions other rulers presumptive had on the land.

That, Mr. Teagarden said, was where things were then. On her own, Triosha was ever the lady, hospitable in public to her lord. Of her husband's half brother she was respectful, but never more than that. She may even have shared a dislike of his Frankish manners and loved only her husband. But no opinion she spoke of her brother-in-law ever entered the legend.

The overwhelming fact was that she was of rare and delicate beauty. Her likeness carved in stone survives in the British museum, Mr. Teagarden told the children. There were several portraits done from that bust in his home town: one in a little museum and the other in the entry way to The Dragon and The Rose.

"She was a very fair miss, I'll tell you," said Mr. Teagarden, speaking of the ancient times. "Very fair, indeed."

"So what happened to her?" asked Katie.

"Well, that's a very bad bit of business" he said, sucking in his cheeks. He made a quick ticking sound, the kind someone makes to warn a little child. He wasn't looking at any of the three, but instead at the far wall above their heads. "You understand I've only got the story to go on; I don't know if it's true or cut out of whole cloth…that means it might be untrue. But the story is that when she wouldn't run off with him, the Rose used his alchemy to change her into a statue. A regular pillar of the community, you might say. Whether she was quartz or marble I never did hear.

"She was seized by the spell in one of the castle rooms, not a bedroom; that might look too suspicious of her good character. Anyway, the Rose was the last one to have left her and when the Dragon walked in at the end of the day and found her standing there, I guess there was a roar or two.

"See, he had a good idea the Rose was behind it and so all the gloves came off. He was going to hunt for his half brother in earnest, no matter the consequences. And he vowed to send a dirk—that's a dagger kind of knife—through each of his eyes."

"What happened to the queen?" asked Brian. "Is she still standing there?"

"She was moved. The Dragon first had her hauled to his bed-room but that was too sad for words, so he had a shrine cut into the living rock. He enlarged a natural cave in the mountain and had her put there, where she stands till this very day. …If the stories are true. Of course, no one nowadays knows where that cave might be, or if he does, he's not talking."

"I sure would like to go exploring," said Reme. "Finding that cave would be a real adventure."

"Yeah," said Brian, "But it might be kind of spooky, too. I mean, wouldn't she be dead or something?"

"Perhaps not," said Mr. Teagarden. "The spell was intended to turn her to stone until, well, until something that the Rose was to do. And then she was to regain her life not one second older."

"Okay, but if the Dragon killed the Rose he couldn't undo the spell, could he?" reasoned Katie.

"That's so, and as it turned out Vrolich the Second never got the chance to poke out his half-brother's eyes after all," said Mr. Teagarden. "In fact, it went the other way. One day while Vrolich was out on a mission for the high king, he was caught in the middle of a clearing by some outlandish folk. Some say evil spirits or jinns. And he was pinned upon a kind of rude altar that had been chiseled out of a great rock. Those spirits were said to be operating at the order of their earthly master, the Rose. As his half-brother struggled against the forces of hell, the Rose said his piece. And heigh! presto! the Dragon earned his name all over again. Vrolich the Second really turned into a dragon, complete with fiery breath and long tail. All the standard accoutrements of scales, eyes that could freeze you solid, a lizard's tongue, claws and teeth. From the castle, he was seen learning his new wings and shedding big tears, dragon tears, which, I understand, are quite like diamonds, already cut and polished."

"I bet it's not even true," said Brian. "The Rose probably just killed him and then told somebody he'd turned his half brother into a dragon. That way no one would go looking for a body."

Mr. Teagarden held his tongue while he studied Brian. The young man was on the verge of disillusionment about so many things in life. Mr. Teagarden had a time like that, too, when he was a young man. But such cynicism wears off, he reminded himself.

"That may be so, young Brian, but the fact remains that the legend persists, that the ruins of the castle are still to be found, that the picture of the fair Triosha—or a copy of the picture—still hangs in The Dragon and The Rose."

Mr. Teagarden paused for a breath and continued. "And what's more, the story goes on to tell of some rather odd sightings of the dragon named Dragon. He left the vicinity of the castle, but he didn't leave Britain until a little more than a century later. He was not one of those treasure-hoarding dragons you've heard so much about. Instead he was a man trapped in a dragon's body, and if ever he had to devour a maiden in the line of duty, it was done with much misgiving and many tears. They say that amongst the Crown Jewels—secreted away, mind you—there's a whole line of his dragon tears all strung together; they call the necklace The Repentance.

"When push came to shove, as it always does with dragons, he was held at peril in a cave in what came to be the cathedral city of Worcester. (That's in England.) He was given a choice—be killed or fly away."

"So, which did he choose?" said Katie. "I'd choose the flying away if I were a dragon."

"And so did he," said Mr. Teagarden. "He launched himself over the wide Atlantic Ocean heading toward the new world.

He was never seen, reported, or heard from again. He probably perished miserably amid the waves."

The conversation was interrupted by the opening of the door. Mr. Teagarden paused to greet a couple coming in for their early evening libation. Katie looked at the clock and said to Brian and Reme that they'd better get to their homes for their suppers. They waited until Mr. Teagarden had served the two their beer and then, with a wave of the hand, bid their host goodbye.

It took a few seconds for their eyes to accommodate to the bright sunlight outside. Squinting, Reme looked at Katie. "It really bothers me when the bad guys win," he said. "It's just not fair."

"No, but, then, who says life is fair?" said Brian. Katie reflected that he spoke as truly as he knew.

Reme went on to his house, and Brian and Katie turned up their driveway to find their mother's car parked; she was home. Katie rushed in and squeezed her mother tightly around her thin waist. The hug was returned with all her mother's strength. Brian came quietly in the door. "Hi, Mom," he said and headed toward the refrigerator once again.

"Brian, first wash up and then come and sit down," she said dishing up plates. "I know you're hungry so I popped a casserole in the microwave...it's your favorite: slimy goo with turkey and peas."

"Aw, Mom," said Brian as he turned on the kitchen faucet and reached for the soap. "I like it okay, but not all that much. And, besides, we had it once already this week." He toweled off his hands and sat at the kitchen table.

Their mother sighed as she handed him his plate. Katie wanted to hit her brother with something...something heavy like a rock... right on his head where it might do some good. It wasn't as if he lived in a vacuum. He knew that Mom had to work as many hours as she could. He knew that sometimes she made meals ahead and that sometimes the meals were pretty much alike. He knew at least a little bit about the load that had landed squarely on their mother's shoulders after their father died; after all he'd had to pick up some of that load, too.

Brian looked down at his meal and laid his left hand over his fork. Only when their mother began to say grace did he stop and look up. Katie had seen that look before, but not lately. The last time had been when his mother told them that their father had died. Katie had immediately burst into tears, inconsolable. Brian just stood there, looking without seeing, and that indefinable expression on his face. He looked like he was almost going to cry. Almost.

Brian said nothing as he consumed his dinner. That left Katie and their mother free to discuss plans for the weekend. Who needed to be where, and when. Neither of the children had plans, but because she was working on Saturday, their mother needed to call Mrs. Robinson in order to arrange day care for them. Then, too, there was the possibility that their grandparents would come and spend Saturday evening.

"Grandma and Grandpa Eames don't get to see you as often as they like," said their mother.

That, at least, was something else for Katie to look forward to. Her grandparents were all such different people. The Eames were her father's parents. Katie knew that she and Brian were the link to her grandparents' dead son; for that reason alone, the elder Eames would value their grandchildren. But there was so much more to the relationship: love, affection, and shared interests. These days they didn't laugh as much as they had before her father had died, but once in a while.... And Katie still shared her secrets with Grandma Eames. Grandma Eames also shared some of hers.

In contrast, her mom's parents lived four states away, and she saw them most often at holidays, and most often when she'd go to see them. Katie remembered only two times they'd come to visit, the last time for her dad's funeral.

Dinner eaten, Katie looked hard at Brian and told her mom that she and he would do up the dishes. Mrs. Eames brightened, stood, tousled Brian's hair and gave Katie a squeeze on her shoulders and walked into the living room.

With hot water running in the sink, Katie took the plates as Brian cleared them, then she rinsed them, and set about washing up. Brian picked up the towel and dried and put the brown-edged dinnerware away. It took all of fifteen minutes, and Brian didn't say anything until the last dish was stacked and Katie was wiping off the table.

"I don't see why they have to come this Saturday," said Brian.

"But, you always like to see Grandma and Grandpa Eames," she said with surprise.

"Yeah, but they get kind of sticky. They're always sniffling and having to excuse themselves. It's kind of...well...creepy."

"Well, we miss Dad, and they do, too."

"Yeah, but they go on and on about it."

Sometimes, she, too, felt sad. Very sad. And lonely. And it helped some when she could talk with her closest friend, Sandy. But while Brian had friends like Reme, he never seemed to talk about what he was feeling, at least not that Katie could tell.

Katie decided that a change of scenery might be enough to nudge Brian's mood; reckoning they had a couple hours of late summer daylight left, she suggested they go down to the end of the street and walk into the woods. There was always something to do there; sometimes they even saw deer. After telling their mom where they were going, they set off on foot, Brian dragging slightly.

To the west, their street ran into town. To the east (and next door) was The Dragon and The Rose. Then came the four corners, a block of houses...and then, within a half mile, the pavement ended and the road was surfaced with gravel. Farther east, the gravel went to sand, the sand went to a two-track which finally faded out in the middle of a meadow. All around the meadow brooded a wood of tall, tall trees...mostly beeches, with a few huge oaks. Down toward the river were ancient cedars. The river twisted through the countryside, circled around the woods here, then snaked around the town of Misty Haven, and, finally, debauched into the big lake, Lake Michigan.

The walk to the end of the road had taken them perhaps fifteen minutes, but they were now seemingly centuries away from civilization. Katie and Brian entered the meadow and fell silent, caught in the stillness. It was like walking into a beautiful and large church, a church with a blue ceiling very high overhead. The trees — always pressing in — had fallen away suddenly and the bright evening sunlight drew up their heads to consider the sky.

"I suppose this clearing was once a farm field," said Katie who often tried to find reasons for events and phenomena. "Maybe from the first settlers or even Indians!"

"Nah," said Brian, who had not left his ill humor behind. "If it was from that long ago it'd all be overgrown again. It's either natural or it might have been a field a couple of years ago. I bet it's natural, 'cause there aren't any little trees starting up like you'd see even in a year. And it's been like this as long as I can remember."

Katie wasn't above rising to the bait: "You mean like two years ago?"

Brian frowned and started off across the clearing. He put his hands in his pants pockets and stared at the ground as he slogged along. Katie let him get half way across before she ran to catch up. When she did she tapped him on the shoulder and kept going: "Tag...you're it!" Brian then started chasing her, knowing that his only advantage was that she would have to turn at the edge of the clearing; otherwise he'd never catch her until she tired. He guessed that she'd veer right when she reached the trees, so he set his course accordingly. That's just what she did until she looked over her shoulder and saw that he anticipated her move. Then, like a rabbit, she took four shortened strides in the tightest circle possible and reversed her direction. Brian was committed and narrowly missed her. He swung out awkwardly in a larger circle to correct his path and then ran full out to try to cut her off again. Katie looked back, knowing she'd have to evade him and outrun him in the circular field; he was headed toward her but was still under the branches of trees at the edge of the clearing.

Once more Katie pounded ahead and after fifty feet or so judged it was time to look again; she glanced over her shoulder and saw that he was twenty feet behind her and gaining. He was angry now; she could see the red pushing up his neck and the scowl on his face. He was driving himself even harder than before, arms and legs pumping furiously, so hard that he was closing the distance. She leapt into zig-zags at the tree line and hoped to evade him for a few more seconds. And then a few more. And a few more.

When she didn't hear him drawing near she looked back once more and saw...

...Nothing.

Brian was gone.

She drew to a stop, bent over with her hands on her knees and sucked in great gulps of air. When at last she was able, she raised her face to where he should have been. Not a blade of grass stirred in the breeze, and the tree leaves stood as still and heavy as if they'd been cast in bronze.

Slowly she approached the woods. He was probably hiding, she surmised, and would jump out from behind one of the giant tree trunks as she passed.

She was so intent looking from side to side she didn't see the yawning hole that opened before her as she approached the edge of the trees. There, just into the shadows, she walked exactly where her brother had run. And just as he had plummeted down, she also fell without so much as an "Oh!"

Chapter 2

IN—AND OUT OF—THE CAVE

Katie landed squarely on Brian, who let out an "Oooff."

"Thanks," he said, catching his breath. "Like I really needed that."

Katie crawled off him, accidently kicking him in the shins. "It must be a cave, and there is a hole in the roof," she said. "I wonder what else is down here with us."

"Well I, for one, don't intend to find out," said Brian with a note of panic rising in his voice.

The light from the hole was bright above them, but it cast little illumination where they lay. They could barely make out each other's face. Ten feet away the gloom dropped to pure black. Katie peered into the darkness, adjusting her eyes. She saw on the floor debris that had fallen in over the years...leaves, pieces of wood. She crawled to the edge of the dark and stared hard at a looming shape, a great, round boulder. Then she turned back to look at Brian, who was standing, trying to grope for roots that hung almost within reach.

"If I can just catch one," he said and leaped to reach above him. He landed with the sound of the air being pushed out of his lungs: "...ungh." He leaped again with the same result. Finally, while catching his breath he explained his view of the situation. "If we can't get ourselves out of here...we're as good as dead. They'd never find us no matter how long they searched. We have air, but we don't have food or water. It'll be a long, slow death."

Katie took a more sanguine view: "I don't think so. In the first place they'd look for us for weeks. And if they go near to the hole they could hear us if we'd shout. We just have to listen very carefully."

As if by mutual consent, they both paused to hear whatever there was to be heard from the field above. A light wind soughed through the hole, first in and then out, like waves on the shore. And there was another sound, too, a deep rumbling, but that came from further in the cave.

"Maybe this cave is connected to the river, or even Lake Michigan," said Katie. "There's something causing that sound."

If Brian heard the rumbling, he gave no sign or answer. Instead, he jumped for the overhanging roots once again. Then he looked at Katie: "You'll have to stand on my shoulders. Come on."

With care, Katie balanced herself, squatting on Brian's shoulders as he knelt. Then, slowly, he stood, and, when he was fully upright, Katie then began to stand, using his arms and hands with hers for support. She imagined they looked like acrobats she'd seen at the circus the previous year. While keeping a firm grasp of Brian's right hand, she reached overhead with her left. Feeling above her she thought of bats that might live nesting on the cave ceiling. She would NOT enjoy brushing against one just now. Still, she kept at her task without looking up. If she did so, she was sure she'd lose her balance. Swinging her arm above and behind, she felt the spring of live wood. She instructed Brian to move back just a pace and then she caught it with her left hand and then her right. The root had enough free play that she was able to bring it down for Brian, too.

"I'll hold it down and you climb up to see if it goes near the hole," he said. It didn't, but Katie followed it anyway to the roof of the cave. There it had branched from an even larger root that stretched across the cave roof and passed close by the entrance.

"It joins another root along here," she said, indicating the direction she'd soon travel. Slowly, she moved along toward the hole, first grasping the root with her hands and legs and hanging upside down, and then, when the root had more branches visibly protruding from the rock and soil above, dangling, hanging only by her hands. She reminded herself that she was especially good at hand over hand climbing both in gym class or at the park. Near the edge of the hole, jutting out from the wall of the cave, she found rings of roots that offered footholds. Grasping on to the roots just above the hole, she pulled herself up and out. With a strain she levered her body onto the ground above the cave. She heard a shower of pebbles dancing on the floor below.

After the darkness of the cave, the sunset—even filtered through the trees—was as bright as having her bedroom light snapped on in the middle of the night. As quickly as she could get herself turned about, Katie poked her head back into the hole and called to Brian to give him advice about the path she'd taken. "If you can't make it, I can always go get a rope."

"If you made it I can make it," he said, and started pulling himself up the root. It took Brian longer to reach the top, but, after a near fall, he, too, clambered above ground. He took a minute to catch his breath and then stood up, a little shaky on his feet. "We've got to get home. Mom's gonna be looking for us," he said, realizing that, while they hadn't been gone all that long, he wanted very much to be home after their close call.

Katie agreed, and they took off at a fast walk. The return trip took them less than a quarter of an hour, and though the sun was below the horizon, the evening was still quite light.

As they reached the side door Brian turned to Katie: "Not a word about the cave or we'll never have a chance to go back."

"Well, how are we going to explain how we got so dirty?"

Both their faces were streaked with grime, and their jeans and tee shirts were discolored with ground-in dirt. Brian looked at his sister and then down the front of his own jeans. "I got it: you slid down the bank toward the river and I followed you...no danger, just bad judgment."

"Bad judgment" was one of the things their father had said when they'd behaved poorly or made a sorry choice. That was the downside; the upside was his praise for wise choices and good behavior. Brian reflected that he'd never again hear praise from his father, and he missed it. Brian reached for the screen door and allowed Katie to precede him.

Their mother was on the telephone when they entered. "Oh, here they are, looking a little worse for wear but safe...thanks, Mr. Teagarden." She hung up the phone and turned to them. "Well...?"

"We thought we saw an animal down by the river, and I went down to investigate, but once I started, I slipped and then slid the rest of the way down," said Katie with mild compunction at telling a lie.

Brian picked up the thread of the fabricated tale: "And I slid down after her just to make sure it wasn't a bear at the bottom of the hill."

Their mother looked at each in turn and closed her eyelids half way. "Un-hunh," she said, her Mom's Infallible Truth Detector registering the lie. "I see. And was it a bear?"

"No. It must have been a deer we scared off," said Brian. "But we got kind of dirty. But we didn't rip anything. I'll go take my shower now."

Mom just nodded and Katie followed Brian as he headed for his bedroom. At the door he paused and Katie caught up with him. "She didn't go for it," she said. "She knows that we were doing something we shouldn't. Maybe we should just tell her everything. She wouldn't blame us for falling in a hole."

"No, but she wouldn't let us go back either," said Brian. "And that's what I want to do tomorrow, only we'll take some flashlights, rope, and we'll wear our old jeans."

"And maybe Reme can join us?"

"Maybe."

Katie knew he'd agree to Reme joining their adventure, but he wanted to give the appearance of thinking it over. She wondered if all brothers were like that or only hers.

The morning dawned foggy, but by the time Katie and Brian were at breakfast, the sun had burned off the last of the haze to reveal a cloudless, late-summer day. Their mother set out cereal, kissed them, and left for work. They were to leave for Mrs. Robinson's house for day care...really more like a safe place to check in while they were coming or going during the day.

So far during the summer they'd worked through six weeks of advanced summer school, and swimming and diving lessons. Added to all that, Brian had taken golf lessons, and Katie had continued her gymnastics. They didn't need much tending through the day, but Mrs. Robinson served a substantial lunch and was always interested in listening to what they were up to. When they were younger she'd been their regular baby sitter when their parents had gone out. But that was before...before their mother had to get a full-time job.

Brian organized all the equipment he thought they'd need and gathered it in the garage. Then they locked up the house and left for Mrs. Robinson's. They'd come back a little later and pick up the gear on their way to the cave. First, though, they'd stop at Reme's and see if he could join them, and then they'd go to explain to Mrs. Robinson that they'd be off exploring for much of the day, certainly until late afternoon, and that they'd likely need provisions...sandwiches...if Mrs. Robinson would help them.

At their first stop they were somewhat disappointed. Reme wasn't home, but his mother told them he should be back about 11. So, they went on to Mrs. Robinson's. She fell in with their plan to spend the day exploring and — with their help — she spent a half-hour supplying the party with substantial victuals. They even made extra peanut butter sandwiches — his favorite — for Reme.

"I'm just going to pack your sandwiches in these," said Mrs. Robinson, holding up plastic containers with snap tops. The sandwiches would be safe from crushing, no matter where they were packed. "Just be sure to bring them back after your picnic."

Brian and Katie packed their knapsacks and spent the rest of the morning playing Monopoly with Mrs. Robinson and her neighbor, Mr. Ramsey. Brian cleaned up on Park Place; for some reason Katie kept landing on "Go Directly to Jail." At quarter to eleven the youngsters helped count up all the money and reorganize it. For all his Park Place antics, Brian did not come out ahead. Instead, Mr. Ramsey — who played a slow and steady game — took the honors. Admitting defeat but promising a rematch, Katie and Brian slipped on their backpacks and started down the street.

Reme was home and expressed interest in going with them to the big meadow. His mother, as mothers are wont, asked their exact destination: "That way if we need to find you we can."

Only after they set off down the street on their bikes did Brian tell Reme something of what they had in store. Reme was all for any adventure. And this sounded like something he'd been dreaming of trying, he related. A cave, a real cave; he'd read about them and seen pictures and talked with people who'd visited them. But to find their very own would be better than anything else. Then he could go spelunking, itself an odd word for cave exploring. That would mean, he ruminated as they rode along, that he would be a spelunker. With each rotation of his pedals he said the word to himself: "Spelunker, spelunker, spelunker."

Once on the sandy road the three explorers had to walk their bikes. Finally, just before they reached the meadow, Katie suggested that they put them by the side of the road.

"Do you think we'll need to chain them?" asked Reme.

"Not too many people come out here," said Katie. "But maybe we'd better, 'cause we're going to be out of sight for a while and we might not see somebody sneaking up to steal them."

They secured all three bikes around a young oak.

Brian carried a coil of rope he'd slung over his shoulder when he'd retrieved their equipment. He transferred the flashlights that he'd put in his backpack to Katie's and the plastic sack of other supplies to Reme's. As they walked into the clearing Reme stooped to pick up a stout oak stick that had fallen from a tree. It was a little taller than he, perhaps five feet, and two inches in diameter. "Just what I need on an adventure," he said, swinging it over his head.

The sound of the stick whirring through the air blended perfectly with the late summer music of the cicadas around the meadow. Brian and Katie stopped to listen, and then they started running across the field to the hole.

Katie made the most of her speed, even with her backpack, and reached their destination first. Because he started slightly behind the other two, Reme arrived last. Brian took out a flashlight, stretched out on his stomach and leaned over the edge of the hole, directing the beam all around the cavern below. Reme, meanwhile, sat on Brian's legs, so he wouldn't fall in again.

"It really doesn't look like much," he said. Katie had to strain to hear him; his speech was directed into the cave. "It's not very big. And there are mostly rocks scattered around." After three or four minutes he scooched back from the edge, turned over and sat up. "We can tie the rope to that tree," he said, motioning to the nearest beech.

Reme tied the knot and both Katie and Brian checked it: "You can't count on the roots in the cave," said Katie. "This way we'll all be sure to get out."

Before he threw the rope over the lip of the cave and into the darkness, Brian tied knots in the rope every foot or so for hand and footholds. Then, with the rope dangling into the black, he carefully inched over the hole, feet first, grabbed onto the rope, and descended. Once he was on the cave floor he turned on his flashlight and Katie and Reme followed. Soon all three of them had their lights switched on and were exploring. The bedrock from which the walls were fashioned looked like stone had been placed upon stone. But the joints were tighter than mortal hand could fashion, fissures resulting from the earth's movements and, perhaps, by the earth's cooling a long, long time ago.

The cave was neither circular nor square, but egg shaped, with an odd corner thrown in for good measure. And it was bigger than Brian first had thought. In fact, it went on quite a ways behind the large boulder that dominated the floor. Brian followed it, letting his fingers graze along its surface, until he met a very sharp corner. There he hesitated. Once he turned that, he'd be out of sight of the others. So, he saved it for later, when all of them could explore together.

Reme was amazed. He kept repeating "Wow" with every other breath. Again and again he called Katie and Brian to see some discovery. Scattered bones lay on the floor, big mixed with little. Some of the big ones showed gouges from being gnawed.

"Maybe they're from Indians," said Reme, who then set about a hands-and-knees search for artifacts. He sifted through leaves and sticks to discover any tools or weapons...any arrowheads, polished stones, glass beads, or silver. "Well, I don't think they're from people...we haven't found a human skull yet. Maybe these bones were just from animals that fell down here like you did," he said to Brian. There was disappointment in his voice.

"I don't think I'd like to be where somebody died and rotted," said Brian with relief. "I mean, think about ghosts. And, the bones. I mean, you're actually picking up those bones. What if they were really from somebody? Wouldn't that be creepy?"

Reme sat back on his haunches.

"Well, if I was in my room alone on a windy night, yeah. But I'm here and these bones are clean and dry, and I can't think how they're going to hurt me. So, for now, no. And ghosts? I don't think so."

"You don't believe in ghosts?" Katie moved nearer to hear Reme's response.

"Well, have you ever seen one or talked to anybody who's ever seen one?"

"No, but...."

"That's what everybody who I've talked to says about ghosts," said Reme and he smiled. "Besides, I don't think these bones are from people, so unless you believe in ghost animals we're probably safe. Here's a little skull. Maybe from a raccoon." He passed the gleaming skull to Katie who marveled at the intricacies of the teeth and bone. Reme aimed his flashlight at the floor and kept working through the debris. "No, if there were humans here they didn't leave anything."

They paused in their search; it was time for sandwiches and drinks. It was, after all, somewhat behind the time for the noon meal and they had worked up a hunger.

"You know," said Reme around a large bite of sandwich. "Mrs. Robinson makes awesome picnics."

"It's the homemade bread," said Katie. "And the cookies are all from scratch."

The best part was that there were plenty of peanut butter cookies for dessert. Even Brian gave grudging respect: "Mmmph, that's good." He swallowed his last morsel. They sat around on a space they'd cleared. The rock floor was comfortable, even warm, and they were hesitant to move. There is something about adventure that encourages quiet reflection.

"I bet Dad would have loved finding this place with us," said Katie. "He was always trying to show us new stuff."

Brian lowered his head and started picking at the label on his drink box.

"Your dad sure was a great guy," said Reme, directing his comment to Katie. "He was always doin' stuff with you...going places, playing catch. My dad's too busy for all of that. But, for your dad, that was fun for him, too."

"Yeah," said Brian with an edge to his voice. "And then he died. I bet that wasn't fun."

Katie looked across at her brother. His reaction made things harder. She wanted to talk about their father in order to help remember him. Brian pushed away almost anything that dealt with his memory. Perhaps, she thought, remembering was too painful. Or, maybe Brian was just being dumb.

They sat in silence again for a time until Brian started talking about football and the practice that was due to start. As he talked he shifted to his knees and resumed his exploration of the cave floor. All at once he paused and then sprang.

"Ah ha!" he said, pulling his hand out from a small pile. First he rolled something between his palms and then he held it before his flashlight. The rays that went through and bounced back were brilliantly bright. "Cool," he said, turning to show his companions. "Is this cool or what?"

Katie and Reme gathered to observe a small, clear stone. Like glass, but not glass, about the size of a robin's egg, but sharply pointed at one end. Smooth all over and crystal clear.

"That's sooo neat," said Katie who thought she might very much like to have it for her own. "Where do you suppose it came from?"

"I don't know, but it's mine now," said Brian as he pushed it deep into his pockets. Then he turned to the large boulder. It was tall enough so that he had to take a running jump and clamber up in order to sit on it. And on it he sat, dangling his heels and kicking them against the rock, which made a drumming sound unlike any other rock Brian had heard. It sounded almost hollow. Reme cocked his head to one side, listened, and then took up his oak walking stick. He advanced, stood poised, drew back the stick... and swung. His stick bounced off the rock and out of his hands.

For the space of perhaps five seconds nothing happened except Reme stood rubbing his smarting palms.

Then, softly, they heard a hiss that sounded like air escaping from a beach ball. After perhaps a quarter minute the hiss grew louder. Now it sounded like a water faucet turned on full blast. Only it wasn't caused by escaping water: there was smoke pouring up from under the boulder. Smoke and steam, curled round their feet and rose in the still air of the cave. The children stepped back. The hiss magnified to a roar, and soon the cave filled with the stench of sulfur; it smelled like burning tires.

Brian grabbed Katie and put the rope into her hand. "Climb! Climb!" he shouted. In a flash she pulled herself up and out. At the top she turned to find Reme right behind her. Brian followed them by a few seconds.

Once over the edge of the lip they turned to look and saw flames glowing through the smoke. If one of them slipped into the cave below now he or she would die in the oven that pulsated at their feet. The cave entrance had turned into a chimney and the hot air that pushed out and over their heads distorted the trees and leaves that were now barely discernible through the heat waves spewing upward.

With one last look back, Brian led them at a flat-out sprint to their bicycles. They fumbled with the lock for a few seconds that—for all they knew—could have been crucial to their safety. At last the lock sprang open. They hopped on their bikes and wheeled out as fast as they could pedal. Not even the sand road held them back.

Once they regained the gravel road they stopped to catch their breath and look back. High overhead, a pillar of white cloud rose in the otherwise clear sky.

They remounted their bikes and tore off to town. By the time they reached the four corners they were again out of breath. Mr. Teagarden stood outside his gate, watching their headlong flight. They turned to him and stopped at the approach to the pub.

"You've been having a race I see," he said with a puzzled expression on his face. "Either among yourselves or...is there something else?"

Brian quickly looked at the other two and nodded his agreement. "That's right. We all wanted to race back into town and it looks like Reme won this time."

"Well, so he did," said Mr. Teagarden. "And now for a celebratory libation?"

All three—hot, tired, and still a little scared—looked at him uncomprehending.

"A small drink of lemonade," he said by way of explanation, and then cast his glance over the horizon in the general direction from which Katie, Brian, and Reme had come. "I see, too, the cloud has returned after all these years."

The children look behind them, and, sure enough, a column of cloud rose high into the sky behind the woods. Reme felt an uncomfortable flutter in his chest. Katie felt a flash of fear and sucked in some air.

Brian turned to Mr. Teagarden. Katie thought he was going to tell everything, but he held his tongue. Instead, Mr. Teagarden spoke. "It's something of a local legend, I suppose."

"Does anything bad happen when it's there?" asked Reme.

"Well, there are stories," said Mr. Teagarden. "That cloud's been seen all the way back to the time of the first people, the Native Americans. Why don't you step inside, and I think we might find some answers."

While he talked he led them into the pub and set up three tall glasses of lemonade. Brian drank his off in three gulps and Mr. Teagarden refilled it. Then he set the pitcher down, leaned back against the bar, and reached for a tattered book.

There was only one other person that the children could see sitting at a table in the pub, and initially he was half-hidden reading a newspaper and eating a sandwich.

"This village was *A Wani Bissa* in the language of the Ottawa or the Odawa," Mr. Teagarden explained. "That meant it was a place of mists. The mist would appear first as a cloud like the one outside now and the next day it would have spread all over the area, unless there was a pretty strong breeze off the lake. The first outsiders kept the name and added to it: Misty Haven. The Odawa took it as a bad sign whenever the cloud rose; all the big animals would vanish. Those early Americans would live on turkey, rabbits, squirrels, and fish, not always an easy catch, especially if the cloud came in the middle of winter. Then, too, sometimes the ground would rumble.

"The Odawa talked to the first traders and, later, the first settlers, about a giant beast that roamed on land and flew in the air, a beast that made the earth shake when he walked. But you know how legends can sometimes be linked to scientific fact, like an earthquake. Some of those big plates way under the earth, tectonic plates the scientists call 'em, they're always squeezing together and up comes a geyser of hot steam. And then the earth shifts.

"Anyhow, the Odawa gave this mythical monster a name: the Thunderbird."

"Did you read that in the book?" asked Katie.

Mr. Teagarden looked down at where the book had fallen open in his hands. "I did. Well, when the work's all done I have a little time left over...and when there aren't any customers...I do a bit of reading. Now, haven't you yourselves come in from time to time and found me with my nose buried in a book?"

They had. He handed Katie the worn, green-covered book. She noted the title: *Misty Haven: Fact and Legend from the Earliest Settlers.*

"That's a rare jewel," explained Mr. Teagarden as Katie handed it to Brian. "I picked it up at an auction a couple years ago. Took it right out from under the nose of a history professor over at the college. He didn't realize it would be up for auction quite so early in the day. I suppose there are copies in the library and elsewhere about town, but finding one you can read is a little bit difficult. The library holds its copies in a special collection...you can only read the book there while someone is watching you. In fact, you have to make an appointment before you get to look.

"And Joe here says the legends are pretty much what the book says they are." For the first time he nodded at the man reading the newspaper. Joe put down the paper, picked up his cup of coffee and turned to the children. Reme noted the copper coloring of his skin, the finely chiseled nose, and the black eyes.

Mr. Teagarden flustered a bit: "I haven't made proper introductions. These are Katie, Brian, and Reme. And this is Dr. Joe Cavanaugh. To the people where he works he's Dr. Cavanaugh. But to us he's Dr. Joe."

"*Boozhoo*," he said to the trio. "That's the Native way to say 'hello.'"

"An Indian doctor?" Katie wondered.

"Nope. A chemical engineer who just happens to be an Indian. Or Native American, your choice. And Mr. Teagarden has the stories about right." He slid off the stool and went to open the door. He stuck his head out and looked out to the east. Then he walked out and let the door close behind him. When he returned he said with some wonder: "It's back! This will be some very important news among my people."

Dr. Joe walked toward them as Brian resumed flipping through the pages of the book, taking care not to damage them. He was looking at drawings and pictures. He paused at one illustration and then started shifting about on his chair, hands in one pocket and then the other. At last he found what he sought and pulled out the clear crystal that he'd picked up from the cave floor.

"I found this while we were exploring," he said smugly. "And here's a drawing of it, right in your book." Katie again found fascination in the way the light shone through the stone, and Brian held it and the book for Mr. Teagarden to examine.

Mr. Teagarden held out his hand, and Brian dropped it in his cupped right palm. With his left, he turned around the book. "The book calls it an Indian Tear. One of the first settlers traded his best gun for one. It seems to have vanished, but the stories about it have lasted... and there's this drawing, too. I think we're talking about the same thing here. ...Or, something very similar."

"Is it glass?" Katie asked.

"Heavy for something so little. Glass? Hmmm." Mr. Teagarden held it up to the light of the window, then before a lamp on the counter. It was definitely a heavy crystal. "Glass...no. Well, maybe. But, here, let's try this." He took a short tumbler from under the counter and turned the stone so its pointed end was against it. Then he scratched his initials in the glass. "No, I'd definitely say that stone's not glass...not a bit of it. It's something else. I know a diamond will do that."

"A diamond," said Brian in amazement. "That means I'm rich. I bet it's worth a ton of money!" He slipped off the barstool, barely able to contain himself.

"Well, I'm not sayin' it is," said Mr. Teagarden with caution and suddenly speaking much more quietly. "I'm not a jeweler or anything. I've just heard that diamonds scratch glass...and this stone is so clear and makes the light seem brighter when you look through it. ...Almost like it has some kind of fire in there."

Dr. Joe had left his sandwich and coffee to stand behind the children. He was overlooking Brian's find when Mr. Teagarden turned to him: "You're the chemist. Can you tell us what it is?"

Dr. Joe picked up the stone between the forefinger and thumb of his left hand, held it to the light and whistled.

"Look at that clarity!"

After a few minutes lost in the stone, Dr. Joe turned it over to Brian's outstretched hand. "You'd best take it home and not lose it. You know what they say: 'Finders, keepers; losers, weepers.' And you don't want to be a weeper." And he paused, considering. Finally he spoke again: "And, Brian, I don't know that I'd go telling a lot of people about this. ...Maybe just your mothers. And your father, Reme."

Brian reached again for the book to see if there was anything else about his Indian Tear. There wasn't, but he enjoyed looking at the pictures anyway. Reme and Katie engaged Mr. Teagarden and Dr. Joe in further discussion that included the cloud in the sky. Dr. Joe had to leave to get back to work and Reme coaxed the book away from Brian to confirm all that Mr. Teagarden had said. In this way they passed the better part of the afternoon.

At last, with their spirits and throats refreshed, the trio left The Dragon and The Rose. First they took note of the still-rising cloud, spreading into the sky. It seemed to pose no other danger than obscuring the view for the next day or so, thought Brian. Then they rode their bikes to Reme's house. There, they pledged themselves to secrecy; not even their parents would know, at least for now. After the secret swearing ceremony, Katie and Brian climbed on their bikes and headed off to Mrs. Robinson's.

Not one of them had noticed a silent figure slink from a booth in the little room at the front of the pub as they left. Nor did they note that same figure scurry to follow them to Reme's. There it lingered down the block examining some shrubs and flowers. When Katie and Brian pedaled off for Mrs. Robinson's, the figure managed to move fast enough to mark the street where they turned south. Their shadow gained the corner and started off after them at a brisk walk, at least brisk enough to see where they went. After Brian and Katie turned up the drive to Mrs. Robinson's grey house, the figure strolled past, confirming their bikes in the driveway.

Chapter 3

THIEF IN THE DAY

"Well, land sakes! I've been about ready to send out the posse to round up you youngsters...you've missed your snack time, and it's nearly time to head home," Mrs. Robinson said as she bustled around the kitchen, retrieving cold milk from the refrigerator and more cookies, which had not long ago been hot from the oven. A seemingly inexhaustible field of cookies was still spread on the cooling racks next to the stove. That stove—like everything else in the kitchen—was old, but clean and in perfect working order.

Mrs. Robinson continued, "And, Katie, you missed out on your chance to lick the bowl. I knew you were going to be gone for a bit...but that bit stretched into a long afternoon. And I'm not sure I should even be feeding you cookies and milk when your dinner will come so soon. That's all I need: to have your mother mad at me because I ruined your appetites."

"Honest, Mrs. Robinson, you won't spoil our dinners. We'll be able to eat now and then," said Brian as he launched into a second chocolate chip cookie. Chocolate was a nice change from the peanut butter cookies earlier in the day, he thought. Katie was too busy eating to comment. Her eyes glazed over as she concentrated on the taste of cookie and milk.

Mrs. Robinson left them in peace to enjoy their snack for a space of about ten minutes before she made inquiries of their afternoon's activities. She had a pleasant way of asking; the kind of asking because she wanted to know, not because she felt she ought to or because she was nosy. Katie felt like Mrs. Robinson delighted in listening to her and Brian describe adventures her own children had shared some twenty years before. They were grown and gone—although they frequently returned for family gatherings—but Mrs. Robinson seemed to enjoy the child-like wonder of discovery. As they talked about their lemonade with Mr. Teagarden, Mrs. Robinson said she was relieved to find that they'd had some sustenance in addition to the lunches she'd packed.

"Did you enjoy those sandwiches?" she asked. "Did you bring back the containers so I can reuse them?" She watched as their faces betrayed a moment's confusion. Katie could think of no answer, but Brian made the attempt: "The sandwiches were great. But we just...um...burned up all the calories," he said, looking at Katie.

Mrs. Robinson looked at each one of them in turn. "And the containers? Did you bring them back, or did you leave them someplace out in the woods?"

"Uh, we forgot them," said Katie, thinking that they were either consumed entirely or had been melted into a tiny blob. She and Brian would have to buy some replacements.

"Are you sure you didn't burn them by mistake? You all seem to have dragged a bit of the scent of fire back with you. I know that smell, but I can't place it. You haven't been playing with matches in the woods, have you?"

"No, ma'am," said Katie with conviction. "We haven't been playing with matches, but there was..." How could she say this without lying? "There was a fire there and we sat around it. We wanted to make sure it didn't spread. But we didn't toss the sandwich containers into the fire."

That, at least, was technically true.

"We know how dangerous fire can be," added Brian. "We wouldn't think of lighting a fire in the woods or anyplace else without a grown-up. It's not safe." Katie nodded in agreement.

"Well, let's leave it, but don't be surprised if your mother asks about the smell, too," said Mrs. Robinson.

"There was some kind of fog," explained Katie. "Maybe we picked up the smell then. I mean, if fog can smell. I mean, not that fog can smell but, uh, the fog can stink."

"That's it. The fog. I've known certain fogs around here to have that same very distinct odor," said Mrs. Robinson slowly and carefully. "But it's been some time. It slipped my mind.

Long before Mr. Robinson died, we used to have the fogs here. And they smelled like you do now; it's funny how I remember that smell. They were the Misty Haven fogs. Now, I wonder where they could have got to all these years? Fancy me forgetting them!"

"And, did you see the cloud to the east?" piped Katie. "Mr. Teagarden said they had something to do with Indians and legends."

"No!" Mrs. Robinson replied. "The cloud? It's been just ages and ages; the cloud that seems to come straight up. I remember when I was a young girl we'd all go cloud chasing. Those clouds looked like they almost rose up out of the ground some place out in the country. Mostly we went east chasing after them. We'd all climb on our bikes — and later on in a car — and tear off out of town on the south road or the old two-track.

"I remember once we got pretty close to the cloud before it rose too far. We found a clearing. Oh, we had to leave the car stuck in the sand and walk, but we found this clearing and there was the cloud. It went up and over our heads, drifting-like, but I remember that same smell.

"My friend Violet — you remember Miss Morrissey — well, Violet was a little bit before me in school, and she claimed that one time she saw it come out of the ground just like a steam pipe had ruptured, a regular geyser. Did you ever hear of anything like that? Come up out of the ground! She didn't live that one down for years and years."

Brian squared his shoulders: "That's what we saw, too. Right out of the ground."

"Can you credit that?" said Mrs. Robinson. She put the fingers of her right hand over her mouth. Above them her eyes suddenly looked tired and a little sad. They watered up as if she were going to cry. "Well, if you saw it, too, then I'd guess it did happen. After all these years I owe Violet an apology. We all thought she was making up stuff. She used to do that, you see, and we'd always just kid her a bit and let it go. Most times she'd see the humor of her own stories and end up laughing along with us. But she stuck by her story that time. She went home in tears rather than admit she'd been fibbing. I guess she was right to stick to her guns."

Brian helped to clear the table and then he and Katie put their things in order and prepared to set out; their mother would soon be home. He thought briefly about showing her the special stone he had found, but remembering Dr. Joe's caution, decided against it.

Mrs. Robinson saw the children down the driveway and on their way home. She stood and watched them as they walked northward toward their street. Katie turned to wave as they reached the corner. They'd be back on Monday.

Katie and Brian forgot all about Mrs. Robinson when they rounded the corner by their house. There in their driveway sat their grandparents' car. Katie broke into a run and, shuffling, Brian followed. Grandpa Eames stood on the porch and stepped down to the concrete walk to meet his granddaughter. Unhesitatingly, Katie launched herself into his arms. Those arms, strong with a lifetime of physical labor, closed tightly around her.

"Hey, Scout," said Grandpa as he hugged her tight, tight. Even when Brian came up to them Grandpa kept on hugging her, saying over and over that he'd missed her so much. When he turned her loose, she was a little dizzy, but happy.

Grandpa reached out to Brian, hesitated a fraction of a second, and then tousled his hair. Brian moved away a little under the rub.

"Hey, Brian, you're lookin' so much bigger...but I bet that's what everybody says. It's true, though. ...And I bet you're gonna be taller than your daddy was." Brian looked at Katie. "Well, hey, what say you give me a hand getting some suitcases in to the guest room? And say 'Hi' to Grandma. She's in the kitchen helping to start supper."

Brian obediently gave the requested hand while Katie wandered in to see her grandmother who was bustling about the kitchen all the while keeping up a running commentary with her daughter-in-law. Katie's mother looked very small against the backdrop of the kitchen. She nodded and smiled as Grandma peeled potatoes and then went to work on a salad. Katie regretted for part of a second that she'd eaten so many cookies at Mrs. Robinson's. But then, she thought, dinner was still more than a half hour away.

Katie had been standing by the door unobserved until her grandmother turned and waved her into the activity. "Well, look at you," she said, pausing while she sliced a cucumber. "Bigger, taller, and different somehow. I guess no matter how hard we try to keep you a little girl you're still going to grow up on us. You are a sight for these weary, sore eyes."

It was something her grandmother always said, although she had neither weary nor apparently sore eyes. They were black, very quick and exceedingly friendly. Like Grandpa's, they were surrounded by silver hair, and were most often accompanied by smiles.

Katie walked over and gave her mom a hug and then went to stand by her grandmother. "I was just telling your momma about your uncle's doings...he's off traveling again. He says this time he won't get lost and have to write home for money."

Uncle Lou had a habit of wandering as far as his money would take him and then would send out letters for help to fund his return trip. Katie remembered her father laughing over one of them as he shared it with all the family. In the end he had sent a few dollars, explaining that it was worth it for the entertainment alone. Uncle Lou had come to spend a month during the summer before Katie's father had died. He was funny, bright, and very different from any other grown-up Katie had ever met. More like a big child, her father had told her. Katie wondered if Grandma and Grandpa liked having a son who would never grow up, maybe never grow older, maybe never die.

Her mother sent her and Brian upstairs to clean up for dinner. Katie got by with a good wash and a change of clothes; Brian needed a shower. Then, as he dressed, they talked.

"You didn't have to be so mean to Grandpa," said Katie with some spirit.

"I wasn't. I just didn't know if I was supposed to shake his hand or what. I don't like bein' hugged."

"Yeah, but that's what grandparents do. It's like something in their genes or whatever. They gotta hug."

"Well, did Grandma hug you? I saw her working at the sink."

"No, not yet, but she will when I go down all clean. I can count on it, and so can you, so just get used to the idea, okay?"

And with that Katie galloped down the stairs and slid her arm around her grandmother's waist. Her grandmother was just setting two big bowls on the table—one of steaming mashed potatoes with a dollop of butter melting in a center well and the other of freshly cooked green beans. When her hands were freed, she hugged Katie back as the young girl burrowed in for an all-day kind of embrace. Only when she pulled away did she see the tears running down Grandma's face. Tears of joy.

"Katie Louise, you are the star in my crown."

That was something else she was always saying. And whenever she said it, she'd crinkle up her eyes, tears or not, and smile. The lines in her face set off that smile as they radiated from her eyes, nose and mouth. Smile lines.

Dinner tasted better than ever before, thought Katie. There were pork chops, too. And, the food just kept being passed from one to another. Even Grandpa took thirds on the potatoes, but Katie wondered aloud why, since he probably ate this way every night. He did not, he assured her. This was the harbinger of a celebration, the start of a grand—but short—visit; they would be gone tomorrow afternoon. Katie started making a list in her head about things she wanted to talk about with them; a day—even with an overnight—didn't seem nearly long enough. Katie looked over at Brian and thought he might find the time entirely too lengthy. Well, that was his problem; he wasn't going to ruin her good time with his hanging head.

After a dessert of apple pie that had obviously been homemade and brought with them, Grandpa corralled Brian into helping clear and wash the dishes. Brian noted that the sink was much fuller than usual with pots and pans, but he shouldered up to the task. First he ran hot water to rinse off dinner remnants into the garbage disposal. Then with the water running hot, just as hot as he could stand it, he filled the left of the double sinks. He added dishwashing detergent and started scrubbing. Pretty soon he and Grandpa—who was rinsing and drying—were talking about baseball, fishing, and Brian's planned attempt at football this fall.

"You're good sized and you're agile," said Grandpa. "I'd think you'd do very well."

"Maybe," said Brian, "but I'm slower than the other kids. I guess I just gotta run time trials or something."

"Every-day practice is a great way to get better really fast. I know because I've done it. I was slower than other guys on my high-school football team, but I just kept running, and I made the varsity team. But it took some determination. That didn't really make it easy, but it made it more worthwhile. I'm gonna bet you'll do all right if you put your mind to it. We Eames are pretty much a stick-to-it bunch."

Brian nodded. His dad was sure like that...if it was worth doing, it was worth giving your very best...in anything. Everything.

The evening concluded with a long walk around the neighborhood...block after block, milk and more apple pie at the kitchen table, tooth brushing, prayers, and bed. Katie reflected on the oddity of the day as she drifted off to sleep with the comforting buzz of adult discussion downstairs. Whatever had happened in the cave out there by the edge of the wood couldn't harm her here.

Sunday morning brought worship at the Congregational church downtown. After church Grandpa said he'd like to take everybody out for a big breakfast at the DeeLux Diner, Katie's most favorite restaurant.

"You can get French toast there made with slices too thick to fit in any toaster," she explained. "And they put whipped cream on it, too, if you want."

They did indeed devour French toast, and waffles, eggs, sausages, and muffins. Karen, their waitress, kept the chocolate milk and coffee flowing, so that by the time they finished they were sated and beyond.

Katie looked up from her plate in mock distress: "Oh, Grandpa, I don't think this was such a good idea." He laughed and knew in a twinkling that it had been a very good idea. He looked at his granddaughter, this too-often too-serious young woman, and half-whispered to Grandma that seeing Katie smile was worth anything. Even Brian, he noted, was a little less withdrawn. The boy had a lot of grieving yet to do but it would take time.

After breakfast they all strolled the waterfront. For a Sunday morning, things were pretty calm, Katie thought. Normally, weekends downtown were hectic, but just now there was time for the quiet walk without throngs of vacationers and tourists. There were other family groups — moms and dads pushing strollers, kids on in-line skates — and, far off, a bicyclist heading out to the pier, but Katie and Brian and their family were not in the least crowded.

Grandma Eames stopped and sat on one of the many benches, and she studied the river as it headed toward the big lake. Katie sat beside her, resting her head against her grandmother's shoulder, and Brian stopped behind the bench. His mom and grandpa kept walking slowly, only to stop at a bench further on.

"This river just keeps on moving," Grandma said wistfully to Katie, brushing a loose strand of fine grey hair away from her own eyes. The wind had picked up and was stirring small waves out in the main channel. "You just can't imagine it not moving, or moving in any other direction. The river always runs to the lake, the lake to an even bigger river, and that river to the sea. Time is like that river," she said looking at Katie. "And, while we might like to go back in time it can't be done...otherwise the river would have to back up. It might overflow its banks. It wouldn't be right. But we can remember the river as it was the last time we visited here. And that memory can stay sharp and clear forever and ever."

Katie sighed deeply and nodded. She understood. Grandma gave her a squeeze and kissed the top of her head. "Your dad would be so proud of you. He loved you so much." Katie reflected how much she had loved her father's approval; when he had told her that she'd done a good job, she had been always overjoyed. She missed that so much now.

Brian, standing behind them, gave no sign that he'd heard or understood the message that his grandmother had delivered. He began to move off, toward their mother and grandfather.

Home again after the breakfast and walk, Brian watched as Grandma and Grandpa busied themselves making preparations for leaving. Every bag was packed into the trunk just so; in the end there was lots of room left over. As Brian was helping, his grandfather paused as he reached his hand under a blanket in the rear of the car.

"Oh, I almost forgot," said the older man. "I brought this for you" and with a flourish, he pulled out a fat book...not big but fat; it threatened to escape its leather binding. ...And old, curiously old. Brian took it from his hands. The brown hide covering the volume was cold, cold and clammy, odd because the book had been in the trunk of a car standing in the summer sun. Very carefully, he opened the front cover. Brian had seen old books before... but they were in a museum. Here was one in his own hands, a book that he believed his grandfather was going to give to him.

"'Of Efquiry, Courtly Mannerf, and Combat,'" he read aloud. "What's 'efquiry?' What's a 'mannerf?'"

"Oh, it's the way they printed in the old days. The 's' looks like an 'f' and if you have two 's'es it looks like 'f-s'. This book is about Esquiry: being a squire or an assistant to a knight, often in training to become a knight. And courtly manners were the ways to behave in ancient time with royalty. And, you know what combat is...but this was in the days of knights and ladies and kings and queens."

"Well, thanks, Grandpa. It's a very old book and I'm sure it's very good." He ran out of words. As he flipped the pages there rose around him an old gingery smell. It tickled his nose and almost made him sneeze. This would be a lot of work to read; there were no pictures, not even any drawings.

"This book was one of your father's favorites when he was growing up. It's been in our family for, well, I don't know how long. But a long, long time. My grandfather gave it to me, and I read it first when I was about your age. It's a good book to hold on to. It tells all about war in the old days: single combat, besieging castles, fighting dragons and the like."

Brian realized that perhaps Mr. Teagarden would like to see it. Suddenly the book had more value in his eyes. He held the volume closed and marveled at how cold it stayed in his hands.

"You know, I've always felt there was more to this book than what meets the eye," said his grandfather appraisingly. "That may be part of its value. And it *is* valuable."

Brian nodded: "I'll take good care of it, I promise. It'll stay in my room unless I have it out showing somebody, like Mr. Teagarden."

Grandpa Eames nodded. "That's a good plan. But it's yours now, however you treat it. If you take good enough care of it, perhaps someday you can pass it on to one of your children...or even to a grandchild."

With a final burst of goodbyes and hugs, the senior Eames were off. Their mom, waving until the car was out of sight, turned and suggested an uncharacteristic midday snack. More milk, and cookies; these their grandmother had baked and brought. Brian had to admit that these visits did have an upside. Before sitting down to their snack, however, their mother urged them to go upstairs, hang up their church clothes, and climb into something more appropriate for playing outside, like jeans.

Katie dodged into Brian's room as he was giving his hair a final brush and check in the mirror. "You did okay," she said. "You didn't flinch a bit when Grandma hugged you goodbye."

"Well, yeah, but that was goodbye," said Brian with seeming indifference.

"Sometimes you ought to just hear yourself," said his sister with some heat. "Do you think you're the only one who misses Dad? Well, you're not."

She turned around and headed for the stairs. Brian raced after her. "Wait, Katie. Please wait." Katie stopped on the third stair down and turned to face him. Her eyes were filling with tears. She wiped one away. Brian could see that she was struggling not to cry.

"I'm sorry. I didn't mean to hurt you...or Grandma or Grandpa or Mom. It's just I don't know what to do. There's nothing I can do to make it better and I miss him all day, every day. I can't believe I'm never going to see him again. I'm sorry. I didn't mean...."

"That I can live with," interrupted Katie. "The fact that you don't mean it helps just a little. But I can't live with the idea that all the rest of us are just getting in your way, taking up your valuable time. It makes me feel that you'd rather we weren't even here, that maybe we should be dead, too. That...that hurts."

"I don't mean it that way. That's an awful thought." He shuddered visibly. "I'm sorry. I'll try not to do that again."

Slowly, they both walked down the stairs and found their mother pouring out the milk. Just as she finished, the phone rang. She grasped it and then cradled it between her ear and her shoulder as she put the cap back on the jug. She put the full glasses on the raised counter that separated the kitchen from the dining area.

Brian and Katie heard only her side of the conversation: "Yes, hello.... Oh...my...that's very serious. ... What do the police say? ... Yes, they're both here now. ... No, that wouldn't be a problem. I'm sure they'll want to help any way they can. ... No. I won't worry about them being there tomorrow, but are you sure you're up to it? Well, if you're sure, I'd be very grateful...and it's less than a month now until school starts. ... Uh huh...yes, well, 'bye."

Brian looked up at his mother and saw her quiver. Katie wondered at the puzzled look on her face as she began explaining.

"Oh, that was Mrs. Robinson. It seems that someone broke into her house today while she was at church and ransacked all the rooms...looking for something. She doesn't think anything's missing, but she's not sure yet; it could be something she wouldn't miss for years. All her jewelry is there, all the silverware, even the television and DVD player. The police said it might be young kids, just creating a mess for the thrill of it."

"Who'd do anything like that to Mrs. Robinson?" asked Katie angrily. "I mean, she'd give any kid a cookie, and she's always really nice."

"Well, we don't know for sure that it was kids," said her mother as she returned to sit at the table. "That's what the police said it might be. They warned her to lock her doors and windows at all times. The police might stop here later on to talk with you both, just to see if you have any ideas. They might even want to take your fingerprints. I told her I thought that would be all right with you. Is it?"

"Take our fingerprints? Cool!" said Brian. Katie was a little less enthusiastic: "If it'll help I'll do it."

"Well, we'll see what the police want when they get here. Until then, what's ahead this coming week? When does football practice start?" Mrs. Eames asked Brian.

"It's in a couple of weeks, but I'm not positive of the day. I have the schedule upstairs in my room. I'll get it. I have to go early to get a uniform and everything," he said as he left a cookie and half of his glass of milk. He bounded out of the kitchen.

As he rounded the turn for the front hall he paused to look out at the street and saw a police cruiser pulling up in front of the house. From the driver's side a uniformed officer stepped out. At the same time a passenger opened the car's other front door and another person—not in uniform—struggled to get out. This man was very tall, Brian realized, as the two men headed up the walk to the house. Not only was he tall, he was thin. And he moved his long legs like a man he had seen dressed up as Uncle Sam, a stilt walker, during the city's most recent Fourth of July parade. That Uncle Sam had displayed unexpected grace as he stood above the crowd. Brian remembered looking up at him to see him gazing serenely over the landscape. He wondered if he'd have to look up as far to make out the face of this stranger, too.

He did, almost.

Brian raced to the front door and answered it before the bell was rung and found that if he looked across on the level, his eyes would rest just above the man's belt buckle. Slowly, his eyes rose to take in the wrinkled brown sport coat, the clean, white shirt, the goofy bow tie, and the trace of a smile on the man's long, narrow face. The eyes were deep set and very dark, and they looked intently down at Brian. The tall man gave Brian the impression that he saw everything.

And the voice fit the face; deep, serious, but not rough.

"I'd guess that you're Brian," he said. Then looking over Brian's shoulder his eyes fastened on Katie who approached from the kitchen. "And you're Katie." It wasn't really a question. He was registering their faces forever. "And now that I know who you are I'll tell you who I am: James Grosskopf. In German it means James Big Head. But as you see, it's not just my head." Katie approached the screen door, fascinated. "I am a detective on the Misty Haven police force. This is my associate, Officer Tom Lujens." He indicated the man in uniform, a young, pink-faced blond who looked as if he, too, was extremely gentle.

"If your mother is home may we come in?" asked the tall man. Their mother, in fact, had come up behind the children. They turned to find her there and then nodded their assent to the almost-giant. He had to duck to come in the door. Brian knew — because his father had told him — that most doors were six feet, eight inches tall. That would mean that Detective Grosskopf was very tall indeed.

Their mother led the guests and children back into the kitchen where Brian and Katie resumed their seats, cookies, and milk. Brian watched as the detective studied their plates and frowned. Maybe he didn't like cookies? Their mother offered water, coffee, or milk to the officers.

"Coffee for me, please. Cream and sugar," said Officer Lujens.

"I'd prefer milk," said the detective. "And, if you might have a cookie or two...? We haven't had time to stop for any dinner today. The cookies we saw cooling at Mrs. Robinson's just kind of whetted my appetite. It's funny: when some people get burgled they go to pieces. Mrs. Robinson said that her first reaction was to bake."

Katie thought that was quite bold of him to ask for cookies. If she'd done that at anybody else's house, she'd be sternly lectured to not appear a beggar. Her mother, though, didn't seem to notice the rude manners and brought over another plate of cookies, a full plate that both officers proceeded to eat, most deliberately, one by one.

They paused only to ask questions: Had the kids seen any strangers around Mrs. Robinson's house lately? Were there any threats against Mrs. Robinson? Had she any enemies? Had they any enemies who might want to get back at them through her? Could the police take their fingerprints? That would help when they were trying to sort out who had been in the house. Once they eliminated all of Mrs. Robinson's own finger prints and Brian's and Katie's, the police could see if there were any left over. Chances are they couldn't catch the burglar right off the bat, but if there were other break-ins, maybe they'd be able to match fingerprints. And when they finally caught the perp — that was the word he used, "perp" for perpetrator — they could charge him with a whole bunch of crimes.

Officer Lujens excused himself to go to the car and bring back the fingerprint kit.

"This is the old-fashioned way," said the detective. "We use ink and cards. At the station we do it all on a glass screen. We digitize the prints right at the source and there's not much to clean up."

The finger printing itself was fun, but messy. Brian and Katie had to scrub a long time to get the ink off their fingers.

The cookie plate empty, the detective and officer stood to leave. "I'll stay in touch," said Detective Grosskopf, looking in turn at Brian, Katie, and their mother as if he had an unspoken message for each.

Chapter 4

KEEPING AN EYE ON THINGS

Brian thought a lot about the detective during the evening and the next morning. For one thing, he'd never met anyone that tall before. And, for another, he was very certain that Mr., er, Detective Grosskopf missed nothing. It had something to do with the way he studied people and the details of places. He took his time when he looked, not in any hurry to move on. Brian believed a burglar wouldn't stand much of a chance if the detective could find even a few clues.

It was Monday morning with only four weeks before school began. Mom had already gathered his and Katie's back-to-school clothes, binders, pencils, compasses, and protractors. They even had new lunch boxes, the kind that stack food containers one on top of another. Brian's was dark green, Katie's, a light sky blue. But there would be other things they'd need.

The pressure of school's approach left Brian very sad. Even though he could be good at it, he didn't like the idea of sitting all day long. And the homework! Katie, on the other hand, loved school: the order, the idea that time was planned out for her. She actually liked her teachers, and she looked forward this year to working with a new one. And, her teachers always liked her right back. Maybe that was it: Brian didn't really like his teachers, and they could tell. They taught him, but they didn't spend a lot of time liking him. He supposed that teachers could only really like so many students, so they might as well like the ones who started by liking them; it was more efficient that way. He wished, and not for the first time, that he could be more like Katie.

When he went down for breakfast, she was already seated at the table.

"Do you think Mrs. Robinson will be hysterical today?" she asked seriously.

"Hysterical? I doubt it. But she'll still be upset. Maybe she won't let us get out of sight. I'd kind of like to get back to the cave today, you know, see what's left."

Katie looked at him and then down at her plate. "I don't think that's a very good idea, especially after what happened Saturday. It might be dangerous."

"Yeah, well, so what?" He avoided looking at her as he poured out his cereal. "I'm going and you can stay or come as you like."

Brian had to admit that Katie was brave enough for almost anything. Sometimes braver than he was. But he wasn't going to show that he was scared, too. This was something he'd face by himself if he had to. But he didn't prefer it that way; he wanted Katie by his side as he stood on the floor of that odd cavern.

Mom was reading the morning paper, standing by the counter. She shook her head in disbelief.

"Wow, that's awful, just awful."

"What is, Mom?" asked Katie.

"There's a story here about a herd of cattle, twelve, that were slaughtered in a farmer's field. They were ripped apart. Somebody or something attacked the heifers and steers right in the field. They think it might have been a pack of wild dogs. Now, that's scary." She flipped the page. "Oh, here's the story of the break-in at Mrs. Robinson's. Boy, that Detective Grosskopf sure was tall, wasn't he? And he sure does like cookies. In fact, I'd better put more on the shopping list, just in case he comes back."

Mom smiled at the thought. Brian thought it was a kind of sad smile, but it beat the no-look-at-all she'd sometimes worn during the last year. He helped wash up the breakfast dishes and then climbed the stairs to brush his teeth and comb his hair.

In the bathroom mirror, he saw a face that most resembled his mom's, at least a little, and that vaguely reflected his father's, or what he could remember of his father's. The pictures downstairs that showed Mom and Dad in formal poses didn't carry very much information. Brian couldn't recognize his father in any of the pictures the way he remembered him: smiling and easy. It was the smile Brian remembered most, a smile that kind of crept over his face as he watched Brian or Katie. To picture that smile exactly, though; well, Brian had been struggling to do that for months. And the more he struggled, the less sure he was of exactly how his father had looked. All he carried now was an impression. Could he ever forget his father? What kind of a son would that make him? He sighed, and the narrow, serious face in the mirror sighed with his. Brown hair, blue eyes, a few freckles.

When he finished, Katie jumped in to get ready for the day. She was wearing old jeans, so Brian was pretty sure that she'd join him. Maybe they'd get Reme to come along, too.

Mom kissed each one of them as they headed out the door. Yes, she'd be at work — sorry, no phone calls except emergencies — and she'd be home on time. No extra hours tonight. And, off they went to Mrs. Robinson's. The walk was only a few minutes, and they had the chance to talk together about the strange goings on. Butchered cows and break-ins.

"I think it's awful about all those cows getting killed," said Katie.

"Yeah, well you eat hamburgers, don't you?"

"Well, I guess, but when they kill cows for meat they do it fast. That's what mom said. They stun them first and then kill them so they don't feel it."

Brian looked at her with some alarm; she knew more about it than he did.

"But this," she said gesturing to the whole wide world, "sounded like something ripped them apart while they tried to run away. At least, that's what the farmer said when the reporter asked him. The cows...or little parts of them...were all over the field."

"Maybe it was some guys who decided to kill the cows and butcher 'em in the field," said Brian.

"I don't think so," replied Katie. She paused to reflect. As she concentrated, Brian saw that she looked a lot like Dad. Far more than he did. She had the same squarish head. The same golden-red hair and the same greenish-blue eyes. And he wondered at the unfairness of it all: How come she was entitled to wear their Dad's features?

At Mrs. Robinson's nothing had seemed to change. She was in the kitchen — as usual — and if the house had been in disarray it had also been set back to rights. Katie was the one who asked if there had been a mess.

"A mess? Oh, land sakes alive! I noticed right away that things had been gone through down here, but upstairs in Donnie's old bedroom everything was taken apart." Donnie was her grown son. "Somebody went through that room like a tornado. I've been meaning for years to get rid of all his old clothes and I had 'em settin' out on the bed. Pants from when he was your size, shirts from high school. And they were all thrown everywhere. All his dresser drawers, all the boxes that he managed to collect over the years, you know, things you decide you want to keep, and then, when you go away to college you decide you won't take 'em with you, and then they stay behind forever.

"Well," and Mrs. Robinson paused to snort. "I guess that room got about as good a cleaning and clearing as it ever did yesterday after the police left. I don't guess Donnie's gonna come and collect some of those things he left behind after all, at least, not any more.

"And, you know, the funny thing, whoever it was went through my jewelry box and didn't take a thing, not a single thing. Of course, I don't have all that much that's valuable; no jewels, not a lot of gold. Whoever it was didn't even bother with my great aunt Sophie's brooch. I guess that's the most valuable piece I have."

Brian asked if her doors had been locked.

"You and that detective!" she said, fixing him with a hard stare. "He wanted to know the same thing. I set that tall drink of water on the right track. Of course I had my doors locked, front, back, and side porch. Whoever it was came in through a basement window after it had been busted out. Mr. Tenny said he'll stop by later this morning to replace the glass. I don't know what it's coming to when a person's house isn't safe. And since whoever it was spent most of his time in Donnie's room, maybe it was some poor, wretched child looking for toys and who's bent on a life of crime."

Brian managed to keep a straight face, but he saw a laugh flicker across Katie's. It was fortunate for both of them that Mrs. Robinson had turned her back and was intently stirring yet another bowl of dough for cookies that would be soon be in the oven.

"I thought," said Brian to her, "that we might have another picnic lunch today. Katie and I want to go for a hike again. When school starts in a couple of weeks we won't have the chance to take almost a whole day for anything else. And then, too, fall will be coming and...." He trailed off as Mrs. Robinson stopped working the dough to consider.

"Well, I can fix sack lunches but I don't know that the freshest cookies will be done in time to send them along. And last week you came back so late that I was worried. What assurance do I have that it won't happen again?"

"My promise?" Brian weakly offered. "And the old cookies will be just fine."

"Hmm."

Katie piped up: "My promise, Mrs. Robinson. I'll stop at home and get my watch, and I promise we'll be back by four o'clock."

Mrs. Robinson's shoulders dropped a quarter of an inch in assent: "Well, all right, but you don't have to go home. I'll let you take one of Mr. Robinson's old watches, the one he wore when he was puttering around on weekends. If it's damaged it won't be much of a loss."

"We might go back that way, anyhow, to see if Reme wants to come with us."

"Does that mean another lunch?" Mrs. Robinson asked, not unkindly.

"Well...." said Brian, hopefully.

With less than half an hour's preparation they were on their way. This time Reme had to find the rope to send over the edge of the cavern. The rope and a flashlight. Brian and Katie's mother had not yet noticed that her household was missing the flashlight, rope, and a few other supplies. Brian thought fleetingly of buying a replacement light; it would cost some money, maybe all he had. He'd need to make time to stop at the local hardware store, just a bike ride away. Maybe he could pick up new sandwich containers for Ms. Robinson at the same time.

The path through the woods and to the clearing didn't seem quite long enough to suit any one of the three children. They expected some scene of devastation: scorched earth, maybe a hardened flow of lava. They wondered aloud how grown-ups could be so incurious as to see the plume of cloud and not want to investigate.

Brian cautioned Reme again and again not to hit anything, especially not a rock: "It was probably some boulder on top of a volcano steam vent and you dislodged it just enough to nearly get us killed."

Reme—also shaken—agreed that he wouldn't do anything, anything except look and listen. And, maybe he'd do that above ground. He wasn't sure about going over the edge this time; it really wasn't safe down there.

Once they'd passed through the trees, the meadow looked much the same as before. They could hear the birds singing over toward the river. Nothing seemed out of place. Nothing, that is, until they approached the hole that dropped into the cave. Around it for four or five feet, the tall grasses were yellowing and right at its edge the earth was burnt dark. Above it, they could see that the leaves from the trees had all withered; many had fallen off. The effect was of a narrow tunnel coming down from the sky. The sun obliged by sending its rays to shine on the hole in the ground. They saw that the rope they had tied to the nearest tree had been burnt off at the edge of the abyss.

With steady care, Brian dropped to his knees and looked down. He saw the shadow of his own head rimmed by the shadow of the hole. Finally, in order to get a better look he stretched out onto his belly and peered into the darkness.

"Wow! There really was a fire down here!" Katie and Reme heard him exclaim. "The flashlight's just a lump. At least I think it was the flashlight. And the big boulder's moved to the other side of the cave. I can't see where the hole was beneath it, you know, where the smoke and steam came from. But there's nothin' moving down there. Nothin'. And it's not hot or anything."

Reme stretched out the new length of rope, tied it to the same tree where the other stub still circled the bark, and slowly lowered it over the edge. Once the remainder was coiled on the floor he stepped back.

After testing the rope, Brian began lowering himself like a mountaineer; hand over hand. Even though the temptation to drop the last five feet was strong, he completed his descent in style and softly touched the cave bottom. He looked around to see none of the detritus of his last visit: the cave had been scoured by fire. Brian's knees shook as he tried to walk around the cave.

Once he'd made as much of the circuit as he could see in the light that streamed from overhead, he returned to his landing spot and looked up at the two small heads. "Did you see anything move?" he asked anxiously.

"Nothing," responded Katie. "Not a single thing. But that rock isn't where it was. And those others, the long ones that stretch out like big beads on a string, they weren't just exactly there before, I don't think."

Brian took another tour of the circuit, closely examining everything but touching nothing. When next he returned to the rope Katie readied to slide down. Before she did, Brian tied knots every foot or so in the rope as high as he could reach.

"That should be enough," he said, "if we have to go back up in a hurry."

Then Katie came down, her eyes wide with fear. She knew this was a bad idea, that they could be trapped down here in another explosion of steam or gas or of a little volcano. But knowing that, she still climbed over the edge. Tentatively, she put her foot on the cave floor. And then she, too, explored the perimeter of the dimly lighted area. She, too, came back to the rope and looked up. Reme, alone, remained on the verge.

"But don't you think somebody should stay up here?" he asked, his voice floating down to Katie and Brian.

"Why, sure," said Katie. "It makes sense to me, just in case there's another explosion. That way you could run for help."

"Or tell 'em where to look for the bodies," said Brian, more grimly. With a look around the chamber he added: "But maybe not this time. There's nothin' left down here. I guess we should come up."

"Then wait so I can come down, too," said Reme. "I want to come down just for a minute, but I don't want to be down there alone. I'll just touch the floor and then climb right back. That way I won't be a complete chicken, okay?"

Katie smiled at the thought; Reme was not a chicken. She, herself, was scared and Brian...well, he looked awfully pale, even in the dim light. His face stood out even in the gloom. Before she had time to look further around the room, Reme was standing by the rope. He had descended as quietly as a cat.

He still held to the rope but moved toward the center of the cavern. "I just gotta touch the big rock," he said, and before Brian or Katie could say or do anything he dashed and very carefully laid his palm against the boulder.

"Hey," he said, keeping it there. "This is warm. Real warm."

After a pause, Katie and Brian joined him. Fingertips first, each of them put out first one hand and then two. At length, Katie laid her cheek against the rock.

In that position she missed what the boys saw, but she heard. She heard the sound like the hot-air furnace makes when it lights for the first time in the morning. And she heard the sound of something inside the rock shifting. But it didn't sound like a rock; suddenly it didn't feel like a rock, either, but like something else. And it moved like one of the horses she'd ridden earlier in the summer. And she heard Brian's intake of breath and Reme's low moan.

And then she took her face away, turned, and looked into two of the most golden eyes she'd ever seen. They were more gold than gold, except for the red at the center; but there were flecks of gold there, too. They dazzled. And she saw the eyes were set about a foot apart and between them was a shape like the bridge of a very long snout. And the snout helped to make up a huge head that looked an awful lot that of a dragon. Katie shook her own head, telling herself there was no such thing as a dragon. Impossible! From the mouth, a tendril of smoke lazily issued and curled against the cave ceiling. Striking out into the light that shone down from above, a giant flickering snake's tongue shot out to taste the air, only to return to its lair. Katie had the vague impression of teeth, too. Lots and lots of teeth, but mostly she looked at the eyes; they looked back at her.

Katie was never sure if she heard the words, or only thought them, but there came to mind odd sounds, words certainly, but not in a language she had ever heard, much less known: "*Memento, homo, quia pulvis es et in pulverem revertis.*"

Chapter 5

A WEE BEASTIE

How long she stood transfixed, Katie never could determine. The eyes that held her in thrall also probed her mind and her soul. Her soul? Oh, yes. Of everything that day, she was most certain she had a soul, for it was weighed in the balance. She saw into herself, but through eyes other than her own, every unkindness, every deceit, every slight — intended and accidental. But she also saw the loneliness, the ache for her father, the night fears, the day fears. Lastly, she saw the goodness: the love she shared with her mother, the love she saved for her father, and even the love she held for her brother. And the hope, and all the good things she had done in her short life, and suddenly it seemed all too short, pitifully short. But she looked death steadily in the eyes and owned up to the fact that if the only sorrow here was that life was too short, it was indeed a very good life, one well worth living.

There occurred to each of the other two the same kind of scouring examination. There was no hidey-hole in which they could escape the searching gaze of the ensorcelling, golden eyes. The more each child looked, the more fascinated he or she became. Each saw the past in the glittering orbs. For Reme, that included a birth and the first few weeks in a far off land he now could only imagine.

At length, there floated a feeling of wonder and these words: "*non nova, sed nove.*"

Very softly Katie heard Reme whisper, trying to explain: "It means 'not new things but in a new way.' I think it's seen a lot of little kids before. Maybe for breakfast, lunch, or dinner."

Katie couldn't help herself: she laughed. Out loud.

The dragon, for that certainly was what it was, sent up a small snort of smoke...followed by another and another. The sulfur smell filled the cave.

The beast was laughing, too, but very softly. The effect was something like the small train at the zoo. Even Brian smiled and then turned to Reme: "How do you know what it's saying?"

"Latin...it's Latin. You guys go to a public school and I go to a Catholic school. That's what I've been studying for the last three years; that and everything else. My Dad says it's unbelievable to find a Catholic school that still teaches Latin, but mine does."

"What did this thing say the first time?"

"You don't want to know."

"Oh, yes I do," said Brian with some heat.

"Well, it's from when they bury people: 'Dust thou art and unto dust thou shalt return.'"

"You mean we're gonna be ashes?"

Reme nodded. "That's what I understood it to mean."

The dragon, sensing the mood, swung its giant head toward Reme: "*Aequo animo esto.*" Reme translated on the spot: "It says 'be of a calm mind'; maybe it gets indigestion otherwise."

Again came the giant snort, but this time, since the dragon had moved closer, its head was slightly averted to avoid scorching clothes and hair. The smell had diminished, as though only in stoking up did the beast give off the stench of rotted eggs. And again the three backed up as far as they could. Katie felt the cave wall digging into her shoulder blades. The dragon seemed to be taking a special interest in her. Extending its great head on an endlessly flexible serpentine neck, the beast first studied her, then closed its eyes and...sniffed. Katie was relieved when the eyes reopened and turned away from her, moving to Brian.

...Relieved until she realized that it might be picking one of them to eat. With a start she jumped between Brian and the dragon. She paused long enough to shout and then flew at the beast's head.

"You're not gonna eat my brother," she screamed as she flailed away. The dragon drew a clear protective lid over each eye but otherwise remained immobile. Not even a hiss of smoke issued from its nostrils.

For perhaps thirty seconds Katie expended her fury and fear. Then, as quickly as she began, she stopped and started shaking.

The dragon drew back the hard, clear nictitating membrane and turned very slightly. "*Pax vobiscum,*" it said, and repeated: "*Pax....*"

Reme peeled his back off the cave wall and approached. "It said, 'Peace be with you.' Like it doesn't want to fight." The dragon nodded steadily.

Brian, somewhat recovered from his own fear and the amazing sight of his sister trying to protect him, moved up as well and put his arm around Katie. She was still shuddering.

"So," said Brian, "Are you pretty sure about this Latin? I mean, if you get it wrong it could be all wrong."

"I've been practicing a lot. My dad has a friend at the college who teaches Latin, and he's been giving me extra lessons. He says I've learned about as much as there is. And then there's practice at school. The Catholics used to use it all the time, but there are still some nuns and priests who know what it means. I practice with them, too, sometimes after school. They're mostly old."

"Yeah, well, either you must be good, really good or...," began Brian.

"It's the 'or,'" said Reme. "It's using really simple Latin like maybe you'd use for a beginner. I know it can understand what we say, sort of. I wonder if it can speak English, too."

"*Minime,*" came the rumble from the dragon.

"Well, that settles that: it speaks Latin but listens English," said Reme. The dragon chuffed once more in reply. Then Reme directed his remarks at the beast: "Are you gonna eat us now?"

The great rock-colored head gleamed in the sparse light from above. It swung from side to side in a wide arc signifying "no."

"Did you eat those cows?" asked Katie. Again its head moved, this time up and down. "You did? Wasn't that a lot to eat?" Again, a "yes." Katie paused to think a moment and continued: "Had it been a long time since you had eaten?" A nod "yes." "Like years and years?" "Yes," again. "Will it be a long time until you need to eat again?" The nod was less emphatic, but was still a "yes."

"So, that's it," said Katie. "It's been asleep. We woke it last week, and it needed a snack. Otherwise it would have just kept sleeping away until..."

"*In perpetuum,*" said the dragon, as sadly as a dragon could.

"It means 'forever,'" said Reme.

"Yeah," said Brian. "I could guess that one."

Katie chimed in: "We've been saying 'it,' but are you a he or a she dragon?"

The giant head bowed to Katie. "Does that mean you're a he?"

"*Ita*," said the beast. "'Yes,'" translated Reme. "He's a he."

"*Oppido*," said the dragon. "'Precisely so,'" translated Reme.

"And now what?" asked Brian. "Now that we've disturbed his sleep what's he going to do? Will he let us go or will he have to keep us prisoners?"

In answer the great beast began slowly to back away. In the process he had to swing his giant cloven tail—the seeming beads on a string—back and forth to accommodate the reverse circum-ambulation. When he had backed nearly to the other side of the cave, the dragon motioned with his head that they should ascend the rope to escape to safety.

"Come on, Katie," said Brian as he approached their means of escape.

Instead, Katie walked across the cave and stood before the dragon. "You wouldn't hurt us. At least, I don't think so. But what would happen if we ran away and told somebody else? Somebody like a grown-up?"

The dragon shrugged his giant shoulders and hunched closer to the floor. Katie had seen cats use the same movement when they were settling in for a nap in the sun. "We won't, you know... tell grown-ups, I mean. But, can we come back? Can we come back tomorrow?"

The dragon nodded and then, very carefully, extended his neck to a point where Katie could easily pat his head. At the first touch of her hand the beast began to purr like a giant cat. So loud was the sound that the walls seemed to vibrate in sympathy. Reme had to cover his ears.

At the last, quite done, the dragon closed his clear eyelids and squeezed out a tear from each eye. These ran down the sides of his cheek and fell to the ground with a 'clink.' Katie bent down to retrieve them.

"Dragon tears?" she marveled examining the clear crystals. The beast nodded. She put them in the pockets of her jeans and turned to the rope. She was the first up to ground level, followed by Reme and, lastly, Brian. Katie returned to the hole and stuck her head in one more time: "We'll be back tomorrow."

In reply, the dragon said, "*Bene valete. Curate ut valeatis.*"

When she reported the words to Reme he translated for her. "'Good bye. Take care of yourselves.' And, if you'll notice, we just met a dragon...a real, fire-breathing dragon. And we're still alive."

All three were infected with a sense that they'd escaped from a very great danger. Their path home was marvelous to behold: their steps were light as they walked their bikes; they sent up great whoops of joy. They even dropped their bikes by the side of the road at one point and ran into the forest. There, finding a downed and dead oak, they sat along its length to eat their lunch. They devoured the sandwiches. And the cookies tasted sweeter than ever.

As they sat, Reme launched into the first of what were to be a series of Latin lessons. His introductory session involved saying hello and goodbye.

After the brief lesson, they ran about for a bit, climbing trees, running along deer paths, jumping over hummocks and running through tussocks. At last, with a little of their wild enthusiasm expended, they retrieved their bikes and rode toward town.

As they neared The Dragon and The Rose, Katie addressed the boys: "We've got to stop here and get ourselves a little more under control. If we go back the way we are—wild and shouting—Mr. Teagarden, Mrs. Robinson, and our moms are going to want to know what's going on. So, let's calm down a little."

"Yeah," said Reme. "I suppose. But did it really happen? A real dragon?"

Katie reached into her pocket and took out the two dragon tears. "What do you think? Here's the proof, all the proof I'll ever need. The same thing Brian found last time, before we woke the dragon. He has his, I'll keep one, and here's one for you, Reme."

Katie handed over one of the marvelous stones, which Reme immediately secreted in his pocket. Then they crossed the street and entered The Dragon and The Rose.

"Oh, back from another day's adventures?" Mr. Teagarden inquired. He was bustling from the counter to the back room. "I'll be with you in a bit; we have a birthday celebration on for tonight, and I've got to get the decorations just right. Mrs. Teagarden's away, and she usually helps.... Say, I don't suppose you could fetch along those boxes just inside the front door?"

With relief at escaping conversation, the three children carried the boxes, opened them and began setting out party favors. Brian asked if he could have a toot on a pasteboard horn.

"Well, I should have just three extras, so each of you shall have one at the end of our labors," said Mr. Teagarden. In all, the setting-up took about fifteen minutes. The children returned with their host to the main room, paused for a quick glass of lemonade, and departed with their noisemakers.

Brian and Katie led the way out the door. Reme followed and moved along in their wake, hanging back a little. He had the nagging feeling that he was being watched. Halfway down the block he stopped and turned to see a figure just leaving the pub. He quickly looked away, and when he looked back again no one was there. Katie and Brian looked only forward. At the corner where they separated, Reme looked around again and thought he saw something...someone, but just for a second. He hurried home, and once inside the house, he locked the door behind him.

Chapter 6

TWENTY QUESTIONS

This time it was Reme's house.

The burglar again had broken in through a basement window while Reme and his parents were out to dinner.

Little in the rest of the house had been disturbed except Reme's room, and there it looked like a whirlwind had tossed everything to the four walls. Every drawer of his antique Empire-style dresser was pulled out and emptied; the drawers were left upturned, thrown down one atop the other. His desk drawer suffered a like fate, and the desk was overturned. All his clothes had been pulled out of the closet and tossed on the bed and floor. Every container was opened; pennies that had filled four jars were strewn about the carpet. Every envelope was ripped open.

Had anything been taken? Reme searched among the debris and gave his verdict: nothing.

Detective Grosskopf received the news with some confusion: "What, after all, is the point of all this? What did Mrs. Robinson not have that the burglar wanted and didn't take or find here? What do you have that wasn't taken?" He drilled his eyes into those of a young man who hadn't fully spoken the truth. The detective detected an omission.

Something *was* missing, but its absence should have been known only to Reme and two others. And admitting its existence would have led from one revelation to another and to yet another. How, after all does one go about vouching for dragon tears?

Reme pondered how he was to tell Katie and Brian, but he didn't have long to wonder; they were at the front door as soon as the police car carried away the detective and his lieutenant. Reme received his friends on the front porch.

He had left the dragon tear in his pants and those were at the bottom of a laundry basket. Reme was going to retrieve it after coming home from dinner. Only after ripping his room apart did the thief think to sort through pockets in dirty clothes.

"It looks like somebody knows where you live, where Mrs. Robinson lives, and maybe where we live," said Brian. "And it sure looks like he knew just what he was after. Who could know? Mr. Teagarden? Isn't he the only one who ever saw the dragon tear, the first one?"

"Well, Mr. …Dr. Joe…Dr. Cavanaugh, too," said Katie.

And it was unthinkable that Mr. Teagarden could or would have done such a thing. That left only Dr. Joe—at least to their reckoning. Only he could have known. Maybe he was the one who broke in; he almost had to be.

"But why would he break into Mrs. Robinson's?" asked Katie at length. "That wouldn't make any sense."

"Was there anybody else there when we were showing it to him?" asked Reme.

"I don't think so," said Reme, "but I'm not positive. You know how sometimes people just sit there in the booths? And there's that little room at the front with a kind of open window into the rest of the bar."

Tomorrow they would return to The Dragon and The Rose and ask Mr. Teagarden just who else might have been there; he would have served anybody who had come in. But tonight, it was getting late, and Reme's father came out on the porch to herd him in.

"What is this conference?" he asked as pleasantly as anyone could whose house had just been broken into. "Do you discuss the *Arcanum arcanorum*?"

Reme smiled and rolled his eyes: "My dad's talking about the 'Secret of Secrets.' Yeah, we were just finishing up with what we were going to tell the dragon the next time we saw him."

A look of pure disbelief passed over the two faces that opposed him. Reme managed to toss off his revelation as a joke, something his father seemed to enjoy. Only then did Katie and Brian realize that the truth would protect them simply because it sounded so outrageous. At least, here and now.

"Well, dragon whisperer, it's time to hang up, so bid your boon companions a fond farewell," said his father.

Most seriously Reme turned to Katie and Brian, raised his hand in benediction and said *"Vale in crastinum* (Farewell until tomorrow)."

They, in turn, returned his salute: *"Valete* (Farewell)!" In each of their ears echoed the rumble of the dragon's voice.

Very briefly Reme's father looked from his son to his friends. Then he nodded and opened the screen door. Gently he patted his son's shoulder as the boy passed in.

The automatic closer hissed as the door shut behind them, and Katie and Brian walked down the steps and then the sidewalk to their own house. They agreed they were going to have to be much more careful.

The morrow didn't exactly dawn. Instead, it just turned from black to dark grey to, finally, a little lighter grey. It was the pro-verbial grey day, something their father had jokingly referred to as a "Grade A, great day, grey day." Brian mouthed the phrase as he looked out his window. He'd need to take a sweatshirt along; it looked like it was going to be chilly.

It wasn't exactly chilly, but it seemed damp on the walk to Mrs. Robinson's house. Would she be kind enough to prepare yet another picnic lunch for three? Mrs. Robinson was more than happy to oblige. Of course there were cookies, too, at least as many as the detective had left in his wake.

"Didn't I tell you?" Mrs. Robinson queried Katie and Brian. "He was here again this morning. I do believe that he sees some connection between the break-in here and at Reme's. I think so, too. And you two are the connection. But what could you have been up to that anyone would think important enough to break into my house?"

Katie looked at Brian for confirmation and then spoke: "Well, we did discover a dragon..."

Mrs. Robinson spent much of her life dealing in literal thoughts and terms. She did, however, possess a sense of humor that, once activated, led to laughter. Such was the case now. She laughed hard enough that she had to use the corner of her apron to wipe tears from her eyes.

"Oh, my. Discovered a dragon! And, perhaps you've hidden it here? Or at Reme's? Must be a very small one. What won't you think of next? "

Katie was relieved that Mrs. Robinson wasn't angry. Katie diverted the conversation away from the dragon theme: "It sure does look like there's something that somebody wants from one of us and maybe our house is next. I'll tell Mom to be extra careful when she locks up."

Mrs. Robinson was by this time placing the sandwiches and cookies into a heavy paper bag, the kind with sturdy handles. Following a careful inspection, she sent them down the street toward Reme's, the bag dangling from Brian's bicycle handlebars.

Reme's mother opened the door with some hesitation. Her face was anxious and her fingers of her right hand kept twining around those of the left. "I'm not sure it's a good idea for Reme to go with you today. It's just a little while until school starts, and I have to take him shopping for new clothes. ...And, it's just not a good day for him to be away."

Reme could be seen behind his mother, shrugging his shoulders and trying to convey something through facial expressions. When his mother finished her explanation, he popped forward to offer something of his own: "Yeah, this has been bad...with the break-in and all, and my dad had to go out of town, so I want to stay around here today. I hope you guys have fun; I'll talk to you later on tonight. After my dad gets home."

"Yeah, sure," said Brian. And with that Katie and Brian turned about and headed down the sidewalk and journeyed from the land of men into the land of dragon.

Without Reme it was different, a little scarier; not that it ever would be without some tinge of fear: imagine waking a dragon in his lair. But that's exactly what they set out to do. Katie was first to reach the rope. From the top of the hole she shouted down and awakened the sleeping monster.

For his part, the dragon looked at her and sent out a very small chuff of smoke, a welcoming puff. The fumes lazily wafted through the smoke hole. Katie slithered down the rope, followed by Brian. The dragon looked expectantly above them at the hole until Brian explained: "He couldn't come today. Somebody broke into his house last night, and his mother is kind of scared today. He wanted to be here, but he needed to stay home."

"*Sufficit*," said the dragon.

Katie looked up at the imperious golden eyes. "Is that like sufficient? Is the explanation enough?"

The dragon nodded and Katie continued: "This Latin stuff is kind of like English only harder?"

"*Certe,*" chuffed the dragon.

"Certainly?" said Katie, and the dragon bobbed his head yet again. "Well, if you can understand what we say, why can't you speak English?"

"*Non omnia possumus omnes,*" he said and turned his head away.

Katie was baffled. "Well, even if I can't always understand, I can guess. Have you ever heard of twenty questions?" The dragon had not. "It's a game where we ask questions and you answer either 'yes' or 'no'. I'll start: are you a real dragon? I mean were you always a dragon?"

Minime.

"Did you once live as a boy or a man? Or maybe a lady?"

"*Certe, certe, minime....*" "Yes, yes, no."

"Did you come from far away?"

"*Certe.*"

"From England?"

"*Minime, Certe.*"

"From near England?"

"*Certe.*"

"Were you turned into a dragon there?"

"*Certe.*"

"Do you...?" she hesitated. "Do you know the story of The Dragon and The Rose?"

A huge chuff of smoke rose toward the cave ceiling. The dragon vigorously nodded his head.

"And, are you that dragon?"

The dragon gave a little nod and a tear ran from his cheek. It clinked to the floor as another gem.

"You mean your brother did this to you? He turned you into a dragon?"

Another small nod; another tear.

"And your wife...the lovely lady, er, I forget. What happened to her?"

The dragon shrugged; two tears coursed down his cheeks this time. Clink, clink.

"He doesn't know," said Katie turning to Brian. "Mr. Teagarden said that the Dragon had moved her into a cave beneath the castle before he was changed. But how long could she last there? Isn't that awful; he doesn't know what happened to her, whether she lived or died. Although I'd imagine she's dead by now — or else she'd be very old. Like a thousand years."

"Yeah," said Brian in a whisper. "But remember, that's how old he is."

Involuntarily, Katie took a step back. "That's right," she said, also in a whisper. "And there's magic. That's bound to goof up time; it always does in the story books."

The dragon, meanwhile, was looking from one to the other as they spoke with lowered voices. It was as if they expected the dragon to quite suddenly have developed a hearing loss, something dragons rarely, if ever, did. At length he gave a small snort and brought their tête-à-tête to a close.

"Well, what are you doing here?" Brian asked. The dragon rolled his eyes, and Brian cringed at his question. "Sorry. Did you come here because there weren't very many people here a thousand years ago?" A nod "yes."

"Did you come here because there were lots of deer and other game to eat?" Another nod "yes."

Katie joined in: "When you sleep, do you have to eat as much?" No. "Had you slept for a very long time when we woke you?" Yes. "And you were very hungry and had to go out to eat a lot?" Yes. "Are you hungry now?" No. Yes.

Quickly Katie opened the lunch sack and pulled out the sandwich Mrs. Robinson had made for Reme. After unwrapping the clear plastic which had surrounded it — something, by the way, that fascinated the dragon — she held the meal out on her palm, much the same way she'd been taught to feed a horse. The dragon snuffled at the bread and meat concoction and tried — unsuccessfully — to get it between his teeth.

Brian stepped up. "I think somebody has to hold it for him because it's so small. May I?" And with Katie's assent he held the sandwich before the great jaws. The dragon opened his mouth and allowed Brian to place the sandwich between the rows and rows of very sharp and very clean teeth. The dragon's breath was a little like a furnace in that it was hot, but, since he was up and running, it wasn't sulfurous any longer. Brian had expected a stench, perhaps the smell of rottenness and decay. But this was like the door had been opened on an oven full of loaves and roasts and potatoes.

The dragon made extravagant work of the little morsel, even to the extent of an "ummmmm" followed by tooth sucking. Katie next volunteered her own sandwich, something the dragon would not take, so she and Brian—after he offered his, too—sat down and ate their sandwiches, but not in silence.

While one was chewing and swallowing, the other was asking questions. In consequence what they learned was this: the dragon had flown over the sea perhaps nine hundred years ago, vowing to return when he could break the spell. Year after year he hunted the wild game here, observed only by the changing seasons and a very few eyes belonging to the people of the place. Then about two hundred years ago there began to arrive some who had the look about them of new people, but from an old land; his old land.

Perhaps a hundred years before the present, the dragon had settled in for a particularly long nap, something he'd done to save his strength and energy. He had awakened rarely and then only to hunt for enough to sustain his limited needs. Dreams don't require much food. Discovery, he knew, might mean another rout—and where was there to go? Hadn't all the world been discovered not once or twice, but three or four times? What was he to do? There was almost no way he could avoid detection in the long run in this day and age. Certainly someone at some time would see him. And that would be a problem. Dragons can be killed.

"Or you might be put in a zoo," said Katie. "Although there would be problems with feeding you. Maybe it would have to be a special zoo."

The dragon hissed his displeasure. He shook his great head from side to side.

Brian held out the cookies that accompanied the sandwiches. At his urging, the dragon ate all of them. Brian had been thinking and realized that things had come to a pass; it seemed a time for the dragon to make choice.

"If you stay here you'll either have to sleep or you'll be discovered," he said. The dragon nodded. "So, sleep?" asked Brian.

"*Non possumus*," he said indicated each of them with his head. He was awake — the children had seen to that — so that ruled out dreaming his life away and to die sleeping.

"And discovery?" asked Katie. The dragon chuffed unpleasantly.

"That only leaves leaving," Katie said. "So, where would you go? South America? A desert in Africa?" The dragon negated each suggestion.

"Home?" asked Brian. The dragon nodded and looked intently at them.

"But things will be very different back where you came from," Katie said. "It's probably just like here. And if you're going back, are you going to try to find your brother…your half-brother? How will you know if he's still alive? What will you do to find him? Surely, he's moved in the last thousand years. And how are you going to go there without attracting a lot of attention?"

Katie was asking so many questions that the dragon finally had to silence her by nudging her in the stomach with his nose.

"Oh, sorry. I just saw all these scary pictures in my mind and I can't imagine how you'd go back and fight. Do you have to do it alone?"

The dragon shook his head slowly from side to side. No, not alone. Katie began suddenly to feel quite nervous as the great golden eyes looked into hers. There was something there, all right, and it looked a lot like a question.

Brian interrupted the stare with his reminder of the time: "We've got to get going or we're gonna be history, too. We'll come back as soon as we can, but it might not be tomorrow. Will you be okay?" The dragon nodded.

"And, whatever you do," added Katie, "try not to eat people. They don't like it."

In pledge, the dragon held up his foreclaw and snorted. Katie wondered if he also was laughing, although she didn't hear his "chuff-chuff-chuff." Maybe he was smiling instead, but a dragon smiling bore an uncommon resemblance to a dragon frowning.

Chapter 7

THE NEXT TO LAST TEAR VANISHES

For her part, Mrs. Robinson had been in touch with Reme's mother and learned that he had not gone along. She had then quizzed the children: "And what did you do with the extra sandwich?"

"You never saw a hungrier dragon," began Katie picking up on her supposed fabrication of the morning. Then she knew she was about to tell a lie; she crossed the fingers of her right hand behind her back. "We were really extra hungry, Mrs. Robinson, and we ate it. Every single crumb and morsel."

"And the cookies," said Brian. "You know, you never have to worry about them going to waste. And they were eaten with a new appreciation."

Mrs. Robinson looked gratified. She blushed as she offered them a fresh plate "Baked just while you were away. I had a suspicion that the detective might come back, and he seemed to like them, too."

Brian didn't hesitate to snarf down a few accompanied with milk; Katie took one and nibbled. She didn't like the idea of lying to Mrs. Robinson, her mother, Detective Grosskopf, or anybody else, for that matter. Her father had taught her that a lie was a bad way to build or maintain trust. An untruth was a poor way to reward someone you liked. But she and Brian were committed to the lie now, and there was no easy way out; the truth seemed too impossible to believe.

They said their goodbyes and walked out the door. Katie and Brian then aimed for Reme's before they went along home. Again, his mother answered the door. She looked more tired, more haggard than before. This time, though, she invited them inside and began to set out milk and cookies when Brian told her that they had just eaten some.

Reme's mother left them at the kitchen table and resumed what she had been doing all day long: walking a path about the house. From room to room, window to window.

Reme told Katie and Brian that she'd been very upset: "She doesn't like the idea that somebody could just break into the house. She's worried about what might have happened if we'd been here. I don't think she slept at all last night and it sure doesn't look like she's going to tonight, either."

"Mrs. Robinson's upset, too," said Brian. "But it's not anything like this. Your mom is really serious about this."

"She and dad used to live in a big city," Reme explained. "But they moved here after something bad happened. That was before I came to live with them, before I was adopted. Dad's supposed to be home in an hour, and I'd say he couldn't be here too soon. He'll know what to do."

Reme paused and then shifted in the kitchen chair. The vinyl squeaked as the exposed part of his left leg dragged across it. "And I'm scared, too. On my way home yesterday I thought we were being followed. I didn't really see anybody walking behind me... just somebody who came out of The Dragon and The Rose. But...."

Katie shivered.

Reme gathered his pluck and smiled a little. "So, what's new with the dragon? Same old stuff?"

All three smiled shyly at the ridiculous thought of a same old dragon. Taking turns, Katie and Brian related all they'd learned through twenty questions. Then Reme added a few thoughts of his own; he'd been busy with ideas all afternoon. "You know how you said the Dragon's bride must be more than a thousand years old. Don't you remember? She was turned into a stone statue. She may be old, but if she's still in one piece, maybe the spell can be reversed. And, maybe she'll only be as old as she was when the Rose cast the spell on her."

Katie and Brian both liked the sound of that. And they related the idea that the dragon was going to do something now that he was awake. Maybe there was a way they could help with whatever he was planning; Katie knew there had been a question in his eyes. With lighter hearts, the two set off toward home.

This time it was Brian who sensed that he and Katie were being observed. He looked about as they neared their house. Maybe, he thought, it had something to do with what Reme had said and he was just being imaginative. Or maybe there were more police in the area and he could sense them watching. He scanned the street to see if there was a patrol car nearby. Nope, nothing. They went up the drive.

Inside the kitchen, their mother began by telling them about the evening's plans: "Brian, you need two more white shirts, and Katie needs a new blouse to go with the school slacks we bought last month. So, I thought after dinner we'd take care of the last of the clothes and pick up whatever school supplies you still need. Then, if we're all really good..." — she said this smiling — "...maybe we can go for ice cream at Pflughler's Drug Store."

Both Katie and Brian thought the plan reasonable, though perhaps a little inconvenient; Brian wanted to look into the book on dragons his grandfather had left behind. There was a lot of reading to do.

Their mother took extra precautions locking the doors before they left. "The break-in at Reme's house has me a little worried," she explained.

Katie agreed: "Yeah, Mrs. Robinson said we were to tell you to lock the doors really well. It sure is funny the way Mrs. Robinson has reacted to the break-in, especially compared to Reme's mom. She's really nervous."

Mrs. Eames looked significantly at her daughter as she climbed into the front passenger seat. "Perhaps if you had been through what Reme's mom has been through, you'd be upset too."

"But what makes her that way?"

"I'll tell you about it later, when you're older." With that, she started the car, and they drove off.

Katie reflected that sometimes adults went out of their way to make things confusing.

Then her mother changed the topic: "I think it was a really good idea for the school to try uniforms last year. Everybody's dressed the same, and it's made my life simpler. That way you can save your good clothes for really special functions. And you don't have to decide what to wear every day."

Katie did have to admit it made getting dressed in the morning a real snap, but there were still some areas where people could show their individuality: "Even though it's a white shirt or blouse," she said, "there's white-plain and there's white-fancy. And some of the guys have these really cool socks: they're dark blue where you can see 'em, but above that they have patterns. I'll show you if I can find a pair."

They found not only a whole rack of them in Steketee's Clothiers but signs, too, that indicated that the socks met the letter of the school dress code. Mrs. Eames initially was not impressed: "Okay, so you can get by with them."

"No, really they're okay," said Brian. "A lot of the guys wear them. But I don't have to have any."

Brian sighed softly and turned away. Just the basics, he thought; that's all we can afford.

He was surprised when his mother looked at him and asked which of the many patterns was his favorite. After he made his selection and the socks had found their way under their mother's arm, she stopped by a rack of sweatshirts which bore the emblem of the school team, the Sea Hawks. Mrs. Eames carefully noted the stitching and garment weight. Then she took one off the rack and held it up to Brian's chest.

"What do you think?" she asked. "Would this be good for after school and just bumming around? Maybe for after football practice?"

Brian nodded wordlessly. It would be better than good. With care, his mother added it to their other intended purchases. "Thanks, Mom," he said very quietly, but loud enough so she'd hear it. In return, she nodded and smiled.

There was something special for Katie, too: a good, dress-up blouse. "You might wear it with a skirt, and it should look nice with dress slacks or even jeans," said Mrs. Eames after Katie picked out the one she liked best.

After they'd paid and left the store, Mrs. Eames directed their walk to a corner where ice cream was dug out of paperboard containers that were hidden in the depths of an old, white freezer at the back of Pflughler's Drug Store.

Mr. Pflughler presided behind the prescription counter and would tell anyone, young or old, whether they'd heard it or not, that the name Pflughler rhymed with bugler. In consequence, he sometimes had to take checks made out to Bugler's Drug Store, a matter that caused tellers at the local bank no small amusement.

Tonight, a high school student — her name badge said Theresa — held sway behind the soda fountain. Mrs. Eames set her packages on the marble counter and then sat on one of the round button stools. Katie and Brian sat on her right.

"Let's see.... I'd like a root beer float," she said. "Those always taste extra special here. What would you like Katie? Brian?"

"I'd like a double scoop of vanilla with hot fudge," said Brian, hurrying to add a "Please."

Katie took her time. She looked at the menu board and then asked her mother: "May I please have a half banana split? Is that too much?"

Her mother shook her head: "No, it's not too much. And, yes, you may have that if Theresa is willing to make it."

Theresa was, and soon all three of the Eames family were either sucking on a straw, stretching out hot fudge, or sculpting whipped cream. All this was undertaken with the most delicious sense that the experience might go on for some time. There was no hurry; everyone was content. Even Theresa who, admiring her handiwork, leaned against the counter, twirling her short, dark hair around the index finger of her left hand.

Soon they found themselves sipping at the water that Theresa had provided and looking forward to the trip home where they'd examine and try on their purchases. Brian realized that his mother had bought only clothes for them and not anything for herself. He wondered if she'd do her own shopping later, or whether there was even enough money for her to buy new clothes.

Once home they entered the fray of unpacking and trying on. Katie picked out a skirt, and the blouse looked just perfect, good enough for parties, maybe a special school function, or church.

Brian put on some newer jeans and found the sweatshirt made a great total look. He was either going to be a Sea Hawk as a player or a supporter. He rather thought he'd most like to be a player. Practice for the football team started soon — too soon. He'd have to do a lot of running then. Maybe he'd get fast enough so he could regularly beat Katie. None of his football friends knew he got beat by his sister; they just knew he was slower than they were.

Such were his thoughts as he turned to his dresser in order to put his new sweatshirt away. He stopped when he pulled out the second drawer. Brian knew he was not an overly tidy kid, but what met his eye when he slid out the drawer was definitely not his work. Or his mom's. Somebody had been through it. He tried the others, all with the same result. He turned to his closet and then the stuff at his desk. Everything had been moved or touched.

"Hey, Katie," he called softly. "Check this."

Katie spent a few minutes in her own room verifying that everything there had been moved, too. "Whoever it was had time to put everything back in place," she said.

"Yeah, but do you think 'whoever it was' might still be in the house?" Brian's question sent Katie's pulse racing. "And, do we tell Mom, or what?"

"I vote for 'or what,'" said Brian. "Especially if there's any chance she'd turn into what Reme's mother is doing. I don't think I could take that. And, besides, we know what he was after." With that Brian dug into his old jeans' left-hand pocket and withdrew his dragon's tear. Katie turned from his room and scuttled to her own, only to return in a minute, crestfallen: "I put mine in my jewel box and he took it," she said.

"Ah, well, it'll be all right. You'll see," said Brian. "At the rate that dragon laughs or cries we'll have more in a couple of days. It's just that I don't like the thought that somebody knows something about what we're doing. And that somebody had to learn about it at Mr. Teagarden's. And you know, I don't think it's Dr. Joe; Mr. Teagarden trusts him. Mr. Teagarden didn't hesitate to ask him about the stone. But it could be him...Dr. Joe. I mean, he knows the story, some parts even better than Mr. Teagarden."

"Speaking of Mr. Teagarden," Katie said slowly. "Do you suppose it's a coincidence that he just happened to settle near where we found the dragon?"

Katie and Brian looked at each other and shook their heads. "I don't know if it's a coincidence; he's been here since before we were born. But I know whoever broke in here, it couldn't be Mr. Teagarden," said Katie. "He'd never...." She paused shaking her head.

Roused, Brian asked: "Well, are we calling the police, or do we look through the house to make sure whoever it was is gone?"

Not the police. Instead, together they moved through the small house, room by room, closet by closet, upstairs and down. At length they were in the basement.

Brian found a misplaced baseball mitt and Katie gained a new appreciation of just how sinister the laundry room could look, but the only sign of their intruder was the basement window that had been dislodged while the intruder was breaking in. It had been closed and locked with a hook, but a sharp kick had disabled the metal fastening and allowed easy access. ...And maybe exit, but sneaking out the side door would have been easier.

"At least he's gone," said Brian after they searched all the basement. He went to the wood scrap pile next to his father's workbench, selected a piece that would do. "Here, let me see if I can wedge this closed." He moved a short stepladder below the window and stepped up to jam the wood in place. Then he climbed down. After they determined that nowhere else were there signs of intrusion, they returned to their rooms.

Upstairs again, they were confronted by their mother: "Somebody's been through my jewelry box. Do either of you know anything about that?"

Katie looked at Brian for a clue and then back at her mother: "Oh, Mom, I meant to tell you: I was looking for a safety pin earlier tonight and I was in a hurry. Did I leave it a mess?"

"No, not a great mess, but I could tell someone had been in it. And, besides, you know I don't keep safety pins there."

"I know, but I forgot, and I was in a hurry."

Mrs. Eames looked at her daughter sharply. Katie's eyes fell to the floor. "Katie, I'm entitled to some privacy, the same way you are. I don't like other people going through my things without my knowing."

"Yes, ma'am," replied Katie quietly, wondering at herself. She was getting awfully good at lying in pretty short order. At the same time, she wondered how her mother would feel if she knew that a stranger had been going through her jewelry box.

And, what if something was missing? What would Katie do then?

"Did I put everything back in the right place?" she asked, hoping that everything was accounted for. Her mother had only a very few good pieces, but these mattered a lot to her, especially her wedding ring. But that would never be in the drawer; she always wore it day and night, except when she was washing dishes or cleaning.

As they readied for bed Brian asked her: "What did you say that for? Why did you lie? Maybe we should have told her the truth."

"I just don't want her to turn into Reme's mom. Almost anything would be better than that."

So, instead of their mother losing sleep, Katie and Brian tossed and turned, imagining every squeak of the old house as a return of their intruder.

Chapter 8

"OF DRAGONS AND THEIR LAIRS"

That was the title of the chapter he was reading in the book given to him by his grandfather. Brian had trouble making out the words for a bit. The tall "S"s looked like "F"s—it took time to work out the spelling, and the words seemed to have different meanings. Right away he guessed that "awefull" didn't mean the same as the "awful" that he was used to. He'd already learned what a squire was supposed to do, and he'd brushed up on his courtly manners...he'd know when to bow if a queen or one of her ladies in waiting entered the room. But he was just skimming the early chapters; he wanted to know about dragons.

Brian had given up on sleep and, instead, decided to read at his desk. The great, ancient book groaned and cracked as he turned the pages. Here were the chapters on the mythical beasts. After "Of Dragons and Their Lairs" came "On the Fighting of Dragons," "Spells and Incantations," "The Perfidy of Dragons," and, lastly, "The Taming of Dragons." Brian wanted to know everything about dragons. But pages seemed to bunch up and wouldn't lie flat, so he put the book open on his desk, stood and leaned down on it. The binding gave a great crack as if after a long strain, it had finally snapped. Brian blanched. Now he'd done it... ruined a family treasure. Brian stopped and looked carefully at the book. The binding was perhaps looser, allowing it to open more fully, but he couldn't see any other damage. Very slowly he raised the book and turned it upside down. In the process, what he took for a piece of pasteboard slipped from between the loosened leather covering and the book spine and landed on the floor. Drat! He'd really done it now. Whatever it was belonged in the book, perhaps as something to stiffen the book spine.

As he set down the book and picked up the thing that had fallen, his own spine stiffened and he sat straighter in his chair. Between his fingers lay a piece of very old...what was it? Pasteboard? Paper? No, at least, not like any paper he'd ever seen. And it was folded and coated with some kind of light glue. With infinite care he teased apart the edges. Good, it was intended to come apart, he thought.

Brian noted that it wasn't printed, but was, instead, written in a very old style of writing, perhaps older than the book.

"Whereas it pleaseth us to reward Robert Eames, Dragon Master, with ownership of Norcross Manor for his work in the Holy Quest to rid our land of the Dread Peril of the Beast that flyeth by day and by night.

"Whereas Robert Eames is himself from a long line of Dragon Masters from time out of mind.

"And, whereas our good Lord Eames has he, himself, pledged his sacred honor and fortune to our cause and pledged his progeny from this day forward, too.

"Whereas he has surpassed even our most hopeful expectation in ridding us of a plague Dragon, to wit the Monster of the Latter Doom. And because he's promised to rid us of all Dragons except the One he is foresworn to protect {that being from his family's former country of the River Wye in the land of Wales and unlikely to trouble us here}.

"Let it be known that Robert Eames and his own, hence forward and for ever more, shall be known as the Dragon Slayers, and shall inhabit Norcross without hindrance or let, from this day forward.

"By the favor of His Majesty..."

And here the document was blackened with age and beyond all recognition. Only the date stood out at the bottom: "*Anno Domini 1233.*"

Brian felt it yet again between his fingers, concentrating on its pliability and thickness. No, definitely not paper.

Brian couldn't think of the best thing to do with the document. Maybe he should refold it and replace it in the book. But, then, it might be broken as he turned the pages. He knew he should keep it out of direct sun. At last he carefully let it assume whatever folded shaped it chose...about half-way open...and he put it on the top shelf of his closet.

He doubted very much whether his grandfather knew anything about it. The book, important and interesting as it was, served only as a cover for this thing that said that, once upon a time, some ancient Robert Eames had been very good at fighting dragons but was pledged to defend one, too.

Brian felt very proud of this remote Robert. Heretofore, he'd always thought that the Eames name was kind of wimpy, a sissy name. Now he knew better. It stood for something. And, for a while at least, the Eames had lived and held a place called Norcross...Brian figured that stood for North Cross. Maybe the Eames family had even served in the Crusades. Maybe someone from the family still held the castle, but his father had never said anything as dramatic as that.

Brian was lost in thought as he returned to the book and slowly turned the pages. The book fell open to the last chapter: "The Taming of Dragons."

He read:

"Tho the natural Dragon be perfidious to the utmost part of its soul, still there is one spell stronger than any other. It is the same spell that maketh the unicorn to lay down in docile obedience and maketh all manner of evil to.

"That is the spell of the virgin.

"Only a virgin without spot can draw nigh with impunity. The Dragon, who doth love our Lord like a Christian, also holdeth in highest regard His Mother. And like the Virgin Queene of Heaven is she who is without spot of sin. This doth the Dragon know, and herein is he true, tho in all else, he may be false.

"But so long as she is pure, she is safe, and the Dragon will do her bidding."

What followed next was a series of suggestions of using young women to approach a dragon in hopes of taming, but, failing that, either banishing or killing the beast.

Brian wondered if anyone ever thought to ask whether the poor girls were willing to be herded along to the dragon's lair in hopes of influencing the awful beasts.

And, yes, they were awful, assured the books; that is, they filled one with awe. That's what Brian had felt as he stood before the beast in the cave. Brian wondered if the fact that he and Reme were safe and still claimed their skins was because of Katie. He decided that it wouldn't be a good idea to go to the cave without her.

And he wondered about what the book had called a "natural" dragon. Was theirs an unnatural dragon because he was an enchanted king? Would that make him better or worse? More trustworthy or less so? The book didn't seem to cover that.

There was more, lots more, but it dealt in spells and formulae.

Tired but excited, he lay down on his bed to think: Robert Eames the dragon killer, whose blood even now coursed through his veins. Norcross. And the incidence — not a coincidence — of a dragon practically in his own back yard....

And he slept.

And while he slept there came a dream.

He found himself high on a misty hill. Around him the country stretched in all directions without interruption: no houses, no factories, no roads. Far away, a man approached, leading something. That something grew into a horse as they neared. The steed was covered in battle armaments. Brian watched closely as they climbed the hill, this man and his horse, both covered with blood and muck, as if they'd been in battle royal. At last they drew up, and Brian was surprised at the size of both man and beast. They were small and very thin.

For a long time Brian and the man looked at each other. There were no smiles, no discomfort at the silence, nothing to indicate that the usual civilities were attendant. The horse looked first at the man who led it and then turned to study Brian.

Brian saw the vaguely familiar droop of the warrior's left eyelid. There was something very familiar about the way the little man stood, too. Familiar and comforting.

Then the man tilted his head back, and Brian recognized with a start that in just such a way did his father prepare to speak.

"You are the latest, then," said the man, bending over to wipe his gore-spattered hands on the grass. He stood and wiped them again on his trousers. "It has been long since one of our blood has opened the sacred seal that affirms for all who see it, that we are, in truth, the slayers of dragons."

Here he withdrew his sword from a bundle of rags and knelt down. He motioned for Brian to join him. Brian fell to his knees.

"See, here I come from my last kill," said the man tossing his head to indicate where he'd been. "Again and again do I come by this path from the last battle. Day by weary day do I walk here and each time I see nothing save the fog and the mist."

Plucking handfuls of grass, he wiped down the blade, dislodging blood and pieces of flesh. The stink of gore was sweetened by the smell of the fresh grass. With exquisite care he wiped off the stones and jewels of the sword hilt.

When he'd finished with the grass he stood, leaving Brian on the ground, pulled a chamois out from a pack on the horse and sat down again, carefully polishing the sword. The horse, obviously used to the routine, dropped his head and began to eat of the fodder at his hooves, jingling all the while the accouterments that surrounded his face.

Words vaguely sounded through Brian's mind: "*Non est vivere sed valere vita est.*" Brian looked back as the man polished and polished the blade.

He nodded at Brian and then spoke: "'*Non est vivere...*' It's the family motto, yours and mine, and has been since the beginning of our line. It means that life is more than just being alive. Life has purpose...mine, yours, even the dragon's. Perhaps especially the dragon's. There is no unkindness in what I do...no ill will or hate. That is not our way. We are to serve a higher good, to be good at need. From my forebears—he who served the Dragon Lord—to me, and now to you...we are called. We are pledged to the Dragon Lord and to the good God whom he served. Our choice is this: answer or not. Which will you choose?" The diminutive man paused and looked at Brian.

There was no urgency to respond. Brian thought of all that a willing heart might be asked to give and he assented. The man nodded and smiled a very little.

"True steel, this," the dragon slayer said at last, holding up a gleaming metal. "It was made to take the place of another that's been lost. The first sword, the true sword, belonged to the Dragon Lord. From all accounts this is a fair copy. And, as such, it's very good for its purpose."

Brian stared at the blade flashing as if it were in the sun while everything else was still in a mist. The three top-most stones on the hilt formed a red crescent.

"Always take care of your blade and it will always take care of you." The man said as he stood again; this time Brian rose, too. "There are other things for you to learn. But you must learn them from other teachers. I am content we have met." He smiled again slightly. "And here you are on perhaps the three-hundred thousandth time I've come this way after the kill. And simply by your presence you come with a message for me that the future is still filled with dragons and dragon slayers.

"This is good news indeed, for dragon slayers we must be. That is our calling, as God has willed it," and here the man crossed himself using the first and second fingers of his right hand. He seemed to tap them twice on his forehead, his abdomen, his left and right shoulders, and then to his lips.

"I see now that your part in this business is as yet begun but not ended," he said looking very directly and calmly at Brian. "For this you must travel farther and faster than the hawk. And where you travel, there you shall struggle with all the evil in Hell before which you must stand. ...You and she who is blood to you and to me. She is stronger by far than the evil that lurks, the evil that waits upon a man to weigh him down. And beyond that evil there is the killing you alone must do, for the death is a delivery, a salvation. I shall be with you—both of you—at the end. Your sword shall be my sword; your hand shall be my hand. For you are the rightful inheritors."

The figure, which had begun to look more and more like his father, sheathed his sword. The blade flashed as it slid into the sheath. It seemed to Brian that the light was suddenly hidden inside the sheath, but was streaming out from every crack or crevice.

The man then turned to grasp the reins of the horse, who unmindful of the impending interruption, continued to pull grass. Man and boy looked at each other again. What the man saw was known to him alone, but he exhibited no dismay or displeasure. The boy saw the warm spark of intelligence, of dedication and purpose. He also saw age upon age of duty and, now, after a battle that had been fought again and again, much weariness. But there was hope, too. At last the man dropped his eyes and smiled.

At a gentle tug of the reins the beast raised his head, shook his mane, and gazed again with interest at Brian. The two moved a few paces off and Brian made to follow when the warrior turned and raised his right hand in salute.

"*Vale, victor!*"

Brian wanted to cry out to him to stay, but he found himself, instead, raising his right hand to return the salute and instead of a cry he uttered "*Vale!*" as the figures of man and horse turned away and faded into the mist.

With a sob he awoke.

Why did he have to dream that dream? His father had been there. It was his father, wasn't it? Why couldn't he have stayed asleep and dreamed more? Why couldn't they have talked? There was so much he wanted to tell him, so much he wanted to hear.

Wiping the tears out of his eyes he looked out the window. Just like his dream, the scene outside was shrouded in fog and mist.

Brian sat for a long time on the edge of his bed, looking out into the dawning sky. There was no hurry, he knew, but he wanted, suddenly, to be about his work, his business, whatever it was. He stood and began to dress.

After he'd readied his room he moved to open his door. Something was wrong with the handle; it didn't turn as easily as normal and before he could swing the door in he had to push out against it. When he did and turned the knob it suddenly flew open toward him. There had been something leaning against... something that now fell into the room.

With relief Brian saw it was just Katie, but Katie wrapped in her blanket.

"You didn't have to do that!" she said crossly.

"Do what? I was trying to get my door open. You had it pretty well jammed. In fact, I had to push out to open in."

"I know. I felt it."

"So, was my door especially comfortable or something last night?"

"It most certainly was not," she said, still angry. "I was dreaming and I just wanted...." She paused and lowered her head so

Brian couldn't see her eyes. He could, however, see the tears as they fell one by one onto the blanket in her lap. "I was dreaming of Dad, and when I woke up I didn't want him to be gone, so I came here."

"Yeah, me, too," said Brian. "I was dreaming of somebody who turned out to be Dad. And there were dragons, and I don't know what all. It's all mixed up, but it sure seemed real. And he was right here with me. Do you suppose that can happen? Was it a ghost? Would Dad come back to haunt us?"

"I don't think so, but I'd settle for it just to see him again," said Katie, sniffling and drying her tears. Brian automatically went back into his room and retrieved a tissue from his desk, where he saw the ancient book open and the charter spread out. What was the charter doing on his desk? He distinctly remembered putting in on a closet shelf. How did it get back on his desk? He'd have to think about that later. For now, he returned with the tissue for Katie and then helped her to her feet.

"Come on in here; there's something I have to show you." He led her to the desk. "I was looking through this book from Grandpa and look what fell out. It's a charter for Eameses to be dragon slayers. Look at the way it's done. Like with flourishes and stuff. Do you think it's real?"

With great care, Katie picked up the document and read it. Then she held it up to the desk light.

"It's on vellum...that's really thin sheep skin. And it lasts forever."

"Yuck! Sheep skin?" said Brian, dropping his hand away from the document. "You mean, that once covered some sheep?"

Katie nodded abstractedly. "That's what I mean, all right, but there's a reason. And this might be what Dad was talking about in my dream. I couldn't make sense of what he was trying to tell me. That's what was so frustrating: he kept saying something about the contract: 'the contract alloweth this, the contract demandeth that.' He never talked like that in real life."

"Are you sure it was Dad? Or could it have been somebody else? Somebody else maybe who looked like Dad but who was a lot older...really ancient?"

Katie started to speak and then paused. "I don't know.... I thought it was Dad, and I wanted it to be Dad. But he didn't seem like Dad. He wasn't friendly like he was happy to see me. He was more respectful, like he was just meeting me, and he didn't treat me like Dad did, and he didn't smile; he was really serious all the time. He said something, well, about 'in light of my virginity.'"

"That, too?" asked Brian. "That's in the book. Here, look. Only virgins can tame dragons, or, at least, the natural dragons. I don't know about the other kind. And it works for unicorns, and against any evil, too."

Katie gave a little laugh, followed by a quick, indrawn breath, and then — almost as if it were against her will — she started laughing very loudly. Brian couldn't help himself, and before they knew it, they were rolling on the floor.

How long they laughed escaped them, but they stopped when they heard their mother: "And what is this?" She stood towering above them. Or it seemed that she towered, but perhaps that was because they were flat on the floor.

Brian stopped laughing first and sat up. "Hi, Mom," he said, wiping tears of laughter out of his eyes.

"What has you guys so deliriously happy this morning?" she asked pointedly.

"Virgins," said Katie, "...for dragons and unicorns." And she started laughing again.

Brian watched as his mother's face went from dismay, to concern, to amusement, until she too was smiling.

"So, anyway, what got you onto the idea of dancing virgins this morning?" she asked.

"It was something I read in the book that I got from Grandpa Eames, about dragons and stuff. You need a virgin to tame one."

"And I had a dream," interrupted Katie, "About that since I was one, I was supposed to..." she faltered. "I was supposed to do...something."

"I had a dream, too," said their mother wistfully. "I'd almost forgotten it, until you spoke of dreams. You — both of you — were supposed to go away and I had to let you. I didn't know when or even if you were coming back. I was so sad. I didn't want you to go. But I was told in no uncertain terms that you had to. The dream seemed so real at the time, but by the time I'd awakened, I forgotten all about it. I wonder what they mean, these dreams?

But I suppose mine could just be one of those things that happens to parents when their children start to grow up."

Katie rose from her seat at the table and stood beside her mother. "Don't worry, Mom. If we go away, we'll always come back to visit. I promise." Very softly, she kissed her mother on the cheek. Brian saw the tears start out in his mother's eyes and wondered if she, too, had dreamed of Dad last night.

Later, much later, he remembered that as one of the best things that ever happened to him. It was innocent, pure, and very happy.

Chapter 9

MR. TEAGARDEN HELPS ARRANGE
A RUSE

Reme's father had returned and managed to give his wife the comfort and support she needed. She was calmed, and by the next day, Reme was once more able to join Brian and Katie as they headed off on another adventure complete with more of Mrs. Robinson's sandwiches.

"Even an extra one for the dragon," Mrs. Robinson had explained, sharing a laugh with Katie. Well, Katie had sort of laughed. Reme had also begged an extra sandwich at his house, but when the three youngsters came together to analyze their trophies—five sandwiches in all—they realized it might still be too little, even if all of them gave up their own lunches. And, while they'd do that before allowing themselves to be hideously eaten by a famished dragon, the resulting hunger was not something to be highly desired.

"I know," said Katie. "Let's stop at Mr. Teagarden's and see if he has any extra food that he's otherwise going to throw away; not that it's bad now, but that he knows he's not gonna serve before it does go bad."

"Yeah," said Brian with a sudden flatness in his voice. "And what do we tell him? Remember that whoever it was that broke into our houses had to find out at The Dragon and The Rose that we had the dragon tears. We didn't show 'em to anybody else"

Reme was mystified. In the end, Brian and Katie both had to explain their break-in and confirm their suppositions, too, that the pub played some role in the unpleasant events at their house, Mrs. Robinson's, and Reme's.

"I know Mr. Teagarden, and he would never, ever, do something that would hurt us," said Reme to Brian. "You know he doesn't break the law, not even a little. And if he wanted the dragon tears, all he'd have to do would be to ask. I couldn't refuse his request even if I didn't want to give it to him. How many times has he given us lemonade or iced tea, or snacks and sandwiches, or just plain water when we've been hot and thirsty? And he's never asked for a penny in return, not even from our parents. I agree that somebody there has been paying more attention than he ought but it's not Mr. Teagarden. And if he trusted Dr. Joe enough to ask him about the dragon tears, that clears Dr. Joe with me, too."

Brian listened with surprise of Reme's forwardness. In the end he had to agree: "Yeah, well, let's go in there, then, and see if we can't figure out who's been climbing into our houses."

Mr. Teagarden was busy preparing for his lunch crowd when the three walked into the common room.

"Do you know? I had just about given up hope of seeing you again," he said as he lifted a tray of glasses to the top of the bar. "I thought I'd done something that displeased you, and that you'd given up on old Amos."

"Oh, no," said Katie with some distress while Brian blushed furiously.

Reme moved forward to speak: "We've been so busy getting ready for school and with the break-ins and all."

"Ah, those 'break-ins' as you call them," said Mr. Teagarden warily. "I've got my own idea about that." He leaned conspiratorially over the bar. "I think I've been entertaining unaware the culprit."

Brian and Katie gasped aloud.

"Is it Dr. Joe?" asked Brian.

Mr. Teagarden looked about in alarm, all the while pushing his hands down on the air above the bar.

"Soft now, soft!" he warned. "No. Certainly not Joe. That's a nonstarter. But I think that somebody has been taking a very active interest in what you've been up to, following you, like, and perhaps trying to steal certain somethings?"

Katie nodded. "And he got 'em, too...at least, two of three we brought home."

"He? Did I say it was a he?" asked Mr. Teagarden.

"Well, who is it then?" posed Brian, in a rather louder voice.

"Shhhh. Shhhh. She's in there, in the snug." Mr. Teagarden had explained before to the children that the snug was a separate section of the bar, set off in ancient days for women. In The Dragon and The Rose it was a little room off to the side near the front entrance. "I wondered what she'd been up to sitting there for hours and ordering just one cup of coffee. I looked in through the service door from the kitchen and saw her watching your approach just now. She was standing at the open windowspace and as soon as she saw you coming she ran back to her booth to sit behind a newspaper. And I know she was in that room on the day you showed us the dragon tear, the very first one."

"But, who?" said Katie.

"Maevis Blenchly," said Mr. Teagarden in a whisper. The name meant nothing to the children. "She's the one who owns the specialty antique shop up the road. It's dark and set off the street, but there's almost always some traffic there. Enough so that Maevis said she preferred to leave her assistant in change and come here for her coffee and to do her books.

"A few days ago she asked me about you three, when you'd be likely to call in and all. She's never mentioned you before and to the best of my knowledge she's never met you, at least not in here. She's not the sort who would seem to like children. She didn't bring her bookkeeping with her. Quite frankly, whatever she's up to is giving me the willies."

"And she's in there now?" Katie needed confirmation.

Mr. Teagarden nodded: "Yes, but I'll bet if you turned to look at the window in the partition, you'd see her face in it, studying us. No, don't turn around, Katie. I can tell you from where I stand right now that she's there and has been for almost all our conversation. I suggest that you move away and begin telling me anything you like, any old story about what you're going to do today. Whatever you do, don't tell whatever it is you have planned. And be loud about it."

Katie moved to a booth farther out in the room and sat down: "Yes, please, a glass of iced tea would be very nice just now, Mr. Teagarden. What about you Brian? Reme? You take such good care of us, Mr. Teagarden, and we have a busy day. We thought we'd walk downtown; I have to get some school supplies and Reme wants to look at some clothes."

Mr. Teagarden brought over their drinks. Katie permitted herself one quick look toward the snug and shivered when she saw the face in profile, turning an ear toward their business. The face was thin, almost fleshless, and the hair — curling and twisted — added nothing of any grace. Katie thought the woman reminded her of an evil bird wrapped in somber feathers. She caught sight of a dark coat with a dark floral print. Dead flowers, she thought. Dead, dead, dead.

Katie kept chattering. Neither Brian nor Reme could join in the pretense, and it was hard work for Katie to keep up her end of the conversation while thinking. When she'd resolved her plan she carried her glasses to the bar and said to Mr. Teagarden: "May we come back at three? We should be all done then." She winked very markedly to let him know they wouldn't do any such thing.

He nodded and smiled: "Until three, then."

The children walked outside with apparent calm and then dashed down the block, into town. About halfway down the block, past Brian and Katie's house, they hid behind a hedge. Sure enough, pushing her brittle way into the sunlight, came a crabbed and dark-cloaked figure that started off in pursuit.

"If she's coming this way, then we'd better cut through the back yard and head the other way," said Brian.

"Right," said Katie.

And that's what they did. Even with their bikes they cut through a yard to a street that ran parallel to their own and then headed back out of town. A little farther outside of town, they'd join that magical road that would take them to the clearing and the cave. They had been delayed briefly in leading their pursuer astray, but they'd get there all the same.

Brian rode silently beside Katie for almost a quarter mile before he asked: "What's so important about three o'clock?"

"Glad you asked," she said brightly. "That's when we're going to pay a visit to her store...and I didn't want her there then. Instead, she'll be waiting for us at The Dragon and The Rose. We'll see if her store's the kind of place where a thief could sell dragon tears."

"Oh," said Brian and pedaled on in silence.

When they arrived at the clearing, Katie was the first to climb down the rope; Brian had explained to Reme the importance of virgins in the process of taming dragons. With some hesitation Brian went next into the hole; he was, after all, supposed to be a dragon slayer who was from a long line of dragon slayers. Brian found to his own consternation that it's one thing to know something of dragon slaying in the abstract but quite another to face the reality of a dragon, and a hungry one at that. Still, over the edge he'd gone. Half way down he let go of the rope and dropped to the cave floor.

The dragon regarded him carefully and hissed a welcome. Then he returned his attention to Katie, who was speedily but carefully unwrapping sandwiches. The dragon opened his mouth just enough for steam and smoke to lazily escape. His lizard tongue rolled out the side of his mouth curling around his teeth in the process. The tongue was bright red with the central strip of shiny black. As Katie fed him each half sandwich, the dragon would close his eyes and make his purring sound.

Brian, Reme, and Katie each had a half sandwich and one cookie. The dragon got everything else. And he ate everything with great satisfaction. At last, when every morsel had been delivered, the dragon carefully shifted position and brought his tail up and around his front paws.

Katie walked up to the dragon and asked: "Did you have enough?"

For reply the dragon belched, ending a puff of smoke toward the roof of the cave and spoke: "*Sufficit.*" That required no explanation, but then he added: "*Vita non est vivere sed valere vita est,*" and cast his eyes at Brian. The dragon's gaze triggered his dream from the night before.

Reme cast the words about a few times. "'Life is...more... than living.' I don't get it." The dragon repeated himself and, as he finished, Reme jumped with enthusiasm: "'Life is more than just living; not just living, but to be lived strongly.'" The dragon snorted.

"It's our family motto," said Brian. "At least, I think it is, and that's what it means."

The dragon nodded.

"I think we have a problem," interjected Katie. With some thought she laid out before the dragon the news that his tears had been stolen, that Mr. Teagarden knew that something was going on out here, and she wasn't sure that the dragon was at all safe. "What will happen if you're discovered? Could they really take you away to a zoo or lock you up?"

"*Minime*," said the dragon. "*Fugit irreparabile tempus. Vincam aut moriar.*"

"No," said Reme. "He's not going to a zoo. He has to do something and time is passing. He says he'll either conquer or die."

The dragon nodded in agreement. He paused and looked at them each in turn: "*Et tu?*"

Reme was last: "And I think he means that we're supposed to help him. He asked if we would."

What followed was a counsel of war. The dragon had mixed feelings that adults knew of his existence from his tears. On the one hand, every time Maevis' name was mentioned the dragon gave out with a small puff of smoke. But by contrast, every time Mr. Teagarden's name came up he purred. He even repeated it: "*Te, le Gardien.*"

Katie was amazed that a dragon that had no lips with which to smile or frown with could show such a range of emotion. Much of it, she realized, came from his voice, but there was something else. Maybe his posture changed, or maybe he emanated some feeling that the children could perceive.

Brian came up with the most workable plan. If they could squeeze a few more tears out of the dragon, something the dragon obliged immediately, they could go to Maevis' shop and — if she was in — offer to sell them. That way they'd be able to determine her interest. If, by chance she wasn't in, as Katie had tried to ensure with the ruse at Mr. Teagarden's, they'd investigate to see if the stolen tears were visibly displayed and maybe even for sale. At any event, they'd return to the dragon's lair and give a report. Then they'd determine what to do next. ...If there was anything to do.

"*Te, le Gardien*," said the dragon again as they readied to leave. "*Patris est filius.*"

Reme translated: "He says Mr. Teagarden is 'You, the guardian.' More, he is his father's son. But we all are...except for you, Katie." And he smiled.

The ride back to civilization was accompanied by plans: who'd say what, when, and how. They determined that if Maevis Blenchly were there, Brian should show her the new dragon tears. If she wasn't, Katie should ask to see jewelry for her mother.

As they approached, the three young people remembered more and more about the antique shop. The meager building had been known to them since they were first old enough to explore the neighborhood. But it held no attractions; there was nothing there for a child, and the unpainted structure offered no enticement to draw them. As usual, there were a few cars pulled into the ungraveled and potholed drive. The building was long, low, overhung by unhealthy looking trees. The brown wood siding was intended to look rustic. Instead, it looked desolate, unloved. The displays in the front windows were accompanied by hosts of dead flies. A hand-lettered sign outlining business hours had faded from exposure to the sun. The glass in the front door was dirty. And yet, customers came.

Brian pushed open the door and held it for Katie and Reme. They all entered and stood in the cluttered aisle. There was junk (spelled "junque") everywhere. Old horse collars, bedpans, and kitchen chairs without seats hung from nails driven into wooden beams that spanned the ceiling. Commodes struggled under plant stands, which, in turn, were buried under piles of old *National Geographic* magazines. Shelves of mismatched teacups and saucers ringed the room. Over everything was cast a pall of dust. The place was a mess.

The three saw that the customers — such as they were — huddled at a glass-topped counter at the rear of the store. An extremely fat woman was haggling about the price of something. She kept waving her hands and shouting about prices and book values. The woman was so broad that Katie, Brian, and Reme couldn't see to whom she was talking until they drew much nearer. With a shudder Katie recognized Maevis. No, it wasn't Maevis exactly. The woman was the same height, had the same predatory look and took the same stance. She even walked the same as she moved behind the counter. The hair was the same, the same tight rolls, looking as if it had been applied only after the figure was dressed. But her face was not as skeletal; the woman was younger, much younger. From any distance, though, she didn't look it.

"It has to be her daughter," whispered Katie, "Or maybe her much younger sister."

The fat woman prepared to depart with a promise to return if she couldn't find what she wanted at a better price elsewhere.

"You do that, Mrs. Ford," said the tired-sounding woman behind the counter. "We're always happy to sell, but we can't give away the shop. It's all mother and I have. I'm sure you'll find our prices very competitive."

"Well," said the fat woman considering, "I'll give you that in some things but not in all. This tea set is almost twice too much. I don't want it that badly, even if it would go with the rest of my collection." She turned to the door and started walking.

"Well, Mrs. Ford, we're always open for you, even after business hours. Just give us a call. And if something else comes in, another set that looks like this but that's cheaper, I'll let you know."

The woman raised her arm in a departing salute and proceeded down the aisles of clutter and out the door. The sales woman looked at a browser who was on the far side of the store and then looked down at Reme, Brian, and Katie. She had been preparing to smile, but that froze in a grimace and then faded to unease as she looked at them.

"And what can I do for you?" she asked nervously.

According to their plan, Katie answered: "We were looking for something special for my mother, maybe some unset stone for one of her rings. She has several that used to have really nice stones, but they got lost or something. We thought maybe you'd have some."

"Er, yes, we have a collection of diamonds and rubies, a few emeralds, sapphires. If you'll step this way, I'll show you a selection of jewelry." She led them to the far right side of the counter and when she had them there said: "Our loose stones are in the safe. I'll be right back with a tray. If you'd like to look at complete settings and stones under glass, here, in the meantime? I don't suppose you brought in the settings so we could get some idea of the size stone you need?"

Katie shook her head no.

"No?" the woman said, "Well, you could bring them in later to see if we can match up any of them. I'll be right back."

The woman was gone a long time retrieving the stones from the safe, but at last she came out holding a flat, velvet-covered tray. She set it down on the counter. Katie immediately noted a dragon tear, but instead of pointing to it, she diverted her gaze to a blue topaz.

"Yes, one of our best stones," said the woman when Katie pointed it out. "But probably much bigger than any setting your mother might have. This is truly a large stone, certainly above the average in size, quality, and…price. Perhaps one of these might be more in line," and she gestured to a group of very dull looking stones. "All first quality, but without the high price."

Katie rolled them about the tray with her fingers and finally brushed against one of the dragon tears. She dexterously picked it up and held it for inspection. "And what's this?" she asked, all innocence.

"You know exactly what it is."

The voice coming from behind startled her. It was like the voice belonging to the young woman in front of her, but deeper, more brittle, and very nasty altogether.

Chapter 10

KATIE IS PINNED DOWN,
THE BOYS CONSULT A DRAGON,
AND MR. TEAGARDEN CONFESSES

Katie, Brian, and Reme spun to see who had crept up behind them and saw Maevis Blenchly in all her malignity. The skin across her brow—normally just pale—was white with fury, her clenched lips twitched ever so slightly at the edges, and her brown eyes snapped open and shut. Her wig-like hair looked as if it was ready to fly off, straight up; the curls had achieved extra buoyancy.

"You know what this stone is and so do I," she fairly spat at them. "*Adamas dragonensis*—dragon diamonds. And rarer than hen's teeth." She turned to the young woman: "That will do, Doris." The younger woman backed away ever so slightly from the children. Her mother continued: "I told you she'd go for the dragon tear if she was the Eames kid. She is and she did. Now put those jewels back in the safe and bring me a dining chair—with ARMS."

Doris turned to put away the tray with a compliant, "Yes, Mother."

As soon as she did, Maevis took two giant steps and stood right in front of Katie. Faster than Brian could move, she grabbed an antique hatpin that had been resting on the counter and held it to Katie's ear. In her other ear she hissed: "And you, my dear, are well advised to stand very, very still, lest I have an accident. Oh, and tell your brother and friend that any movement on their parts could be bad for your health."

Brian and Reme froze in their tracks. The needle, fully four inches long, posed menacingly less than an inch from Katie's ear.

Katie tried to shift her eyes to see exactly what was threatening her. In response, Maevis snapped it briefly before her eyes. "Now do you see? How'd you like THAT in your head, eh?" Her hand quivered slightly as the tip of the needled danced again about Katie's ear.

Brian felt a sudden rush of rage, an anger that threatened to take him over. Reme, sensing his friend's reaction, laid his hand on the crook of Brian's arm and said, "Don't."

Doris returned with a straight-backed dining chair with arm-rests and a roll of silver duct tape. "This should hold her," she said as she slid the chair behind Katie's knees. Doris then pushed down, hard, on Katie's shoulders and forced her to sit. She started peeling off duct tape to secure her ankles.

"Why are you doing this to me?" she asked, bewildered. "What did I ever do to you?"

"It's not so much what you've done but what you're going to do," hissed Maevis uncomfortably close to her ear. "You know what this is," she said holding out one of the tears on her palm. "And you and your idiot brother know where and how to get more. I've been watching you very closely. You go for a walk and come back with dragon tears. *Ergo*, there's a supply of them someplace out there and you know where. I want them. All of them."

In the midst of everything, Katie found herself thinking that Maevis Blenchly was a bad dream; a sad, bad dream. While she couldn't see Maevis, she could see Doris, who Katie realized must be a most devoted daughter to comply with the evil and ill-considered wishes of such a mother. What would it be like to grow up with a mother like Maevis? Katie was sure Doris would do whatever Maevis told her. But that didn't mean that Maevis would be grateful or even kind.

"Tighter, tighter," Maevis said harshly to her daughter as she wrapped duct tape around Katie's ankles and the chair legs. All the while, Maevis kept an eye on Brian and Reme.

Katie could see that Brian still had a wild look in his eyes; so she very slightly shook her head back and forth to signal "No." Brian got the message; his shoulders relaxed.

"Smart move, brave boy," said Maevis. Then, distracted by the thud of the roll of tape escaping from her daughter's hands and falling to the floor, she turned to verbally attack Doris: "What's the matter with you? Get her hands taped to the chair arms. It's a good thing you called me like I told you. Otherwise..."

Katie could feel Doris' hand give a shiver as she played out the sticky tape. "I called," she pleaded, "just as soon as I could, as soon as they asked to see stones. I had to use the office phone."

"If you'd messed up this chance you'd have remembered it for a long time, a good long time," said Maevis, with menace. Then again she turned to Brian and Reme. "Your smart sister will be staying for a visit. Until we're bored with her. You'd just better hope that you're back on time."

"Back?" said Brian.

"Yes, back. You know where these perfect little gems grow, so I suggest that you go harvest all you can find and bring them back."

"What's to stop us from going and harvesting the police?" said Reme coolly as he stepped forward.

Maevis jerked the hat pin a little closer to Katie's ear. Reme stepped back just a little and was relieved to see Maevis' hand relax an inch or so, too.

Maevis redirected her venom to Reme: "Well, your little girlfriend is going to be in the back room, and the police would need a search warrant to find her. And, after all, who'd believe two snot-nosed kids? What will you tell them? A story about stolen diamonds? More likely they'll want to talk with you about the break-ins, especially if you bring them back and I tell them I had midnight visitors and show them something one of them left behind...say, whatever you have in your pocket. Got a knife, boy?" She looked at Brian. "Something with your finger prints all over it?"

Brian dug his jackknife out of his pocket and reluctantly handed it over. He knew he had to in order to help his sister.

"That will do," said Maevis. "So, if you bring our friends in blue back with you, you're in trouble and something very bad might just happen to your sister."

Both of Katie's arms and legs were now taped securely to the chair. As a finishing touch Maevis shoved Doris aside and tore off a length of tape and pressed it over Katie's mouth: "That way we won't be distracted by mindless chatter." Then she turned to the boys: "And what are you waiting for? I want the diamonds in less than an hour or bad things start to happen."

Reme tugged at Brian, who stood glaring at Maevis. "It's no good," Reme told him. "Let's just go and get what she wants."

Brian tore away from Reme's grasp and glared at Maevis: "How do we know you'll turn her loose?"

"Oh, I'll untie her all right," said Maevis. "You don't think I want to put up with her, do you?"

"But you might kill her just to keep her from talking."

"Talking! Hah! That's good. I won't need to. Who'd believe her? Or you, for that matter? Three silly children who claim their diamonds were stolen. Who'd believe 'em?"

Brian reflected that Maevis had made a very bad mistake: she assumed that just because no one had ever trusted her, no one would ever trust him...or Katie...or Reme. Brian could think of four or five people right away who'd believe him, starting with his mother. He knew Maevis wouldn't understand him, though, if he said as much; she'd just grow angrier. He heeded Reme's tug on his shirt sleeve. Slowly, at first, then gathering speed, they moved away from the counter, down the aisle and then out the door. They retrieved their bikes from the yard at the side of the building and took off riding toward the dirt road that led to the meadow.

They started moving off at a flat-out pace, and ten minutes later they approached the entrance to the dragon's lair.

Brian paused, patting his jeans. "I've still got a couple of dragon's tears in my pockets. I'm surprised she didn't ask if we had any more with us. You think we should try to get more?" Reme nodded. Brian continued, "I suppose it's easier that way. I hope she doesn't demand to know where the diamonds came from. I don't want to tell her if I don't have to. And the dragon might not like it, either."

"Besides," said Reme, "It might not be our decision to make. Let's ask the dragon what he thinks we should do."

With a shout of warning, Brian dropped the rope over the edge of the hole and then slid down into the darkness. Reme followed as silently as a shadow. Neither one had a light, and only by the deep red glow that surrounded him, could they tell—and that barely—that the dragon was there. Until he opened his eyes. Then it seemed there was plenty of light, light to spare.

"Quid novi?"

"He wants to know what's new," explained Reme.

Brian tried to gather his thoughts before he spoke. And then, most deliberately, he told of their venture and Katie's danger. When he described the hatpin being held to her ear, the dragon began to breathe faster and harder. Soon Reme and Brian had to bend down to stay out of the smoke that was trapped against the roof of the cavern and deepened toward the floor with each exhalation. When Brian's story was completed, the dragon gave a final snort and turned, lumbering toward the back of the cave. There, he rolled aside a rock and waddled along a passage, his tail sweeping from side to side. After watching in amazement as the beast actually moved, Reme and Brian trailed after him.

They came out, far down the bank and much closer to the river. The passage to the cave entrance was overgrown with vines and creepers. The dragon held his breath as he thrust these aside for fear of wilting them with his heat. The dragon—that previously they had seen only in the dim light of the cave—no longer appeared dull and grey like the rock that had surrounded him. Now he took on the mottled green of the leaves and vertical stripes of brown, mimicking the trunks of the oak trees.

Once they stood on the hillside, the dragon gave vent to his rage. He hissed, spat fire, and—from what Brian could deduce—said some very nasty things. One such: *"Anguis in herba,"* which Reme translated to "A snake in the grass."

After additional chuffing and snorting, the dragon looked about him and then beckoned with his head that the boys should climb on his back. To make the process easier, he squatted down.

Reme was the first to clamber aboard. He seated himself at the top of the arch of the dragon's back, just behind the wings, straddling the beast with one leg on either side. Brian joined him, stepping up on the dragon's elbow before hopping on behind. The plate-sized scales on the dragon's back gave them handholds. The only response the dragon gave was a flick of its tongue. When the boys were seated the dragon rumbled into a low clearing. There he gave a few flaps of his wings. Brian hadn't realized that they were so large; they'd been effectively folded to take up very little space when the dragon was in the cave.

With each flap, dirt, leaves, and small sticks and stones flew around them. Brian had to close his eyes in the rush of wind, and when he opened them again they were aloft. And not only aloft: they were moving. Fast.

Brian looked down. They were well above the trees. Instead of the dirt path, the dragon followed the older route, the river. From above, the dragon took on the coloring of the river below. Reme wondered if from below he took on the blue of the sky above, sort of like a super chameleon.

Brian found that the dragon would respond to his leading if he applied pressure with his knees. The only problem was that things looked different from the air. At last, just over the city limits, the unfolding map beneath them began to make sense; there were orderly streets toward all four points on the compass. It took a hard poke to get his urgent message through the scales as Brian directed the flying giant to the roof of the antique store.

Brian marveled at how few people there were about. There were no travelers on the road ahead of them. That was probably just as well. The last thing they wanted just now was to have an unidentified flying object report filed and the attendant response of police cars and gawkers.

The dragon stopped flapping his wings, and holding them out to catch all the air possible, he silently glided into the tall grass behind the store. With sinuous grace he slid, lizard fashion, behind the building, just to one side of the back door. He turned his head around 180 degrees in a neat maneuver and whispered to the boys: "*Mox nox in rem.*"

Reme translated: "He says: 'Let's get on with it.'"

The boys jumped off and ran to the front. Before they entered, Brian looked at Reme and wondered if his own eyes were shining as brightly. They nodded at each other: Now. Brian took a deep breath and entered the door first. He walked straight back to the glass-topped counter. Maevis Blenchly came out from the back room to meet him. They had moved Katie, he noted, probably into the same back room where, doubtless, Doris stood guard.

"Your pockets better be full," Maevis said to Brian.

Brian put on a mask of fear and shook his head from side to side. "There weren't any more there on the ground, but I brought the thing they came from."

"'The thing they came from,'" said Maevis in a sing-song parody. "What kind of nonsense is that? The thing they came from indeed. Everybody knows that diamonds are formed deep underground. What did you do? Bring a little planet?"

"No, honest," began Brian. "I'm sure there are more inside, but I can't get them out. Maybe you can."

Maevis harrumphed and followed Brian and Reme outside, but only after she shouted to Doris to watch the girl "like a hawk on a chick." Then she permitted herself to be led around the corner of the building.

Whatever Brian had expected was very little like what happened next. He could understand the shock of seeing a full-grown dragon, nose to nose. And, indeed, Maevis stopped and stood stock still. Then she started shaking, moving as if some power outside herself were trying to get her attention. The shaking went on at such a pace that Brian could see two of her in different places, almost as if she had developed a shadow body.

Then she was standing beside herself and there *were* two of her. With a heavy sigh, one dropped to the ground — the more vague one — and the other, more distinct, stood suddenly quite still, with its head lolled forward. Then slowly the distinct one raised its head and opened its eyes. At the same time, the still standing Maevis raised her arms over her head, fingers toward the dragon and shouted: "*Ave, Draco. Alea iacta est.*"

Reme translated on the fly: "'Hail, Dragon. The die is cast.'" He paused for a few seconds and then added: "I think maybe they know each other."

In response, the dragon sucked in bushels of air and gave out a fiery blast. Instead of consuming the body before him, the fire merely burned away her clothes, the hair that looked like a wig, and the red lipstick. What was left was a pale marble statue, a body in stone. But it wasn't that of Maevis. Instead it was a semblance of a beautiful and innocent young girl, nothing like the brittle, wicked shadow woman who vacantly lay unsinged on the grass at the feet of the statue.

Still the dragon roared and flames licked around the stone figure, flaking off layers of stone. At length, the dragon paused; the form revealed had changed from a young woman to a coiled snake, poised to strike. And it changed in color from grey to brilliant green. It moved. With a great hiss it drew itself up taller and larger and then it spoke: "*Animum debes mutare, non caelum.*"

Again the dragon gave out a searing blast, at last consuming the snake. It writhed, hissing and bubbling in the immolation. And vanished.

Where it had been, the air shimmered; beneath it lay the remnant body of Maevis Blenchly, who — otherwise unscathed — was returning to consciousness.

"What do you think that was all about?" Brian said to Reme.

"I'm not sure. The snake told the dragon that 'You must change your soul, not your sky.' It sounded like a warning to me."

"Do you suppose something took over Maevis' body."

"Yeah," said Reme. "But she was a perfect candidate. The priests say one of the first things is always that the body has to be willing."

"She'd fit that part," said Brian. "After what she said she'd do to Katie who, by the way, we'd better find before Maevis wakes up and tries to do it all over again."

Whatever had possessed her had passed. Maevis sat up and backed toward the building. In answer the dragon approached and stood over her and carefully, just above her, extended its massive head to the corner of the building. The jaws opened and then closed on the wood planks of the back of the shop. With the sound of splintering and nails shrieking, the dragon tore a gaping hole.

That was all it took to galvanize Maevis. She dodged out from beneath the dragon and the rain of debris and started running off down the drive. When she reached the street she paused, trying to determine which way to go. Finally, she chose the path to the left, back toward The Dragon and The Rose.

The dragon spit out a second mouthful as he tore away the back of the building. Revealed inside were a quaking Doris, too afraid to move, and Katie, still taped to the chair.

The boys scrambled through the opening and while Reme took the hatpin from Doris' quaking hand, Brian ripped off the tape. He had to go slowly with the last piece that covered her mouth; but that didn't help. Katie screamed in pain as it came away: "Ow, ow, ow, ow, ow. Wow, does that hurt!" She put her hands to the skin around her mouth. As the sting of the pain passed, she stood, flexed and stretched.

"What took you so long?" she asked Brian with a smile. He shook his head in response.

Reme, who stood guarding Doris, piped up: "I think we'd better do whatever it was we were planning to do pretty soon. If they find Maevis running the streets like a madwoman, they'll be here for her daughter and her stuff when they lock her up. We don't want to be here, do we?"

Brian turned to the dragon, who was still breathing hard: "Thanks for saving Katie. I don't know if Maevis was really gonna hurt her, but she said she would. So, is it back to the cave?"

In response the dragon rumbled: "*Non.*" Then he turned to Reme, and with a gentle thrust of his head, to indicate that he was to tell Brian and Katie he said: "*Nunc aut nunquam.*"

"'It's now or never,'" said Reme. "I think he means to fly back to where ever he came from."

"*Certe, verum habes,*" said the giant beast, nodding. He then added: "*Et vos?*"

"'And us,'" said Reme. "He wants to know about us. I think we're supposed to go, too."

"Of course you are," said a familiar voice from behind them. All three children whirled about to see their friend Mr. Teagarden standing there. He'd quietly come up behind them. At a gaze from the unruffled dragon he dropped to one knee in a motion of respect, his head bowed, and the cap that always adorned his head whenever he was out of doors, clutched between his hands.

At a single chuff from the dragon, Mr. Teagarden raised his head, stood, and bowed: "Your Majesty. I am your humble servant Amos Teagarden...*le Gardien.*"

Mr. Teagarden turned to the children to explain. "I am all you know me to be. And a little more. For generation upon generation, the members of my family have been the guardians of the memory of Vrolich the Second. Whether in human form or as this monster, my people have either cared for, or cherished the memory of, this great soul."

The dragon signified assent by a shake of his head. Then he closed his eyes and delicately pushed his great head toward Mr. Teagarden, who stood very still and without any signs of panic. The dragon breathed in the smell of Mr. Teagarden, and expelled a great "ahhhhhh" along with his breath. Only a little smoke curled from his nostrils at the end. When the dragon opened his eyes again, there were tears standing in them, tears that he quickly shook away.

"Yes," said Mr. Teagarden, "there is great joy at this meeting." And he turned to the others, Brian, Reme, Katie, and the paralyzed Doris: "Generation after generation of my family has waited for this day...to see Lord Vrolich. It's been a long, long time. And it's time to be about our business. It's not all mine you know," and here he turned to Brian and Katie. "Believe it or not, we're cousins of a sort. Maybe not by blood, but your ancestors also served The Dragon. You, too, are his defenders."

"You mean we're all supposed to go back to England. Or Wales? Or wherever?" asked Katie.

"Indeed I am—as is His Majesty—and, if you're at all willing, you, too," said Mr. Teagarden looking at them hopefully. "You are needed in the struggle that lies ahead. There's more than you know about the anticipated return of this particular dragon. The Rose will be there as indeed I saw he was here only moments ago. And only with your help can the rightful king regain his throne and his bride."

"I'd like to go, but my Mom..." said Reme, looking stricken at the thought.

"Oh, she'll know, believe me," said Mr. Teagarden. "As will yours, Katie and Brian. Mrs. Teagarden has it all arranged that if I don't return this afternoon she'll know I'm off on what she calls 'one of my jaunts.' And she knows that all three of you are with me. Here, look, I've even brought my passport, although I doubt we'll be going through customs on the way in. We'll have to face the rest of it when we leave. If we leave. There is danger, and it's not small."

He turned to Katie: "Were you scared when Maevis held the hat pin to your ear?" Katie nodded. "You should have been. Not one of us could have saved you had she decided that you should die. If The Rose had taken her over completely, you might be dead now."

"I knew I was in trouble," said Katie. "And I was scared but I knew that if she killed me at least she wouldn't get away with it. Brian would set it as right as it could be."

"Well, that's what we're trying to do: set things to rights," said Mr. Teagarden. "And there are some things worse than death.

The Rose is one of them. I cannot promise that you will be safe. I do not know what he intends. But I do know that if you consent we will battle the force of the Rose. And perhaps, just perhaps, we shall win."

Chapter 11

ON A WING AND A PRAYER

The most difficult part was to figure out who went where…
and all in a hurry. Really, when traveling on a dragon's back, rid-
ers want to make sure they don't slide off, especially on what's
sure to be a transoceanic flight. And this dragon was not so big
as to easily accommodate a large retinue; from end to end he was
perhaps thirty feet, tail and all. Mr. Teagarden was assigned the
hindmost seat, with Brian, Katie, and Reme in front of him. They
accomplished the seating with a few junque pillows from Maevis
Blenchly's store tossed in for good measure.

Through all the settling-in Doris had stood transfixed: she
hadn't tried to escape, she hadn't tried to speak; she just stood
and watched. She whimpered, though, when the dragon first
spread its wings and then reached out for her with one clawed
hand. Katie heard the brief cry of fear, but it came only once. With
infinite care Doris was clutched between the sharp talons; it was
the only place remaining for her.

"Why is she coming with us?" asked Katie. "I don't think she
wants to."

"I have no idea," said Mr. Teagarden with perplexity. "I know
he must have some reason."

With a lurch, the dragon turned himself around on three legs
and Mr. Teagarden had to shout "It's too late now to ask him
about it. HANG ON!!!"

The dragon began by stretching his wings to their fullest and
then running them through their range of motion. In seconds,
debris was swirling around them in a windstorm, and they shut
their eyes. Only when the blast of sand and leaves ceased did
they open them again.

They were far above the ground. Looking down they could see a crowd of people marching toward the antique store. In the lead was a little figure in black, probably Maevis, who was jumping and hopping and running around the crowd from one side to the other. In the distance the children could see two police cars, lights flashing; one heading to join the crowd and the other vectoring toward the store from another direction.

"It looks like we just made it," said Katie. "Another minute and we'd have been in the middle of all that."

The dragon soared for a time, rising on the updrafts along the lakeshore. The view out over the expanse of water was stunning, the glitter of the afternoon sun on the water, the sand dunes beneath them. Cars were now tiny toys that moved along highways and streets. The dragon circled round and round, higher and higher.

"I suspect we'll be amazed how far he can glide once he's in the high air," said Mr. Teagarden.

"You suspect, but you don't know?" asked Reme with some hesitation.

"Well, not by my own personal experience," explained Mr. Teagarden. "Everything I know about this particular dragon has been passed down to me. I've never seen a dragon in the flesh before, but I know probably more about them than any other living person. I'll tell you the story, if you like, as we fly. But first, how are you all faring? Reme? Katie? Brian? Are you comfortable?" They were. "And Doris? Has she regained her composure?"

The children directed their attention ahead to the maiden in the two-handed clutch of the dragon. She lay there, her clothes flapping madly about her. The tight hair—so much like her mother's—had loosened and streamed out behind her to an amazing length. Her head was moving, taking in all that she saw beneath her. Katie was at first alarmed at the smile that covered her face very nearly from ear to ear. Then she realized that it wasn't the face of a mad woman, it was the face of a woman who was smiling and laughing, perhaps for the very first time in her life. Along with the rush of the wind, Katie could hear a crooning, a singing, but she couldn't quite catch the melody. And the words—if there were any—were swept away in the rushing air.

Katie, who was still quite angry about her recent treatment, had seen enough. She "harrumphed" in disgust and then turned to back to Mr. Teagarden. "So why DID the dragon bring her?" Katie asked, motioning ahead to Doris.

Mr. Teagarden hunched his shoulders together. He didn't know: "If nothing else, perhaps out of pity. What do you think Maevis would have done to her if she found her at the store with all that damage and the pillows missing? Sure as anything she'd have found a way to blame it on the poor girl. This way, well, this way she has a chance to live a life, even if only briefly. I don't know if she'd have willingly come, though. I suppose our dragon is guilty of abduction and that's a very serious crime in civilized lands. But you know he's not a tame dragon; very little respect for our laws has this old dragon. Very little respect for most persons, too, I'd judge."

"Us, too?" asked Brian.

"Oh, no," said Mr. Teagarden and then paused as the wind blew about him. "The Dragon drew you to him. There's no other explanation for it. He's a canny old beast, too; knows what he's about. He knew you were the right ones.

"And, you're safe, at least, from any danger Lord Vrolich might represent."

"Yeah, but dragons are very dangerous, aren't they?" asked Reme.

"That they are," said Mr. Teagarden. "But perhaps not as dangerous as you might think. They understand loyalty, for instance, and love. And duty. Dragons don't just go out to see how many peasants they can roast on any given day. That's just some idle chatter. Of course, there are dragons and there are dragons: natural and unnatural. This one, for instance, is an unnatural dragon and has a better moral sense than most, but that will take some explaining, too." And he paused.

Katie jumped in: "What I want to know is how you came to be at the store right when we needed you."

"Oh, that. You didn't need me," said Mr. Teagarden. "You and my Lord Vrolich were doing just fine on your own. But I can tell you how I came to be there. I knew something was up when you signaled me about our pretend three o'clock rendezvous. Maevis was in just before that and glued to a booth. She started fidgeting at three-ten, and by the time her daughter called for her at three-fifteen, she took off on a dead run.

"I knew she was up to no good. And I knew it had something to do with you. So I followed."

"You knew all along that we'd found the dragon?"

"From the first," said Mr. Teagarden, brightly. "I knew as soon as I saw the dragon tear. It's the sign among those of us who serve the dragon. And I had proof positive when the cloud rose in the sky."

"But you never followed us, did you? You know, to see where we were going?" asked Katie.

"No, that wouldn't have been very nice...and I didn't need to worry. It was destined that you were to find him and you did. If I'd been sneaking around after you the magic might not have worked. For all that you think you found The Dragon you were really found by him. He called you—in a sense—and you came."

"But he was surprised," interrupted Katie. "We woke him up."

"That's true. And he'd been asleep for years upon years. Dragons, like cats, sleep more and more as they age. That's IF they don't have anything in particular to keep them awake. That's one of the very real dangers: they fall asleep, get to dreaming, and forget to ever wake again. They pass from sleep to death."

This dragon was most certainly alive. Reme watched as he adjusted the wing tips to catch the best of the air. When he flapped there was a sound like a whip being cracked.

The dragon had circled, rising on thermal currents, and then turned away from the sun and headed toward the east. They were sailing over land, leaving behind one great lake. Brian wondered how soon he'd see the next, Lake Huron, as they approached the other side of the state. It wouldn't be long. He knew they were moving rapidly; he'd flown before, and his sense was that while they were lower, they were moving much faster than in a conventional plane. And the air moved with them. In a plane—if they'd had a window open—the force of the air would have flattened them. Something about the way the dragon sailed allowed the air to wash over them and then follow along with them. They were in a pocket of breeze, not a blast of arctic wind. Of course, it might help to have a dragon with central heating, thought Brian; they were not likely to freeze, even when it came time to cross the

Atlantic. His seat and the inside of his thighs were comfortably warm.

Reme interrupted his thoughts with a question for Mr. Teagarden: "Well, he was asleep when we found him. But, was he in any danger of sleeping until he died?"

"He was in very grave danger of doing exactly that," said Mr. Teagarden. "It had been a score of years since he'd been awake."

"But you said he called us? How could he do that when he was asleep?" posed Katie.

Mr. Teagarden collected his thoughts before he spoke. "I think it might have been this way: He knew the danger of sleeping, but he couldn't help himself. And part of his mind wanted to go on sleeping, or to follow wherever that path led, perhaps into death. He was very tired of being The Dragon and a dragon... he'd been one for so long—almost a thousand years. But another part of his mind wanted to fight for life; to continue the struggle to regain what had been won and lost. And I believe that it was with that part of himself that he sought you out and called you even as he slept."

"Why didn't you find him?" asked Reme. "Did you know he was there?"

"Oh, I suspected he was there and not wholly dead. It takes a long time for a dragon to die; very tough, they are. But I wasn't the one he called, nor did I expect to be. I thought it might fall to a young child. Innocence is great protection against the evil that can be stirred up in a dragon."

"Did you know it would be us?" asked Katie, and then she added, as if dreading the answer: "Is that why you always were so nice to us?"

"Oh, no," said Mr. Teagarden with a chuckle. "No, no, no, no. If that's what's worried you, put that to rest. Mrs. Teagarden and I love you very dearly. I am delighted it was you that the dragon chose, though; I couldn't have asked for anyone better or circumstances more fitting because it allows me to be here, too.

"Does that mean," pondered Reme, "that the dragon could have awakened and you might not have gotten to see him?"

"That's exactly what it means. There were no guarantees. When we—my family, that is—thought it best I come to the States we only vaguely knew where. Others of our line had tried to find him over the centuries. All we had were rumors and the urgent necessity of rousing the dragon if we were able. Mrs. Teagarden was perfectly willing to stay in Britain with me after we married, but when she told me of the tales of Misty Haven I started urging that we come to the States. ...All the more so when my sister heard the tales, too. We're the last of the line, the last of the guardians."

"But don't you have children? Doesn't your sister?" pleaded Katie.

"I do. We do," explained Mr. Teagarden. "But you know how kids are: they have their own minds. They think we're daft when we talk about the dragon. I can't really blame them. I remember being their age and trying to come to grips with what my old dad was telling me about our work with Lord Vrolich. In the end I almost didn't do it. It took all the old books and scrolls and then some before I'd even open my mind that it might be possible. The tellie — excuse me, the television — has made culture the same everywhere. If it didn't happen on the tellie it didn't happen anywhere. So it's no wonder that all the history we try to convey to them, this private history, this story of just one family, falls on deaf ears. No, love them as I do, I cannot convince my children otherwise and I cannot demand that they believe in the dragon. The world, as you imagine, is not hospitable to the idea of such a thing, especially since everyone knows dragons only happen in fairy tales."

"This is a pretty real fairy tale," said Brian. "Look, there's Lake Huron on the horizon. Wow! And is that night over there?" Ahead the sky turned from day to evening, and in the far distance, to night.

"That's where were going," said Mr. Teagarden. "Into the dark."

Within fifteen minutes they were over the great deep blue water of Lake Huron. Then, for league upon league they flew higher and higher. In the darkling, Reme and Brian and Katie could identify concentrations of inhabitation by the glow of lights only. The night was clear and fresh, and tired as they were, one by one the children dropped off to sleep, each relaxing in his or her turn against Mr. Teagarden.

Brian awakened when he felt something change in the flying. No longer was the dragon trying to gain altitude; instead he was dropping. Brian opened his sleepy eyes. He still wished he were dreaming. He hadn't slept like that since he was a baby, maybe. Careful not to disturb the others he moved his head to study the ground. They were still a goodly way up, but they were settling downward in a gentle spiral.

As the dragon began using his wings to break his speed, the rest awoke.

"Look over there," said Mr. Teagarden, pointing in the direction they had been heading. "It's the sea. We're nearly prepared to start across."

Brian looked down through the darkness, relieved now with a bright and full moon and all the stars arrayed in quiet splendor. He saw the land run to the east and then the change to the rhythmically undulating and free open water of the sea. "So, where are we?" he asked.

"My guess is that we're on the coast of Labrador, just getting ready to cross the big water. I believe that our dragon must refuel, and I don't mean with paraffin. Sorry, what I mean to say is that he doesn't run on jet kerosene."

Brian again looked down and spied a small group of cattle highlighted in the moonlight. They were still, very still, unaware of the doom that was descending upon them. From Brian's point of view the ground seemed to be rushing toward him. He knew that reality was somewhat different: he was approaching the earth. At the last minute the dragon flapped against the pull of the planet and they settled gently onto the sloping turf.

The Dragon, Lord Vrolich, loosed Doris from his clutches. She continued to lie where he'd put her. With great effort against sore muscles cramped from long disuse, Katie swung her right leg over the dragon's back and slid down to land on two feet. It felt wonderful. Then she walked ahead to see if there was anything she might do for Doris; she didn't want to, but she felt an obligation. She knelt down to find the woman asleep, peacefully asleep. Gently she shook her awake.

"No, no," she said, her eyes still closed tight. "I'm having the most wonderful dream. I don't want to wake up. I was flying, carried by a dragon." Her eyes came suddenly open and she looked directly into Katie's eyes. "It's true. It wasn't a dream, was it? You're the little girl. And that's the dragon." She sat up, her eyes flashing in the moonlight. "I was doing something terrible to you, I remember, and then the dragon came and made me stop, and then he carried me here." She paused to think.

Meanwhile, the dragon rumbled off toward the standing and staring cattle.

Mr. Teagarden, who was standing with the boys, said rather pointedly: "You might not want to watch this. My Lord Vrolich must eat before he continues, but at the manner of his eating you might take offence. How, after all, does a dragon eat?"

How, indeed? Even Katie turned to watch, expecting carnage. She hoped that she wouldn't have to sit in gore if they were to continue over the sea.

The dragon slowly approached the cattle. Brian watched them sniffing the air to check for danger. Apparently they sensed none. But slowly they moved away in a block.

The dragon reared up on his hind feet and then lunged, landing in the mass of the beeves. With lightning speed he used his claws to slit several of their throats. Within a minute four of the animals lay dead where they'd fallen.

"Wow!" said Reme. Katie was surprised that she felt little but wonder. On principle she opposed the killing of living things. But even more she opposed their torture. And there had been none of that here. The dragon was tearing into the warm flesh, devouring every bit that he could pull free.

The feeding was less pleasant to watch. But the children turned away not so much from revulsion as from a sense of providing privacy for the dragon.

And they found, to their astonishment, they also were hungry. Mr. Teagarden motioned them to follow him away from the feeding dragon, away from the sea toward a group of stunted trees, the remnant of an ancient orchard. "They'll be wormy, no doubt, but there are some early apples there or I've fair mistook my eyes. I spotted them as we were landing."

Katie wondered how anyone could see apples in the moonlight from perhaps 200 feet in the air. Yet, as she studied the trees, she found she could just make out the globular fruit. The apples seemed to shine out at them, perhaps reflecting the light from the moon and stars, or perhaps broadcasting their own inner light. The group moved, not unlike the beeves, toward the trees and found enough ripe fruit to sustain them, at least for a short while. All three children took extra fruit in their jeans' pockets.

Mr. Teagarden looked around to see if there was anything else. "What I'd give just now for a pint and my pipe," he said, chewing around the core of an apple.

Reme looked at the dragon which was clacking his jaws together as he ate, moving now from one dead beast to another. He heard some uncomfortable crunches and snaps as bones broke under the pressure of the mighty jaws, always followed, eventually by the sound of the teeth coming together like giant castanets. Dragons do not have lips to silence their eating. In that regard they are much like cats, Reme thought.

In the end, the dragon dined far longer than did the children. They stretched out on the grass at a fair distance and watched. Again, there was something cat-like in the way the dragon hunched over his food and ate. As he chewed, he would tilt his head back—while still crouching—and then he'd swing up a foreclaw to better handle a piece that was hanging out of his jaws. At length he'd swallow, and then sniff the ground for anything he'd dropped.

Katie had lost track of time. Brian broke the spell by nudging her. "If we're going directly on it's going to be a long time before we see land again," he said. "I was so stiff when I got off the dragon's back that I need to stretch out my legs. What about you?"

Katie agreed and together they got up to wander the pasture. "Do you think Mom's okay? I mean, do you think she'll be worried, really worried?" he asked. "She wasn't planning on us being gone or anything other than that dream."

"She'll be fine as long as Mrs. Teagarden tells her that we're with her husband. What I want to know is what happened at Maevis' shop when the police got there?" said Katie. "Do you suppose that Detective Grosskopf arrested her?"

"Yeah, I'd like to see that. But I'm worried, too, about what's happened with Reme's mom. If anything is going to be bad, that would be it."

Reme had come up behind them while they walked and they were startled when he spoke: "She's gonna have real trouble with this. I found out why, too."

Together they walked toward the apple trees again.

"When my mom and dad first married they had a baby. They named him Ben. And, anyhow, Ben was about a year old and someone broke into their apartment—they lived in a big city then—and robbed all their stuff, including Ben. The thing of it was my mom was there, but she was sleeping, taking a nap. I guess after that she went kind of crazy. The police and everybody looked and looked. They advertised in the paper; they were even on the news. Nobody ever found Ben. Nobody brought him back.

"After a while, they found they couldn't have any more babies and then they thought about it for a couple years and then they adopted me. So, when somebody broke into our house—I guess it had to be Maevis—my mom thought it was all happening again. I don't know what she'd be thinking now, but maybe it's not as bad as before.

"Last night she had a dream. She told me about it this morning. She said she saw me going far away and coming back again. Away and back. If Mrs. Teagarden tells her we're with Mr. Teagarden that might help. I have to believe it will help." He dug in his pocket and took out a phone. "There's no way we're going to be able to make a phone call from wherever this is." He paused to think and then added: "I hope she's right about the coming back part."

They'd all stretched and used whatever facilities nature offered before they returned to Doris and Mr. Teagarden. They were sitting quietly in the grass, talking. Mr. Teagarden turned to them at the approach.

"I doubt that he can lick himself clean," said Brian, "but I really don't want to sit in blood and stuff. I mean, he's probably covered in it."

"And how did his lair smell?" Mr. Teagarden asked calmly.

"Fine, just fine; like dry earth."

"That's because he has his own ways of keeping clean. He's getting ready now and—if everything is true—this should be something to watch."

The dragon began to purr, the sound of it rolling across the field. Soon, in addition to the sound, there came smoke curling round his jaws and up through his nostrils. Then came flame with each exhalation. The flames grew from a yellow flicker to a steady roar of blue, and using it like a blow torch the dragon washed his claws, his legs, his belly, and—craning his neck—even his back in fire. At the end of a quarter hour he let the flame die and, in ungainly fashion, undulated back to the group; a dragon walking is nowhere nearly as graceful as a dragon in flight. He stood before them, docile enough, replete, but evidently anxious to be gone.

"*Fugit hora*," he said, and then added in his first rough attempt at English: "Thee...hour...flies." Not too bad considering he had no lips, thought Brian.

Katie was the first to put out a hand. The dragon's hide was warm, dry, but not hot. "Neat," she said, and clambered aboard. Within minutes all of them—including a willing Doris who again climbed between the dragon's talons—were ready for the next leg of their journey, a trip over the Atlantic.

"Is this gonna take days and days?" asked Reme. "If it is, we're gonna want to stop sometime for a bathroom break or something. But there isn't any place, is there?"

"We'll come to Ireland first," said Mr. Teagarden. "And you're right: that's a long way away. I'm not even sure we'll stop there. We'll have to make do without any of the usual flight amenities. Bathroom breaks will have to be on the fly, so to speak. But we may be surprised to find out how fast my Lord Vrolich can move when needs must."

With the stretching of wings, the dragon kicked up small stones, sticks and grass and set them swirling about. His passengers closed their eyes and were airborne again before they knew they'd left the ground. When Brian looked out they were spiraling up and out. Up and up, ever higher, and out over the waves crashing against the rocky shore. The salt taste in the air became even more pronounced.

Katie turned to look at the receding shore. "I hope we come back some day," she said wistfully to herself.

Dragons have many powers, among them fascination. They can look deep into the eyes of almost any man or natural beast and cast a deep spell. So it was during the flight. The great beast swiveled his massive head to look at each traveler. One after the other dropped into a sleep so total, each dreamed of nothing.

To the travelers it was only minutes before they began to stir, to awaken refreshed.

"I must have dropped off to sleep," said Katie, rubbing her eyes and stretching one arm at a time. The rhythm of the dragon's wings had so far entered her soul that she no longer thought it odd that she was sailing a mile and more over the sparkling blue of the ocean. Katie felt the others waking, too.

Mr. Teagarden's first conscious act was to consult his chronometer. In addition to time it also kept track of dates.

"We've been out of it for a day and a half!"

The sun was rising up to greet them.

"Look, just at the horizon. Can you see it?" asked Mr. Teagarden. "I'll be bound we're at the approach of Ireland, that ancient and fierce island."

Soon they saw her jumbled coastline, waves smashing against rocky shores and throwing spray what must have been a hundred feet in the air.

"Ah," commented Mr. Teagarden, "It's a brisk day on the coast. Chilly down there, too, I shouldn't wonder. Humph... that's another advantage of flying dragon express...heat," he chortled.

It was as Brian had theorized; the heat of the dragon warmed them throughout and surrounded them against the icy blast of the upper atmosphere. Without that warmth they would have perished. The west coast of Ireland, now drawing beneath them, presented a rugged beauty and greenery unrivaled anywhere else on earth.

"There's a reason they call it the Emerald Isle. And you're seeing it," said Mr. Teagarden. Before them rose a series of mountains. "That'll be Carrantuohill, just at the east of Ireland. It's the highest point for many a mile, in fact, in the whole of Ireland. Three-thousand feet and then some. And, to the north, that inlet of water is Dingle Bay. If my guess is correct, we'll be cutting across the southern tip of the island."

Which, indeed, they did. The children saw what Mr. Teagarden told them were the Lakes of Kilarney and Blarney Castle—where the Blarney Stone is poised high in the battlements. They saw all these things, but not even Mr. Teagarden could say for sure what was what; castles look mighty small from a mile above. When Katie looked east again—directly ahead—she saw the shimmer of the sea.

"St. George's Channel," said Mr. Teagarden. "And some hundred miles across we come to Wales. That's when I start to feel again at home. But we're getting there. We're getting there."

Getting there was only a short while, perhaps some thirty minutes, and they had crossed the legendary deeps between Ireland and Wales and approached the coast.

"St. David's Head," said Mr. Teagarden of a finger of land and an island as they approached landfall. "We are now over the land of my birth." With that he took in a bushel of air. "It smells like home, even at this high remove. But we've a ways to go yet, further inland and upland and almost to the border."

Reme had been studying the advent of land, but he raised his head to look toward the sun. Then he put his hand in front of his eyes and squinted through his fingers. "I thought I saw something," he said. "Could it be eagles this high?"

"Oh, aye," said Mr. Teagarden. "They soar forever high, it seems, sometimes just for the sport."

"These don't look like they're soaring," Reme said, as he more intently studied the objects in the bright sun. "It looks like they're headed our way."

Mr. Teagarden likewise raised his hand to screen the sun and looked. "They're not eagles. Nor any other bird I know. Look how they flap their wings. And they ARE coming right for us."

They beat against the scales on the sides of the dragon to alert him, but there was no need. He had already sensed the intrusion. His lizard's tongue flicked in and out twice, tasting the air, and he veered left, to port, and flew more strongly to gain altitude. With the dragon's lateral move, the flying things were out of the direct line of the sun. Brian saw that they resembled nothing so much as pictures of gargoyles that he'd seen in books: they were black, repulsive, and ungainly, but fast for all their lack of grace. And they were coming their way.

"Wh..wh...what are they?" he asked.

"I do fear — and greatly — they are the welcoming committee," said Mr. Teagarden. "The Rose has knowledge of our coming. He was there — in one form or another — at our leaving, and he sends these to greet us. To stop us. Hang on."

The words were no sooner out of his mouth than the first of the harriers came in for the attack.

Katie saw him coming, ducked, and then heard the "whoosh" of wings and the "clack" of claws snapping on the empty air just over her head. She also heard a raspy cawing that sounded like insane laughter.

Then came the second and the third. With each attack the dragon shifted just in time. The great beast swung his tail to ward off the enemy, but for the most part all he could do was evade. In his front claws, his primary defense for this kind of fighting, lay the maiden, Doris. Katie watched as the dragon's razor-sharp talons closed more tightly about her. If he forgot for one instant, she thought, and closed his claws like a man might close his fist, Doris would be cut to bits.

As the fourth, fifth, and sixth attackers tore past them the dragon unleashed his throaty roar. Flame caught the last of them and the black flier folded his singed wings and fell straight down. He uttered no cry as he plummeted to earth.

The remaining five made ready for another attack. Brian felt cold sweat break out on his forehead. To meet their onslaught, the dragon flapped higher and then dove directly at his pursuers.

Doris, aware of her danger, clutched herself to one of the dragon's forearms and freed herself from the other. In addition to his tail and flames he now had a slashing weapon. Gently, he folded Doris' body against his breast with the single claw. The other opened and closed several times in quick succession, snapping shut on the air. Doris was hanging on for dear life, yet there was no fear evident. From underneath the crook of his elbow she looked up at Katie, and a faint smile played over her lips.

With one foreleg freed, the dragon took out the lead attacker, who then somersaulted into the second. There was a sickening crunch as the two bodies collided. From his vantage, Reme could feel it. He saw their black eyes go vacant as they began to fall, inert.

But the remaining gargoyles kept up the attack and shifted their strategy. Instead of flying in to strike with speed at the dragon, they now clustered around like little birds after a crow. The dragon twisted and squirmed in midair, trying to protect and fight back. Two of the black devils kept at his face while one withdrew to the right, the starboard. Then the odd creature dove in directly at Katie.

She had already ducked and dipped as deeply as she could, and the scaly beast knew exactly her entire range of motion. She saw the open claws, slid over the left side of the dragon and felt the leading edge of the beast's foot push her all the way off.

With an intake of breath, she marveled how quickly she moved away from the dragon on her flight to the earth. And then she laughed remembering the old joke: It's not the fall that kills you; it's the sudden stop at the bottom. And despite telling herself it was no laughing matter, she began to giggle as she fell. She commended her soul to God and thought of her mother and father and Brian.

How long would it take before she crashed? Would she die immediately? Would it hurt? She would have thought the land would reach up to her much faster than it did, but she knew that she was rushing with ever increasing speed until she reached terminal velocity.

Looking directly at the ground she couldn't see the dragon's last evasive maneuver that knocked two of the harriers from the sky as the last flew off. He then dove, adding wing power to gravity.

He closed on Katie. Mr. Teagarden urged him on. Brian screamed for his sister, and Reme closed his mouth to lessen wind resistance.

Katie could see the trees beneath her growing much larger when the dragon's foreclaw snagged the back of her jeans. In an instant her downward motion was pushed sidewise, and then reversed.

She felt the jeans tug in her crotch as she swung through the arch. She hoped the fabric would hold. Brian caught sight of a farmer who had seen the whole rescue. The man stood in his field, his hat between his hands, his mouth open in wonder. At his feet, a crumbled black form lay smoldering.

And in a flash they left the scene behind. Brian wondered fleetingly what such a man would make of such a sight. Then his attention was drawn again toward Katie. The fabric had held but there was no way for the dragon to restore her to its back. Nor was there any other way she could be more comfortably carried.

The dragon, after regaining some altitude, scouted out a small clearing in a wooded area and made to land. He glided over the clearing twice to make sure it was uninhabited, and then amid the usual flurry of debris he set down, releasing at last Doris and Katie. The others, cramped from their straddling ride, took a few moments to slide down.

To their surprise, Mr. Teagarden's first action was to drop to his knees. Katie was breathing in great heaving sobs, but she knew clearly enough that his words were prayers of thanksgiving. Crying now with all her heart, she, too, joined him. Then Reme and Brian. Last of all, Doris got to her knees, just in time for the shared "Amen."

When they stood, Katie moved toward her. Doris didn't flinch away as she might once have done. Instead she opened her arms and enfolded the young girl.

"Thank God you're safe. I prayed and prayed that it might be me and not you who was falling," Doris said. "I prayed for the first time in my life. I asked God to spare you because I needed to beg your forgiveness. I haven't yet asked for it...not really. I did terrible things to you."

"But that was what your mother had told you to do," reasoned Katie, who was still quivering and clinging very tight.

"Yes, but you see, I didn't have to enjoy it so much. I wanted to do bad things. I wanted you to stop smiling. All I saw was that you belonged. You belonged to your friends and to your family. You belonged in the world; you had permission to be there. You were cherished, and I wanted to ruin all that. And now I understand how very wrong I have been." Tears were coursing down Doris' cheeks, falling on to the springy turf after they left her face. "And I'm so glad you're safe."

"You never had a brother or a sister?" asked Katie, looking up at her.

Doris shook her head in the negative.

"Or friends...? Boys or girls?"

Again, the head went from side to side.

"Your mother...?" Katie began.

"She didn't want me, but she didn't want me to have anyone else. She was all I needed, she said. But I knew that wasn't so. I was smart enough to see who and what she was. But I wasn't brave enough to stand up against her. It was so much easier just to go along, to become more and more like her...year after year after year."

"Well," said Katie. "It can't happen again. Now you have friends. Friends of your own."

Doris smiled, and the power of that smile, so recently practiced, was enough to light the clearing. Katie could feel the warmth. The two women, one a young woman, and the other a girl, had wandered aside to the edge of the trees. There they continued talking after a brief pause for needful and necessary functions. Very carefully did they examine the neat cut in Katie's jeans where the dragon had snared her. The material had almost been completely severed. Katie had been hanging by a band of fabric less than a quarter-inch wide. Doris put her finger under the loop and tugged. The fabric teased apart into threads.

"But it was enough," Doris said wonderingly. "Just enough."

Doris and Katie walked back to join Mr. Teagarden and the boys. They were kneeling over a map scratched into the dirt. The dragon, which had assumed the protective coloring of the field, looked on over their shoulders. Katie had to hold herself from laughing; they looked so intent.

"Here's where we are now—or at least hereabouts," said Mr. Teagarden. "And here's where we're going." With a stick he drew a long line inland. "And in between are some of the harshest lands known to mankind. Civilized? These are the places men used to live and gave up because they are too wild. Mountains, crags, valleys that fall into nothing. There are no roads. There can't be: too steep up and down the hills. And when we get there you'll wonder what all the fuss was about. That's something you'd have to know by being born to it, belonging to it."

Katie looked down at the scratchings. "This is Wales, then," she said.

"Oh, aye," said Mr. Teagarden. "We're on this side, the far west, and we need to go to the border land on the far east: Hay on Wye. That's where all this dreadful business is pointing."

"And that's where you're from?" Katie asked. She knew it was so and Mr. Teagarden confirmed it with a nod. "Will we see the other Dragon and The Rose? You know, the other pub? The first one?"

"I shouldn't wonder," said Mr. Teagarden. "At this rate we'll be there long before nightfall...but I wonder if that's best?" He looked up at the dragon and continued: "You know, it might be better to move into the surrounding woods and wait here during the day and travel by night. They already know we're on our way and their defenses will be secured. They'll get no stronger by the wait and it might unsettle them."

The dragon chuffed a dry laugh.

Brian piped up: "Exactly who do you mean by 'they'? More of the kinds of things that came over the water to greet us?"

"Maybe that and maybe worse," said Mr. Teagarden. "It's hard to tell exactly what the magician will send; indeed, if he'll send anything. The Rose was a very strong thaumaturge, and his arts were dark, the kinds that consume you once you start. In the end, you become them completely. We may say that the Rose has all the powers of Hell at his disposal. But I'm guessing that sending us those flying hellions took a fair amount of power and magic out of him. It may have been all his strength or only a fraction. How many greeters and of what kind is something we can't know until we see them."

Katie shivered, remembering the feel of the air pushing past her as she fell.

Chapter 12

A SAFE LANDING AND A WARM WELCOME
IN THE NEW CENTURY

They waited until nightfall to leave the shelter of the wood. In all actuality, the time of evening was smokefall, that time after the sun sets when the air pressure changes, and smoke from a peat or coal fire—instead of rising from a house or cottage—rolls downward from a chimney and hovers close to the ground. As it was, Mr. Teagarden, sensitive to such phenomenon, noted the difference in the air and roused himself from a nap. All the others were sprawled out beneath the big trees, the dapple of sun through the leaves dancing over them.

The children alerted immediately when they heard him moving about. He walked to Doris first of all. He'd said nothing to her since their landing on this side of the Atlantic, but he smiled as he squatted on his haunches.

"Are you restored?" he asked with evident concern.

"Yes. Entirely," she said calmly. "In fact, that's exactly what I've been: restored...made whole." She smiled up at him. "I don't know when I have ever before been so much myself. I don't even know the full scope of what we're doing or why we're here. And I don't need to know. It wouldn't make any difference."

"Oh, but it's important in its own right," he said as he launched into the explanation of The Dragon and The Rose and the great enchantment. Katie, Brian, and Reme drew up to listen again. Even the dragon cocked a tympanum, the small exposed hearing surface at the back of his head. When Mr. Teagarden came to the part about the turning of his young bride into a pillar of stone, the dragon wept, tears coursing from his eyes, splashing onto the ground in a crystalline hail. No one bothered to pick them up.

With a heavy sigh from the dragon the others knew it was time to move on. They resumed their seats, or in Doris' case, the dragon's paws. Again they closed their eyes as they ascended through the whirlwind.

Then they circled up and up and up, until they could see that the sun had yet to set in the distant west; but it was only a matter of minutes. They sailed over rough country, and although they couldn't judge the heights of the peaks and the depths of the valleys, they knew it was for the most part unpeopled: there were no roads and only the faintest foot paths and drovers' lanes. Only rarely would they catch a glimpse of the light of a fire kindled by a hardy soul in the middle of nowhere.

They flew deeper and deeper into that ancient land that has grown so tired or so angry it's given up even its people.

As the dark settled in around them Katie had an uneasy feeling of what might lie ahead. She knew that she was here of her own accord; she chose this and would never turn back. But that didn't make it less scary. She thought of what it might mean to face all the forces of Hell. All of them, and all at once. She knew that on her own she was no match.

She shivered again, and Brian turned around to look at her. "Are you cold? No? Are you scared? Me, too. I mean, here we are flying along on a dragon, getting ready for an enormous battle, we don't have any swords or guns or anything. In fact, we don't even know what we're supposed to do, and yet, here we are. If we didn't know we were supposed to be here it might be really scary!"

Katie smiled, relieved that she wasn't the only one who was unsettled at their prospects.

Mr. Teagarden, for all his being a grown-up, shared in their unease: "We'll face more frights, I'd imagine. We don't know what's going to be asked of us. I pray we keep our souls. But I might not give a penny about our bodies. We may not be coming back from this adventure; that's out of our hands. We have been called, each one of us. And, to our credit, we've answered that call with speed and all the honor we can muster. I pray that we are good at need and fearless in the attempt."

"Good at need," repeated Katie slowly, rolling the words around on her tongue. "Good at need...."

Brian added: "It means that when the call comes we will answer it with everything we have."

Mr. Teagarden resumed: "It's the idea that whatever we have we'll give all of it and trust it to be sufficient to what is needful, just at that moment, just in that circumstance. 'Good at need' means that whatever we have will be enough, just enough, to answer for what's demanded. I don't know what my Lord Vrolich will need from me. Perhaps a sword arm, or a spell reader, or even an acolyte. I am ready to do any one of those things—or any of a hundred others—as it's needed. And though I don't know what's to be demanded, I know I'll try to fill it. For now, what counts is the willingness to be ready for anything, to be good at need."

He fell silent, but his words found purchase in the minds of all three children and Doris.

Reme knew that his hour was upon him: he'd find out just what he was made of. He was afraid of so many things, even though he never let others know. His mother's fear had been almost infectious. On his own he feared the dark; feared what other people thought of him. He feared the resumption of school. He feared death. He feared most of all what was ahead of them now.

Brian felt for a moment that all this was happening to someone other than himself. He seemed an onlooker, not one of the main participants.

And Katie screwed up her courage and pushed aside any doubts. She knew that whatever the danger, she'd face it with these friends.

Over the hills and mountains they sailed, rushing into the dark. They kept a wary eye for any further attacks, but in the black of night there was little to see. The dragon flew on without slackening his speed, until several hours later, he began to glide. In large lazy circles he began his descent.

Far beneath, Katie could begin making out lights. First a dim glow, and then one or two bright spots poked their way through the foggy gloom. Then she could see reflected lights on a river that crawled through a valley and a small city. That settlement was poorly lit, but there was enough illumination to reveal a sense of order: streets, lanes, and houses. There were no cars moving along the narrow streets.

In his final pass, the dragon skimmed over the top of the largest buildings and a clock tower. If anyone had been abroad and looked up he would have seen the black outline of wings, perhaps, but would definitely have heard the "whoosh" of the wings cutting the air. With a final flapping of his leathery wings, the dragon braked atop a hill right next to a parking lot and several hundred yards from a nearby castle. The foggy dark completely hid them.

Again there came the need for delicate stretching; dragon riding demands a lot of leg muscles. But in a few minutes the children and Mr. Teagarden were stomping about, the feeling returning to their feet. Doris bent from side to side, loosening her back.

Mr. Teagarden was undertaking another exercise as well: first he would sniff the air and then he'd take in great breaths of it. After holding it for fifteen seconds or so, out it would come, and the process would begin all over again.

Katie walked up to him and watched. After several cycles of breath he noticed her watching him and he laughed. "It's the same air, the same taste and smell. It's the air that I've longed to breathe. Don't get me wrong: there's nothing ill about the Misty Haven air. But this is the air of my home, my youth. It has just the right combination of air coming up from the River Wye, the air coming down from the Black Mountains, burning coal, and peat."

Rapidly chilling after her heated ride, Katie sniffed and could agree that it was different from any other she'd ever smelled. It carried a tang, but it was pleasant, cozy. She longed for one of the fires that she could smell. To be sitting someplace inside where it was warm would be wonderful.

As if he had read her mind, Mr. Teagarden turned to the situation: "We'll need a place for the night. It wouldn't do to sleep out in the open curled up to a dragon. No, my Lord Vrolich will find one of his old lairs and perhaps a meal. We ought to do the same. Follow me and I'll give you the midnight grand tour of the ancient and honorable city of Hay on Wye."

To Brian it sounded something like "Ham on Rye" and he realized just how hungry he was. Down the hill and past the castle they walked until they came to the beginning of a narrow street. "Castle Street this is," said Mr. Teagarden. "Imagine that."

This they followed further down into the town. They passed Boar Street and turned left on Lion Street. All the storefronts were shuttered against the dark. Only through the cracks of the great wooden planks could they see an occasional light.

"These used to be various manufactories, schools, and church-es," said Mr. Teagarden. "Now they are all—each and every one—used book stores. Something very strange has happened here. These canny Welsh have discovered specialty niche mar-keting. And Hay on Wye is now known as the rare book capital of all of Great Britain. Collectors from all over the world used to flock here to browse and pick their way through vast collections. Now I suspect most of their business is over the computer. Change, change, change."

He had stopped outside the imposing facade of a large build-ing. The ashlar surface glowed faintly in the mist. Its white paint seemed to sparkle.

"This is the New Century Hotel. I'm not sure to which century it refers—certainly not this one— but for tonight, perhaps, we'll find a meal if we can beg one at this late hour and beds, unless you've an objection?"

The thought of a meal drew everyone toward the door.

Just as Mr. Teagarden reached out to grab the handle, it was pushed out at him, violently. The sound of argument flowed around them, and out came a hurtling figure, great, vast, and bulky. A women's voice, raised in full alarm, followed the form.

"Out, out you great lurking lout!" she screamed. "You and your filth have no call to rest by my fire."

Katie could see the woman, broomstick in hand, flailing the large man, who cowered before the blows, his arms upraised. With a final swing, the woman took aim at his head and the man, dodging swiftly, ducked the stroke and grasped the handle. Then he stood to his full height. He was immense: tall and broad, but somehow all wrong. His shoulders hung at odd angles, and even though every muscle was tensed he looked loose. After grabbing the broom he swiftly grabbed her wrists. She struggled to slip free.

"Aye, drive me oot athwart your broom ya witch," said the man with clear menace. "The day is coomin' when you'll pay for it, and damn yer een." He pushed her away, straightened his coat and descended the four steps, brushing past Mr. Teagarden and the youngsters. When he reached the bottom he stood before Doris. He looked her square in the eyes, stooping even as he talked. "And belike you'll be another one for the pot before we're through. ...You and your sister there." He tossed his head toward the woman on the steps; her face was aflame with rage. She raised the broom and made to descend the steps. The big man sneered at her and spat on the steps before he walked off into the fog.

The woman with the broom sighed and regained the door to the inn. She pulled open the door and flooded the steps with light. She looked younger than they first surmised. She was younger than Doris, perhaps in her early twenties. And, with the light behind her, they could see the aureole of dark reddish hair, some of which had escaped her cap. She raised her chin and looked down her pert nose at them.

"If you've a mind, you'd best come in out of the damp night before you take cold," she said as she turned brusquely and left them standing alone, the door swinging shut, plunging them into the dark again.

The children had heard warmer welcomes, but their hunger drove them on. And, once they crossed the threshold, they were drawn irresistibly to the fireside and its gentle glow. They settled themselves around the grate and soaked up the smells. There was a savory meal warming somewhere. They could taste it through their noses. And bread, too, perhaps. And ale for Mr. Teagarden and milk for the children.

Katie could scarcely believe that it was the same woman they met outside the inn who now appeared to serve them. She was no longer enraged; instead she was calm and held a hint of a merry smile that played around the corners of her generous mouth. She was indeed young, very young. And petite, dainty. Her freckles stood out in marked contrast to the rest of her milky-smooth skin.

She addressed them at first in something Katie took for Welsh, and noting their lack of comprehension, switched to English of a sort. "It's after time, but you'll be wanting dinner," she said with a singing quality to her voice. "We've simple fare here, plain food and not much variety, but it's good and filling. Will that suit?"

The children agreed. Mr. Teagarden nodded as well, but held his peace. This may have been his hometown, but he was playing the Simple Simon. He looked warningly at his charges; they were not about to let out anything that didn't seem most necessary. Still, he and they smiled when great bowls of mutton stew were carried to a table near the fire. The children had their milk, Mr. Teagarden and Doris foaming mugs of ale. The bread was brown, coarse, and very tasty. It came to them in thick slices, already covered in fresh butter.

After they were served, the young woman spoke to them again. This time she came and hunched down by the fire with her back to the flames. "My name is Fiona, and I'm sorry for such a harsh greeting. It's unfortunate that your introduction to the New Century was marred with such a fashing. That man is one of a breed who—ever overbearing—now has become more so. There seems to be no accounting, but the bad people here have got suddenly worse. It's as if they think they own the place. Sometimes we have to set them straight."

"Will he be back?" It was Doris who asked. The children watched as she shuddered involuntarily.

"Oh, aye. Sooner or later, he'll be aback. And if he acts nicer, he'll be allowed to enter. If not, well, he and his kind have been tossed out of better places than this. And to think that I once walked out with that young man! He's become very like a mean pig. ... And look at you, your bowls are empty. You'll have a second helping?"

They would. They did.

"Well, it's time for me to see to your rooms." She bustled away to check that the beds were made up and ready for guests.

When she returned she inquired about their car and their luggage.

"We didn't drive," Mr. Teagarden explained. "And we've everything we need right with us, so there's no extra luggage."

"Fancy that," said their hostess. "Hikers at this time of year? And no backpacks? Hmmm."

Still, if she thought it odd, she didn't press the point. She did, however, take the time to make room allocations, the three men in one room and the two women in another, all on the second floor.

And then, stuffed to the very gills, the transatlantic travelers toddled off up the stairs to their rooms. A shared bath at the end of the bedroom corridor served all the rooms. The children missed their toothbrushes, but made the best of it by rinsing out their mouths and by using their fingers.

Each in his or her bed, sleep was inevitable and swift.

The great clock somewhere below had chimed one when Mr. Teagarden struggled to awaken himself. There was something terribly wrong; he could almost taste it. He could smell it: the acrid bite of smoke and a fire. Shrugging himself awake he sat up, and found that the smoke was curling under his door. He drew on his pants and sounded the alarm with a loud shout. First, he felt along the door to make sure it wasn't hot, and then he carefully opened it a crack. The hall was thick with smoke. There was no doubt: there was a fire in the New Century. Up and down the halls he roused sleepers: his charges and a few others. With everyone on the floor accounted for, they crept down the stairs into even thicker smoke. The fire was someplace at the back of the building; nothing barred their escape. Coughing and trembling, they tumbled into the street. No one else in the city had appeared to notice that the hotel was on fire.

"Fire, fire," Mr. Teagarden called into the night. He ran to the nearest building, an ancient stone house that was affixed to the north side of the hotel and banged on the door. Its occupant, a fat man, came to the door in an old-fashioned nightshirt and cap.

"A fire? I'll raise the brigade," and with that he rushed off into the house to dress, but not without first slamming the door.

Mr. Teagarden's apprehension was mounting. He, Doris, and the children could see the glow of the advancing fire through the front windows now. The flames were like arms reaching up to scratch at the walls. Mr. Teagarden squinted at the vacillating shadows and shook his head abruptly.

"I fear," he said to Brian, "that not everyone is out. Someone's trapped back there. If I wait longer the consequences will be very grave, very grave indeed. But you stay here to tell them where I've gone once they come to fight this fire." And with that, he ran up the steps and through the doorway.

Chapter 13

A RESCUE, A MEAL, A RHYME

The stone walls of the hotel would not burn, but the roof timbers beneath the slates, the floors, the interior walls and all the furnishings were aflame. The crackle of dry wood and the roar of fire drowned out normal conversation. Anything said had to be shouted.

By the time the full fire brigade was on hand the most important job was to assure that the blaze didn't spread to adjoining structures. The firemen could see the conflagration was going to gut the hotel in a matter of minutes.

Brian shouted to one of the first fire fighters on the scene that Mr. Teagarden was inside the building looking for others who might be trapped. The brigade organizer ordered emergency supplies—oxygen tanks, fireproof blankets, and a stretcher—brought to the command post near the entrance of the building. Sparks and cinders were falling all around them, and the roar of the fire edged up another notch.

Katie could see fantastic shapes and forms in the smoke billowing out through the front door. She imagined each one was Mr. Teagarden and was disappointed until—through a seemingly solid wall of roiling smoke—she saw a foot and then a leg poking through. But these were chest high and Katie could make no sense of them until the rest of the young woman's body poked through with Mr. Teagarden carrying her. His face was black with soot, his white hair singed and in complete disorder. Even the back of his shirt was smoldering. Once through the wall of smoke, his knees began to sag and his burden began to slip from his grasp.

Just in time the others—the fire fighters—came to his aid. A fireman lifted the young woman from his care and Mr. Teagarden, too, was laid on a litter. Katie hurried to his side and listened as he gasped for air. One of the rescue men slipped an oxygen mask over his face, and he sucked hungrily at the concentrated relief within the canister. After a few moments, his breathing slowed and he opened his eyes. Squarely, he fixed Katie's face in his gaze, and she could see the corners of his eyes turn up in a smile. He tried to speak but coughed instead.

"Don't try to talk just now," said Katie. He nodded, resuming his more frantic breathing for an interlude. "I'll go to see if the woman is all right," she continued. Again he nodded.

Katie shuffled to the next stretcher, some ten feet away. An emergency crew was working over the woman. As one of the medical workers shifted Katie could see that it was Fiona; her eyes were open above the oxygen mask, but she was not taking in any of the activity that surrounded her. Katie edged closer and asked: "Will she be all right?"

"Too early to tell," said the lead paramedic. "The burns aren't so bad, but the smoke inhalation can be really rough; that's what kills most people. Still, she's breathing on her own, and she's conscious. Just a bit in shock." Still kneeling he turned to Katie. "If it hadn't been for your friend there, she'd be dead. And I would hate to lose my cousin; Fiona is one of the best we have."

He turned to tend the young woman, and Katie walked back to Mr. Teagarden. Doris was holding one of his hands, stroking it gently. Reme and Brian were taking turns watching him and the fire, which had peaked and was now diminishing. From the rear of the building came a deep explosion—it sounded like a "wham!"—the flames briefly shot up again through the roof.

"Must be the cooker tanks," said a bystander.

The roof timbers collapsed, sending a shower of sparks into the night sky. The fire fighters strove mightily to contain any burning brands that fell on houses in the vicinity. Two roofs that weren't clad in metal started to smolder, but the emergency crew knew just what to look for and then what to do with a spray of water.

After an hour, the blaze had dwindled substantially. Fiona had been removed to a building nearby where she could rest. By the time they carried her off, she still had not come to recognize anything that was going on around her, but her pulse and breathing were unlabored.

Mr. Teagarden—by contrast—was sitting up and taking a glass of water. His lungs were wheezy, but aside from the odd cough and some singed black globs at the ends of his white hair, there was little sign of long-term damage. His eyes twinkled and, after his restorative, he wandered around, approaching and walking away from the fire. Several of the firemen came up to him. Their leader, the same who spoke with Katie, grasped Mr. Teagarden's hand warmly and reiterated much of what he'd told her.

"There are not many men who'd do what you've done this night. Your courage has saved my cousin's life. Fiona is by far the fairest flower of our straggling lot; without her we'd no more carry on. I thank you from the very warmest of my heart."

Mr. Teagarden said something Katie couldn't understand, but she knew it was in Welsh, for the other, at first surprised, volubly responded. After a bit he paused and looked at Mr. Teagarden very carefully. "Duw!" he said. And then in English for Katie's benefit: "Tis true? You are also my cousin, but several times removed? Ain't you the Yank? Tu…? *Te…Gardien*? Of course you are. I see the family resemblance to me mum now. Well, then, *Te Gardien*, you've done a double good night's work here: you saved a stranger who is also your family.

"I suppose I'd best introduce myself, too. I am Michael Owen."

He again extended his hand, covered though it was with dirt. Mr. Teagarden, still seated, met it warmly. "*Te Gardien* is the old name, and somewhat French at that," he said. "For most people, including my young friends here, I'm Teagarden, Amos Teagarden."

"Your sister's no longer here? Nor any immediate family," asked young Mr. Owen. Mr. Teagarden shook his head in the negative.

"Well, what brings you and all this lot back?" Mr. Owen continued. "No, wait; perhaps it's better that I don't know. Or, maybe I already know."

A change in his expression puzzled Katie until he went on: "You are here about The Dragon and The Rose. I can read it in your face. …Of course, of course. Why else would the New Century—that has sat here for more than these two hundred years—suddenly take it to mind to burn to the ground? They know you're here. So, not only did you save Fiona, but in a way you started the fire, too!"

"Our presence might have some effect," said Mr. Teagarden, "but we—none of us—would do such a thing. I believe it's true that the power of The Rose understands that we're here, all of us."

"Vrolich, too?"

"Vrolich, too. My lord is still a changed man, and I shouldn't wonder if rumors soon start to fly."

"And not just rumors," the other nodded in agreement. "There'll be much preparation by their side, then. I don't doubt we'll find this fire was set. I suspect I know by whom, too. Fiona said last night she had to drive out that clod Llewellyn. He and his gang of rowdies have been kicking it up pretty fierce these last few months. It's like they've got it into their heads that they can do anything. I shouldn't doubt we'll find their mark on this night's work. I know they've been watching."

He paused to indicate a small group of figures standing between buildings on the opposite side of the market square. One of them took a cigarette butt out of his mouth and flicked it into the middle of the street, a good twenty feet. Then they laughed and sauntered away, following an ancient bypath that led down to Newport Street and then out of the town.

"Well," said Michael Owen, "There's precious little left of the night, but what there is left, you'll spend with us? My mother will be up and fixing breakfast. She'll know that the fire at the New Century is out and that we'll be returning, and she'll put on the big feed for the likes of all those who labored tonight."

With care, Michael Owen and an associate named Andrew helped Mr. Teagarden to his feet and down the way to Bridge Street. After a block or so they and all the retinue turned in at the low red door of a two-story stone house. Michael, though, was the only one who had to duck, and that he did with practiced ease.

Inside, Katie was struck by the tidiness of the place. Old and faded it might be, but there was a certain determination to fight against disorder. They passed through the front sitting room, doilies on all the overstuffed furniture, through the dining room, where the table was set for at least ten, and into the kitchen, where a small, neat woman bent over a stove. She was cooking a mess of bacon and potatoes. At the sight of so many—and some of them strangers — she threw the full of the apron that was tied around her waist over her head in mock surprise.

"And what, Michael Owen, do you intend? ...Bringing all of the world in to see my kitchen?"

"Hello, Mother," Michael said and leaned in to kiss Mrs. Owen on the cheek.

She bustled all the more furiously, caught Katie's eye and winked. Then she looked at the boys, and at length at Doris. "Ah, good," she said. "You'll do, and no mistake. Here, lass, will you carry in the coffee and scones? When you come back I'll ask you to fetch plates and glasses of milk for the wee ones. And then we'll serve."

At this direction Doris fell into action. Mrs. Owen took a moment to study Mr. Teagarden. She looked at him as though she expected something. Before she said anything, though, her son led him to the washroom behind the kitchen so he could clean up. Reme heard the running and splashing of water. The fragrance of lavender soap mixed with the smell of the food.

Brian had stationed himself by the kitchen sink and was instructed to draw a pitcher of cold water.

"Fighting fires is thirsty work," said Mrs. Owen. Katie was entrusted with toasting bread and spreading it thickly with butter. The jam would be applied at table.

In a great flurry, the food came off the stove and onto serving plates, which were carried steaming into the dining room. Within a minute the whole of the gathering was seated around the table.

Michael dropped his head and clasped his hands before his face: "Oh, Lord, for all thy bounty we give you thanks. Protect us from the evil one and strengthen us in your service. In Christ's Name, Amen."

The grace had come so quickly that Brian's head was still at the level. As he dropped his eyes he noted that Michael Owen looked like a very young man indeed. It had something to do with the way he was praying: the way a child would, trying to summon just the right words to speak to God.

And with the "Amen," the food was snatched off the table and passed round the gathering with amazing speed and enthusiasm. For perhaps five or seven minutes, the only sound was the scraping of the silver across the worn plates.

Michael was the first one done. He set his silverware down on his plate, wiped his mouth with his napkin, and pushed his chair back just a little so he could stretch out his legs.

He openly studied Mr. Teagarden's face, now much restored after a quick wash. He turned to his mother and interrupted her covert glance at her white-haired guest. Michael smiled. "De ye ken him?" he asked. She shook her head imperceptibly and waved at him to hush.

"You mind your manners and don't be embarrassing your mother," she said with mock anger.

At length he ventured: "Oh, I think you know him. He's a Yank now, and he's not come as a tourist" And he turned to Mr. Teagarden: "It's really going to happen after all this time?"

Mr. Teagarden looked up and nodded almost imperceptibly.

"You'll need good men and true if I don't misread you. I'll see what I can do among the good lot."

Mr. Teagarden nodded again.

Mrs. Owen, now openly stared at Mr. Teagarden, regarding him carefully. She chewed her mouthful, ruminating.

The more she looked at him, the more slowly she chewed and the wider grew her eyes. The children watched in fascination. At long last she swallowed and then set down her napkin.

"Amos? It is you, isn't it? I thought there was something familiar about you," she said nodding her head. "It took a bit but I can recognize you through all the years. And you haven't changed. Well, maybe a little. Now, do you remember me? I was Godwyn Jones afore I married Mr. Owen, God rest his soul."

Mr. Teagarden nodded in his own right. "Oh, aye, I kenned from the moment I saw you with your son."

"It's been a long time, indeed," she said. "You've never come back for the odd visit like so many others have done, not even to see us who are your family."

"I've come back to Great Britain before, but not to here."

"And now you have. Michael looks pretty firmly fixed, ready to act for you. And that would mean there's just one thing that's going to happen. Like we've dreamed of all these sleepy years."

"'Old wrongs will be put to right'..." Mr. Teagarden began.

Mrs. Owen picked up the chant:

'...If there's strength in pow'r of light;
and Satan's bane will come again
with child and man on darkling plane.
And twixt the twain in dark and gore
With mighty struggles, force and fore
The days of love for she who sleeps
And he who as a dragon keeps
Again will come to mountain side
To take his place by rightful bride.
And hell will have its own full score
Of those who love the sorcerer.
Death comes at last for every man
Who loves the Lord in this dread land.'

"You have not forgotten, then, Godwyn?" asked Mr. Teagarden.

"Forgotten? Nay. I've taught my own and, even my own youngest who has no wife or children," and here she indicated Michael. "All those years ago that you set me to learn those lines and spread them on? Wasn't that what you had in mind?"

"Ah, Godwyn, you are as good as your name: 'God's own,'" said Mr. Teagarden with a smile. "And now, well, who knows if the rhyme is true? If it is, there may be very hard times ahead. And if it isn't, the times might be worse."

Chapter 14

KATIE DREAMS AND BRIAN FINDS SOMETHING OF VALUE

Godwyn Owen pushed her chair back a little and looked at her son. She nodded her head when he met her gaze, and then she looked back at Mr. Teagarden.

"It's a cause worth a fight," she said with some asperity.

For his own part, Michael sat without moving, but with a small smile playing across his face. At length he spoke: "I used to think it was all fancy tales. I mean, that The Dragon and The Rose ever were, much less still are. But about four years ago I started my own researches, and I studied closely the foundations of the old castle. Not Hay Castle, but the one farther up the hill. Really, it is the remains of a Roman fortification that Vrolich's ancestors built on. And I've mapped some of the caves that open here and there. Mind you, there's nothing in them now—at least the parts I've uncovered. But they're there, the underground network of caves that go God only knows where. When I put all that together I realized that the old stories might have more than a grain of truth in them. I don't know about sorcery, but I'm not fool enough to disbelieve in evil—or in good either, for that matter. I am gratified that it might fall to me to help you in this cause."

It was a longish speech for the quiet Welshman. When he'd said his piece he sat silent once more.

Again, his mother picked up the thread. "Michael will be able to round up a couple of other lads to help. But where do you start?"

Mr. Teagarden sipped a bit of the strong tea in his cup and reflected. "The caves have more to do with this than the open places. But I doubt we'll find what we're seeking through the open network you've found. I recall the passages well, for I was drilled in 'em as a lad. I know the fort, and indeed it was later built into a castle and it was from there my Lord Vrolich ruled his demesne. But there is another opening, there has to be. And a narrow pathway that leads to yet another series of caverns. It has to do with another verse."

Here Mr. Teagarden rose and stood behind his chair, each hand on a rising finial. His eyes looked across the room at a level gaze and with a focus far, far away:

> *Behold the maid—no spot or shade*
> *Behind her is the gloaming.*
> *She, carried there beneath the stone,*
> *Her safe keeping now her dooming.*
> *The Rose, The Dragon ever war*
> *Their battle still a-raging.*
> *While men above their toasts do raise*
> *And set to with their waging.*
> *Follow them and follow down*
> *The path in darkness treading*
> *To swing the sword, the only blade*
> *That full foul Rose is dreading.'*

He fell silent and sat again. Katie squirmed in her chair. Mr. Teagarden looked at her with interest.

"Do you have an idea what it means?" he asked. "I never could cipher it out."

"Maybe," Katie said at last, "it means something simple."

"It could well be," responded Mr. Teagarden. "Not everything has to be difficult."

"It feels as if we only could think hard enough that we'd know where to begin," she said. "...That there is a beginning. Say it again."

Mr. Teagarden obliged and Doris then took up the thread. "It would seem there is at least some kind of sense to it all, if only we knew the key. We're looking for a key, a Rosetta Stone."

"Oh, I've no doubt there's a key. And maybe more than one," said Mr. Teagarden. "This is only the first bit, but the rest makes no sense without this first part solved. So we're at a dead stop there, at least for now."

It was a dismissal, a gentle benediction. He stood, as did Michael Owen and Doris. The children stood last of all for the brief prayer to conclude the meal. That concluded, the men sat again at the table. Doris and Mrs. Owen together determined to take on the scullery duties. Before Mrs. Owen vanished into the kitchen amid the sound of hot water in the sink, she urged Katie to explore the parlor—a sort of room set aside for company.

Mrs. Owen opened the glassed door and ushered Katie into the room.

"There will be plenty of time to see you in the kitchen later," she said. "But for now amuse yourself with the books in here. Mr. Owen was by way of a bookseller, and these he kept back for himself. He said it was his insurance policy, worth a princely sum. But I've not had the heart to sell a one of 'em since his death. They remind me of him. But good books like a good read now and again, so you might want to take a look." And with that she bustled out of the room and back to her chores.

Katie walked along the shelves of books. They ranged from floor to ceiling on three of the room's four walls. There were leather bound books, cloth bound books, even some in boards. She slipped out a brilliantly colored tome and found it was in German. She pulled another from a shelf and found it was in Italian. And a third book was in French.

Finally she took out a great, tall book full of pictures and drawings. It was a book on architecture, and as she turned the pages her eyelids grew heavier and heavier.

She was asleep and yet dreamed of being awake. The book before her had grown so weighty that it was impossible to support any longer, and yet she was powerless to shift it. Moreover, the book—now it was a stone, a great, white stone that covered her—had weighted her down for centuries. With all the effort of her being, she opened her eyes and looked about the chamber. It was no longer the best front room in Mrs. Owen's house; instead it was all of stone, a cave. What light there was came reflected from far down the passage. Someone was coming, someone who was singing and roistering, and swinging a torch from side to side. Here he was now, a swaggering young man, full of drink and tripping over his own feet. With him were companions as ill suited to good manners as he.

They shuffled into the chamber and made mockery of kneeling before Katie.

"Braich y Bedd," said their leader, and instantly Katie knew this was the old Welsh language. "Arm of the Grave," he had said and then went on... "She who stands as though awake but in eternal slumber, it is I, Llewellyn, the Lion, come to tame you, who are already tamed."

The more he spoke, the more he laughed—as did his comrades. Anger rose hot in Katie's throat. If only she could shift the stone cloaking, she could stand. Once standing she'd set them on a different tune.

...And then she shifted, this time leaving the stone behind. Katie was out of her body, floating with the fumes from the torch. She was wafting along the passage in the direction from which the louts had come. She was smoke running along the roof of the passage, seeking a way out. Turning after turning, but always rising until at last, she found her way to a passage that opened above her.

She rose and found her way partially blocked with a flat stone. The men below her had moved it aside just enough for them to descend into the tunnel. As she curled around the stone and out through the hole, she found herself in a cellar. Above her, floorboards creaked with the custom of trade. There was discordant music coming from above, as if many tunes were being played and sung at once. She rose further, past great kegs and barrels, and up the stairs. Through the crack in the great cellar door now she wafted. She spun around as smoke will do and saw that the little room was a pub, and there were people from all ages and all generations crowded together. There were hundreds—perhaps thousands of people—layered one atop another in a room that might, in a squeeze, hold fifty solid citizens. Some of their images wore clothes from the recent age. Others wore leathern breeches and homespun shirts. There was short hair, long hair, unkempt hair, powdered wigs. There were clean bodies and bodies whose next washing would be at their death. And the sound of them singing and talking nearly deafened Katie. "Wi' me own een I seed 'im...." "The bastard right enough took it off me...." "*Vox populi, vox dei....*"

Katie felt the smoke of her substance pushed and packed into a tighter and tighter space until she could no longer breathe. She, too, was being overlayered.

With a start she awoke, finding the open book pressing against her chest. She looked around at the uncrowded certainty of Mrs. Owen's front parlor. Closing the book, she stood and stretched, and then left the room, carrying the volume with her. Everyone except Doris and Mrs. Owen was still at the dining room table, talking with some animation. Well, not everyone: Reme and Brian were asleep in their chairs. Katie looked over at the clock that ticked away on the sideboard. Five a.m.; no wonder she was dazed.

"We have to find the entrance for the cavern, though," protested Michael. "No matter who I bring, it won't do any good unless we know where we're going."

"We'll be shown," said Mr. Teagarden calmly. "This is a matter of signs and wonders. And we wait for the signs; the wonders will come presently."

"I don't doubt that we might wait for a goodly bit," said Michael. "But I think we might do better to follow some of those lads who've been skulking about. They know something. And what about The Dragon? He could tell us, couldn't he?"

"That may be," said Mrs. Owen, coming into the room with a pot of hot coffee. "But you'd have to know that even here a dragon might seem a little odd in broad daylight or by lamplight. I think we can count on The Dragon to stay out of it until the final fight."

"She's right," said Mr. Teagarden. "This is up to us now. My Lord Vrolich would no more appear to guide us than he'd take the town by storm. He would not bring more danger than necessary to Hay on Wye. It is up to us to find the way now and he will join us in a little while. For now, he waits."

Katie moved up to the table and stood beside Mr. Teagarden.

"I know how," she said, still slightly dazed from her dream. "First you have to go into the basement. There's a stone there in the floor. ...I mean there are lots of stones in the floor, but one of them hides the entrance. And you pick up that stone, go down underneath, and then follow the passage. And she's there. But she feels like she's trapped and can't move."

"No more can she," said Michael. "She's been turned to stone by The Rose and has been the marble maiden all these years. But where is this, child? What sort of place is this, and how do you come to know of it?"

"I fell asleep in the parlor with a book on my lap." She looked down and saw that she was still carrying the book she had been reading; she had closed it but not put it down.

Mr. Teagarden had turned to her slightly. He reached out to examine the book. "Oh, it's Freemantle's *Welsh Pubs in History*. Now, which one were you looking at?" He flipped through the pages until he came to a sudden stop. "I wouldn't wonder if it was this one," he said, spreading the pages before her.

Katie read aloud: "'The Dragon and The Rose, one of the oldest pubs in the world, sits upon Broad Street in Hay on Wye. Its origins are obscure but no small amount of legend surrounds the naming of the pub, which is thought to be on the site of a ruined Roman outpost.'

"That's the place I saw in my dream, but it's different, too. And it was full of people, but there were some there I could see through, and the music was strange, some very different than anything I'd ever heard before. Some of it was old, and some of it new...but it was all playing at the same time."

"Aye," said Mr. Teagarden. "Somewhat different from The Dragon and The Rose at home isn't it? Here's the original, the first. Compared to this, mine is but an afterthought. And it's here you say, that we get into the cavern where the lady waits?"

Katie nodded.

"It makes sense that the place was always something I was to remember, and it makes sense with the poem..."

"Say it again," begged Katie. "I don't remember it."

"Nor would you," said Mr. Teagarden. "But here it is again:

'Behold the maid—no spot or shade
Behind her is the gloaming.
She carried there beneath the stone
Her safe keeping now her dooming.
The Rose, the Dragon ever war
Their battle still a-raging.
While men above their toasts do raise

And set to with their waging.
Follow them and follow down
The path in darkness treading
To swing the sword, the only blade
That full foul *Rose* is dreading.'

"Yes, that makes sense if the place described is the pub," concluded Mr. Teagarden.

"And some waging it will be, too," said Michael. "The Dragon and The Rose has been pretty well taken over by Llewellyn and his band of thugs. It'll take us some doin' to get inta' the door, much less down the stairs and to be takin' up the flags on the floor."

"Ah," said Mr. Teagarden, "but it's a place to start. If I know this type of lad you describe, he's at his best about midnight, not so much in the morning. So we'd best plan the trip for early morning, just as soon as we can get in the pub."

"Well, I can tell you that," said Michael. "They make deliveries starting at about nine in the morning, bringing in the barrels, kegs, and bottles. And that's only four hours from now."

"So, nine tomorrow morning—THIS MORNING, rather—it is," said Mr. Teagarden. "We're just going to see what we can see, to reconnoiter. In the meantime, can you raise your band of lads, have them standing by? I doubt we'll need them this morning. But there will be another morning, and soon."

Michael pushed himself up using the table and stood calculating. "Two lads: that should do it I think; any more than that and we won't fit inside...assuming we get there."

Mr. Teagarden nodded in assent. Then he turned to the children—Reme, Brian, and Katie: "For your part today, first, I want you all to take a nap, but a short nap; you've had less than half a night's sleep. And if you can sleep for a few hours it will be to your good. Then, after you are awake and have had something to eat." He paused to look at Mrs. Owen. She nodded. "I want you to spend the day to become as familiar with this town as you can be. Start by taking a look at the map and finding the ruins of the fort and castle—the old castle. Then make it a part of your day to go there. But also go up and down all the streets if you have time. There aren't that many and you should know this place above ground and its streets within an hour. Then, I want you to go out and listen to what people are saying. They might pay you some attention, especially if you speak and they pick up the accents; but you'd be amazed where a quiet child can go and what he can overlisten. That's your job: to be spies, but spies for the good side."

"Shall I go with them?" asked Doris. "I could keep out of the way but be close enough in case they find trouble."

"Well, now," said Mr. Teagarden, thinking. "You have a point, but they must face some of this on their own, too. I guess I'd think it wise if you accompanied them to the castle ruins. Perhaps you could take one of the little books that shows the layout of the rooms, and you could guide them through. But after that come back here and let them skulk through the town on their own. I wouldn't wonder that I'll have another assignment for you by then.

"Michael and his lads will go with me to study The Dragon and The Rose. After the deliveries we'll just be about watching.

With yawns, the children bedded down on various couches and sofas throughout the first floor. Mrs. Owen provided blankets, pillows, and throws. And though they slept soundly, by noon they were up and ravenous. They sat at the table and consumed a full meal of savory beef stew and brown bread with butter.

At their meal Mrs. Owen handed Doris a slim booklet that described the old castle. At the front door, Mrs. Owen handed Doris a covered basket of snacks for the mid-afternoon. As unobtrusively as possible they left and walked through the town to the site of the ruins. They passed Castle Street, Hay Castle — which was not nearly a ruin although very old, the craft centre, through the car park, up the hill and over Forrest Road and again up. Reme could barely contain himself. The day had turned out fine, and there was every reason to jump, hop, and skip. Not to mention shout. But he didn't. With the others he walked along with apparent calm until they approached the castle ruins sticking through the green hillside; then all three children took off at a dead run. Doris, watched them scamper and laughed aloud, something new and delicious for her.

Doris drew up to them eventually as they scrambled up piles of rubble and over mounds that once were parts of walls or ceilings. She set the basket down on a great square block that might have been a foundation stone, took out the booklet and called the children to her. Then they retraced their steps a few hundred feet until they stood on a small berm about forty feet away from the main mass of rubble.

"This was the land moat," she said. "The front entrance through a portcullis would have been right about there." She pointed a bit to the left, and started walking. The children flanked her as they crossed the entry threshold. Consulting the booklet they entered the great hall. At the far end, the fireplace had commanded the focus of the room. It was, Doris read, a fireplace for heat, light, and cooking. Now, there was simply a great stone that had been weathered to a hollow, perhaps the hearthstone.

To the side of the great room were chambers of state, smaller and more private places where treaties had been hammered out, where sensitive conferences had been held. Foundation and wall stones jutted through the grass giving scant outline of the chambers. Above the great hall and smaller side rooms, records and drawings showed there had been three floors of private apartments, or private rooms. That arrangement also coincided with the most common pattern for castles of this type and age. That's where the kings, queens, their very extended families and servants lived. The soldiers would have been quartered within the great, thick walls of the castle itself, both below and above. The castle had two clearly demarcated areas: the inner castle and the defending walls. The latter were honeycombed with tiny rooms, tight passages, and stairs. The soldiers, who were closest to the edge, were most ready to respond to any attack from without.

Brian and Reme traced the narrow confines of the soldiers' rooms in the stones that pushed through the grass at their feet; there was barely enough space to lie down stretched out.

"They must have been crammed in here like rabbits in a too-small cage," Brian said at last.

"How many of 'em do you suppose there were?" asked Reme.

"I don't know, but I'd bet enough to make it count. And I'm sure there were others who could be called from the village. I mean, the village was probably here from when this was a Roman hill fort. So maybe they'd have ten or twelve soldiers who were always on duty and enough others who could come from the town if there was need."

There certainly wasn't much more room than for a dozen or so men.

They turned from the outer walls to the inner court, what had been the great hall in another millennium. Reme looked around with a high degree of interest: "Where do you suppose the steps leading to the dungeon were?"

"I don't think they'd have been in this area," said Brian. "That's not the kind of thing you would put right in front of your dining room. I'd think it would be off to the side someplace, maybe in the walls. If it was below ground, it's probably all caved in."

They had wandered and lost sight of Doris. Reme climbed a stack of stones and espied her. She and Katie were bending over a well, now mostly filled in with rubble. Doris stood at their coming.

"Doris, you have the map? Does it show where the dungeons were?" asked Brian.

In reply Doris handed over the booklet. Brian thumbed through the few pages in only seconds. "No dungeons," he said.

"Well, there might have been," replied Doris, "but maybe they haven't found them yet. When this place fell, it probably came down with a 'thud'. That might have filled them in. Who knows? We might be standing on the roofing right now."

Brian looked around, returned the pamphlet with his thanks, and then moved off with Reme to further investigate. They halted again in the center of the great hall. The air shimmered about them. Fleetingly, they saw around them intimations of what might have been.

"If I were king," said Reme with his eyes now closed, "this is where I'd sit, someplace where I could see and feel the fire, but someplace where I could see whoever came in the room. Kings had to be very careful."

"Yeah," added Brian. "I'd sit here, too. And if my throne was there I'd want to make sure my valuables were right beneath me."

Almost idly he began kicking the turf that had overgrown some large flat stones. Within minutes his kicks grew in intensity and purpose, but a purpose he would not then have been able to define. In a few more minutes he and Reme were on their knees, scraping away the overgrowing sod to find the edge of the largest slate.

"There," Brian said at last, exposing the margins. "Now we need a stick or something."

Reme took it upon himself to search out a stout dead branch that would do for the purpose. It took both of them. All the while each knew that this was not something for which they were likely to be praised: ruining a ruin. But there was something pulling at them, perhaps nothing more than imagination. With a last great heave the stone moved from its bed from where it had lain century upon century. Brian kept leverage on the stick to keep the stone from dropping again to its bed.

Beneath it lay gritty sand and white chalk.

"Nothing here," said Brian with a sigh.

Reme looked at his friend and then at the area where the stone had lain. He sighed, too, squatting down. "But it should have been right here," he said, smacking the sandy surface where the stone had lain with his flat palm.

Reme had to struggle to maintain his balance as his hand passed through a thin crust of earth into a void beneath.

It was all Brian could do to hold up the stone, but if he dropped it, the great slab would come down on Reme's hand, and perhaps even his arm and shoulder.

"Wow!" Reme said, regaining his balance and poising uneasily on the edge of the hole. "Look at this." He leaned over the hole and some of the edge crumbled and gave way into the pit. The boys could hear the clatter of small stones almost immediately striking a floor below.

"It can't be very deep," said Reme as he looked over the edge. "It looks like there's something down there and...."

"Quick," said Brian. "It's slipping and I can't hold it."

Reme ducked back just in time to feel the stone brush past his cheek as it slammed to earth. But his close call didn't seem to faze him. Instead, he turned a pale face up to Brian.

"I think I know what I saw there, and I didn't like it," he said. "It's a skeleton all dressed in leather and stuff. And it's holding a stick."

"A skeleton?" asked Brian. "That's pretty scary, but I think we ought to look again, and we might need help from Doris, maybe even Katie." He looked up to see them walking toward him.

"What have you found, you two?" Doris asked as she approached and knelt beside them.

"There's somebody under that stone," said Reme.

"He means there WAS somebody under that stone," added Brian. "And he left his skeleton behind."

Doris looked from the one to the other. "In usual circumstances if you find anything—a body or an artifact—you have to report it immediately to the bureau of antiquities, or the historic commission or some other such board. I've read about big trouble people have found when they've gone digging in the United Kingdom. So, normally, we'd go get the authorities."

She paused to consider and then resumed. "But this isn't normal by any means. First of all, there's a dragon loose in the hills. Second of all, there's a maiden who's been changed to stone. And third, we've found that some kind of help almost always turns up at the right moment. Maybe this is more of that help.

"Is the body doing anything?" She looked intently at Reme.

"It's kind of dressed and bones are sticking out. And it's holding something."

Doris nodded. "Holding something? Maybe even holding it for us, do you think? Well, you managed to pry up the stone once. Can you do it again? What about it, Brian? And we'll put something under it so it doesn't fall on us or slip back into place. So...Katie, will you run and see if you can find a stone? Remember where you get it from so we can put it right back. It should be about this big." And she held her hands about nine inches apart.

Katie returned first, carrying a white rock cradled in her arms. She dropped the rock and then joined the boys on the turf.

"Was it a real skeleton? I've never seen one of those in person before. This could be really neat," she said.

Doris positioned the stone to one side of the flagstone, a couple of feet from the edge of the hole.

"If you can pry up the flat stone again I should be able to balance it and move it over," she said.

Brian bent his back to the work. Reme came round and helped him with the stick. The flagstone came up smoothly, evenly and teetered just a bit. Then Doris took the upper edge of the stone and walked it aside, the boys having come to help her. They carefully rested it on the stone Katie had brought. She let out a breath of air and told the boys they could relax. The great flag was removed and the hole was now completely exposed.

"Wow!" said Brian. "You're strong."

"I've moved a lot of furniture with my mother. Neither of us looks very powerful, but we know how to lift."

She dropped lightly to her knees and bent over the hole. "Let's see who we have here." The children approached with hesitation to see who or what was in the pit at their feet.

The hole was about a yard deep and at most two feet across. Revealed within was something more of a mummy than a skeleton. Certainly the skull—almost at the top of the hole—showed through around the eyes and at the back of the head, but looking down on him—and it had been a man—they could see wisps of reddish hair still attached to the scalp. He was squatting with his knees drawn up, the only position the tomb afforded. His hands, holding a long brown object, rested between his ankles. He was dressed in some sort of long cloth shirt, probably wool. Over that was layered a leather vest, the kind that would slip over the head and offer protection both front and back.

"Why would he be buried with that stick?" asked Katie.

"I don't think it's a stick," said Doris, "even though it looks like one. I think it's something else, something we might need."

Brian leaned closer, almost to the point of losing his balance. "No, it's not a stick. There's metal of some sort along the length and at the tip. And for all that time underground it's not rusted. Maybe it's gold. It shines like it. And maybe the stuff that looks kind of like wood is really old leather. It looks like the thing that goes over a sword. A...scaaa...something."

"Scabbard," completed Doris. "That's what I thought, too. And look how it's held, straight up, even in death. If this man was buried after he was dead, those who put him here thought that scabbard and maybe the sword it contains were very important. And if he was buried alive, he knew how important it was. Important even in death."

"Buried alive? That would be an awful way to die," said Katie.

"But that's just what some monster would do: bury his enemy right under where his throne sits," said Reme. "That way, every time he sat down he could think about it and smile."

"Twisted," said Brian. "What kind of crazy man would do that?"

"The Rose," said a soft voice behind them.

No one had heard Mr. Teagarden walk up. When he spoke they all were startled. He stood there now beside them, looking down into the pit. "It fits. It all makes sense. Do you remember I told you there was more of the verse about the maiden of stone? The next bit runs on about the sword and the sword bearer:

'The sword remains in his cold hand
Who dead tho living seemeth still
Beneath the arras keeps his watch
For him who comes next to kill.
But one may try, all others cease.
It falls to him whose work is given
Great dragons of the earth to slay
Whose rest at last will come from heaven.
Beware his grasp when you do reach;
Take it firm between your own
Or he in turn will clasp your hand
And carry you living 'neath the stone."

"One of us must grasp the sword," said Reme with a shiver.

"Yes, one must. And just one," said Mr. Teagarden. "And he knows who he is."

Brian stood and looked up at Mr. Teagarden. He said no word as he stared into the older man's eyes. After perhaps two minutes he looked away, and then, after a deep breath, fixed his eyes down. The others withdrew from the edge; they had done their part.

Without hesitation, Brian lay on the grass and leaned his upper body over hole, his arms into the tomb beneath. From above ground the only thing the others could see was that he seemed to be tugging again and again, twisting his body to get better purchase. He called out to Mr. Teagarden and Reme to hold his legs as he moved further into the hole.

Within the pit the scene was somewhat different. Brian found he was looking directly into the face of the dead man, but at an angle almost upside down. He did as he had been told: reached down and took the man's dead hands between his own. They were cold, but flexible.

Brian almost let go when he felt them move under his own, but he knew what that would mean, so he held on even more tightly.

What ensued was a brief struggle, the dead man trying to escape Brian's hold. The body jerked and turned in the limited space, and Brian moved with it, barely keeping his advantage above ground. Brian glanced up from his hands and then looked deep into what had been the man's eyes. There was something there, a flicker of red. And it grew from dull to bright, and then, when Brian felt he could hold on no longer, suddenly dimmed again. At the same instant, the hands under his relaxed completely and fell away from the sword hilt. Into Brian's right ear came the hissing as of a tortured breath, long held, now released. The scabbard and the sword within it came away in his hands.

He lifted the sword above his head outside the pit. Doris took it a laid it on the grass. Then, using both arms at the edge of the hole, Brian lifted his torso out of the pit.

Katie rushed to his side. "Boy, that must have been stuck or something."

"He was holding it," said Brian. "For me."

"What do you mean 'for you?'"

"This is what the man told me about," he said to Katie. "The man I saw in my dream from when we were at home. He's the dragon slayer. This looks like the same sword. Look, here is the crescent of stones in the hilt. It's supposed to be the original, and it was buried with Lord Vrolich's man. I'm almost positive. This was what the book from Grandpa Eames was all about. This was what my dream was all about. This is somebody who's part of our family. Or was."

Mr. Teagarden drew near. "This was the armor bearer of The Dragon. He was a soldier above all other soldiers in The Dragon's service. His loyalty would be above question. It would be likely, then, that The Rose would single him out for special attention, like being buried alive with The Dragon's sword."

"But why this sword?" asked Reme.

"The Rose wasn't the only one who knew enchantment," explained Mr. Teagarden. "There's a story about this sword and its strength. This is the most potent weapon we can dream of against the power of The Rose."

The sword was set aside at Mr. Teagarden's insistence. Then, with infinite care, the flat stone was replaced. Reme and Brian busied themselves trying to refit sod that had been cast aside.

Katie returned her rock. They restored the grave as completely as possible. Mr. Teagarden took off his coat and wrapped the sword. It wouldn't do to brazenly walk back through the village with the exposed blade of The Dragon. Before they set out, though, Mr. Teagarden knelt and invited the others to kneel, too. It was a matter of seconds before all the retinue was at prayer. He delivered a requiescat—a prayer for the dead. Part of it was in the wild Welsh tongue, part in Latin, and some in English. The Lord's Prayer was definitely in English, right to its "Amen."

One by one they stood.

"The first time," said Mr. Teagarden.

"The first time what?" asked Katie.

"I was reckoning that this is the first time that anyone has said prayers over this body. He was not buried in the conventional sense, certainly not on consecrated ground, and I doubt The Rose would ever have said a word to comfort the soul of his enemy or to seek forgiveness or pardon. No, I'm certain we are the first ever to mourn this warrior at his grave, the first ever to know where he lay and to mourn his passing. Others missed him, to be sure—wife, family, friends. But no one outside The Rose, and now us, knew where he lay. This brings a finish to part of our calling."

Chapter 15

SWORD OF STRENGTH

They turned to walk over the heath and toward the town. They arrived unmolested, but not unobserved. A little man, twisted and bent, had seen their leaving and had run on ahead and summoned others—a motley crew. Each had some deformity, however slight. Some were hunched, others had casts in their eyes. One had ears set very low on his head. In the center, stood Llewellyn. He broke through the ranks of what were obviously his minions and strode out to meet Mr. Teagarden, Doris, Reme, Brian, and Katie as they set foot on the cobblestones of Belmont Road.

"And where have you been and what have you been up to?" Llewellyn snarled. His lips drew back over space where several teeth should have been.

Mr. Teagarden brushed him aside and kept on walking. The others of his party followed. Enraged, Llewellyn charged around to re-encounter Mr. Teagarden. As the white-haired man walked toward him, Llewellyn raised his arms to grasp Mr. Teagarden's shoulders and held him in place.

"Unhand me," said Mr. Teagarden.

Brian saw him shift his load; the sword was carried vertically now, still wrapped in the coat. He knew that if pushing came to shoving, the sword would most likely be revealed. He stepped up beside Mr. Teagarden.

"Get out of our way," said Brian. Reme, Katie, and Doris crowded very close behind. Doris insinuated herself between Mr. Teagarden and Katie, a move to protect the girl if a fight broke out.

The thug took his right arm from Mr. Teagarden's shoulder and swung it to give Brian a clout on his ear. He probably would have knocked him senseless if Brian hadn't ducked in time. As it was, Brian not only ducked, but rolled into Llewellyn's legs and knocked him backward. He fell onto the hard stones and, shouting as he rose, slipped and fell again. There was something wrong with his balance.

"You blasted little bastard. I'll spill your guts for this." He reached around behind him and brought out a knife. Painfully, he got to his feet and stood.

Mr. Teagarden slowly began to unwrap the sword, but was halted by a shout from down the street, further into town.

"Hallo.... Help's on the way." It was Michael Owen. Behind him, Katie could see a half-dozen or so others, running at full speed.

Llewellyn turned and looked back at Brian. "Another time, you fatherless bastard." He spat out the "bastard" like a curse and then repeated himself: "Another time." With his fellows he shambled haltingly down an alley that gave way off the street. Katie watched them disperse at the other end of the throughway, all in different directions and at different speeds.

Michael drew up, breathing hard. "I came as fast as I could. They were spying on you, and I think they meant to do some real harm. But I had a lookout of my own and he alerted me to your distress." He paused. "The thing is, I don't understand why. I mean, I know the larger picture, but what have you done today that put them in such a temper?"

Mr. Teagarden peeled back the edge of his coat and the sun struck the gold of the hilt. The flash was blinding. Michael looked away, averting his eyes.

"The sword, then. You've found the sword." Only after Mr. Teagarden again wrapped the weapon did Michael look toward him. "It's no wonder those hooligans stopped you. They knew something that could stand against them was arriving. What amazes me is that they waited at all before they tried to take it from you by force."

Mr. Teagarden looked aside to Brian, who was calmly standing by his side. "That's due to Brian, here, and his attack. He bowled over that Llewellyn fellow before things got rolling against us." Then to Brian he said: "I would not normally encourage your fighting. But you'll have to do many things on your own authority before we're through here." Brian nodded and smiled shyly.

Katie had watched her brother all through his escapade. And now that he smiled, she noted his face at ease.

Michael and two others escorted the five back to the Owen household. At intersections of alleys and streets, Reme caught sight of shadowers who were moving in the same direction, a block or so over. The movements were furtive, and, even at the remove of several hundred feet, threatening. Each one of the party could feel the stalking and, in response, hurried faster down Broad Street.

They paused outside the Owen front door.

"Wait here," Michael said to the assembled party. "I just want to make sure that only Mother is inside."

He opened the door, entered, called out a hello and—in a few moments—returned to usher in his guests. Again they filed into the dining room where Mr. Teagarden returned the scabbard to Brian. He handed it over with a measure of ceremony. Brian then laid it carefully on the table cloth.

"This is it, then?" asked Michael. "The very sword of The Dragon, our Lord Vrolich? And here all the time in our own back yard?"

"I believe so," said Mr. Teagarden. "This sword figures into legend more than once. Yes, it was supposed to be Lord Vrolich's, and his father's before him, but it goes much further back than that. There is a story that this sword was the one that a disciple—probably Peter—used in the Garden of Gethsemane when he struck off the ear of one of the soldiers who had come to arrest Christ. Do you remember the tale? Even as he was betrayed, Christ healed the wound of one who would do him ill. And there are other spells and enchantments laid on the sword, too. It's supposed to have power against evil."

"For all the good it did that poor man in that hole," said Reme.

"Aye," said Mr. Teagarden. "But put this blade one-on-one against The Rose and the story might have been different. There's no telling how many it took to overpower the armor bearer."

Mr. Teagarden paused.

Brian laid his hands on the flaking scabbard. Then he unsheathed the sword; the gold chasing on the blade sent out dazzling sparks of light even in the dim room. In sunlight it would be blinding. He turned the blade from one side to the other, tracing the designs with his right forefinger. He picked it up and handed it, hilt first, to Mr. Teagarden. Before accepting it, Mr. Teagarden bowed and held out both hands. Then he straightened, offering the sword to the attention of the other members of the group.

"It may be that this is the very sword that our Lord Christ put aside with his own hands to forestall further violence. It was this sword that Lord Vrolich used to rule with a just hand. And it was this sword that The Rose wanted hidden away for all time; it would never serve him. In fact, if tales are true, he couldn't even touch it for fear that its merest brush against his skin would result in his death. He was that evil, and this sword was that good. But The Rose knew it could serve his enemies. That's why he had it hidden. And now it's recovered.

"Brian and Reme: I know you were led to this; we've been led all along on this questing. But, how did you know where to find it?"

The boys looked at each other. Brian shrugged his shoulders. Reme spoke: "We were looking around, and it seemed like we could almost see the way things used to be—where the throne would sit, where the fire would be, and tables and chairs. And then we figured out—I think we figured out—where the Rose would keep his most valuable possession. Or what he wanted to keep most hidden. And there it was after a little digging and stone moving."

"...And there it was?" said Mr. Teagarden. "Something for which we've been searching for hundreds of years? There it was? You have found The Dragon and you have found the sword."

He turned to Katie: "And, thanks to you, we think we know where Queen Triosha might be."

Katie looked at her toes for a minute. Then she looked directly into Mr. Teagarden's eyes. "We go there tomorrow," she said softly. The memory of her dream was not terribly pleasant, but she knew she would go with them anyway.

Mrs. Owen, who had been standing behind the young girl, put her hands on Katie's shoulders. Then she bent and whispered in her ear: "The fear will be less with the morning. You'll be brave enough for the task."

Then to the others she said: "I've prepared a meal and then you'll find your beds ready. That's the good part of having a big house: there's room. So, let's sit down for dinner."

Mrs. Owen led the way, calling out to Doris, Brian, and Katie for help to bring the steaming bowls and platters to the table. There was ham, potatoes, pickled onions and pickled pickles, spinach, bread, butter, and jam. And for dessert there was a three-layer vanilla cake with rich chocolate frosting.

During the meal conversation went 'round the table. Doris explained her presence to Mrs. Owen: "I was part of the reason they were in such danger," she explained. "My mother—I don't understand it—was so intent that she threatened to kill Katie simply to get some diamonds. I know they were worth a fortune. But never in all the time I was growing up did I think she'd do something so violent, so evil. She had always been distant, even cold, but never had she committed such an act of true aggression. I'm ashamed to say that I didn't stop her. I couldn't."

"Not then," said Katie. "But I think you could now."

Doris nodded. "Yes, but I am ashamed that I didn't then. I didn't even think about doing it or the fear you were facing."

"Evil," said Mr. Teagarden, "makes us all less than what we should be. Just look at the lot that accosted us this afternoon. I thank God you didn't have the opportunity to explore the town as I'd asked earlier. If they'd have found you alone—any one of you—it would have been worth your life."

"And, what's the matter with them anyway?" asked Reme. "They're all misshapen. I saw Llewellyn when he fell...there is something wrong with his legs, something that he didn't want us to see."

"Wasn't always like that," said Michael. "In fact, it wasn't till about a year ago that anything was wrong with any one of those men. I've known 'em all. Llewellyn and I went to school together here. We were close friends, the best friends sometimes. And then—all of a sudden—he's changed. The rest of them, too. They were all fine and friendly men. But they're different. And in the space of about a year. There were no thugs in Hay on Wye. The stuff they've been doing around here was simply unthinkable more than a year ago. I tried to talk to Llewellyn and it's like he doesn't even hear me. He just stands there and smiles that smarmy smile, a tough guy."

"But he wasn't hard to knock down," said Brian. "It was almost as if he fell down of his own accord. All I had to do was start the process. And, then, there was the smell. I didn't think of it till now, but he sure didn't smell very good. And it wasn't just that he needed a bath. There was something rotten about him."

Mr. Teagarden had taken out his pipe, packed it with tobacco and lighted it, and now sat puffing on it. He raised his eyes to meet Brian's. "He really didn't have much strength when he tried to stop me," he said. "And, yes, there was the smell. It's a smell I know too well: cadaverine. I just caught a whiff of it, but I'm sure it was the smell of the dead. And, too, there was what he said to you, Brian. He called you a bastard, and the way he repeated it was as if someone had told him what to say. Almost like somebody knew what would hurt you most."

"I heard him," Brian replied. "But I'm not a bastard. My father is dead, that's all."

Katie felt the tears mount in her eyes. She stood up from the table and walked to her brother; she needed to be held, comforted. And Brian, for the first time since his father's death, obliged. He turned in his chair and hugged his sister, almost squeezing the breath out of her, tears running down his own cheeks.

And when, at last, Brian let go of his sister, he looked around him at his friends; friends who understood because they, too, had faced losses too big to endure alone.

Mr. Teagarden spoke first: "You've done well, Brian. And you, Katie. And Reme," nodding at each in turn. "And there will be need for all our strength together, so I'm for an early night. We'll need to be up with the sun in order to storm the gates of The Dragon and The Rose. Michael, I saw today that you have a band of able young men. You said you've picked two to join us tomorrow?"

Michael nodded.

"They should all carry something in case there's a fight," said Mr. Teagarden. "But it won't do to have them roaming the streets with guns and the like. A stout staff should be enough. There's likely to be bloodshed before all this is done, and, even if it's ours, we want no loss of life laid to our credit."

"I just hope the other side feels the same," said Michael, shaking his head doubtfully.

"Whether they do or not is up to them only. And we'll find out tomorrow. Now, I pray each of you a good night." With that he rose and, guided by Mrs. Owen's direction, ascended the stairs and to his bedroom.

The others — most of the others, that is — followed shortly thereafter. Mrs. Owen progressed with her arm on Katie's shoulder. Michael and Doris lingered and stayed at the table to talk. One by one the lights went out in the house until only the dining room light cast a weak flicker through the glass in the front door.

Chapter 16

DOWN, DOWN, DOWN

The night passed without incident and the first rays of morning — accompanied by the shrill cries of birds — found Mr. Teagarden pothering about in the parlor. He had ordinance survey maps spread over the couch, travel guides stacked on the chair-side table, and picture books open on the floor.

Mrs. Owen entered her parlor to inquire how soon he'd like breakfast and remarked the chaos: "A right fair mess!"

"Yes, I know it looks that way, but I'm trying to see where and how the caves might interconnect; there are probably hundreds of tunnels leading in and out," he said. "I know that Katie has seen one way, but that doesn't tell me how far or in what direction. I was trying to figure out the possibilities based on the landforms. I remember this section of the caves," he gestured to an area east of the village. "But I don't know where or how it intersects with the cave under The Dragon and The Rose. We are likely to need a back way out. It's one thing to get into the pub at this early morning hour, and it's another altogether to attempt to get out sometime later in the day when we'd likely be outnumbered by the forces of The Rose. If numbers were to be the sole determinant, we would not win."

"Surely they can't be," said Godwyn Owen. "If that were the case the fighting would be all over by now. The power of the Rose is strong, malignant and his determination is fierce. Still, I believe in the power of good and God's promises far more than I believe in the threats of evil. Today's battle may be — if we're blessed — the end of a struggle that was ancient even before you and I were born. But the struggle matters. And, I entrust my son to this fighting. He is the last I have to give. I think I would serve better here, praying and waiting. And preparing for whatever comes."

Mr. Teagarden stood and smiled. "...Whatever comes. I am most worried for the children. They are none of them at an age to consent in joining such a battle. But we need them, and they have as large a part to play in this as any of us. Your prayers will serve us well, I think."

Together, like the old friends they were, they chatted amiably as they progressed to the kitchen where Mrs. Owen, again in her element, began preparing a meal fit for—if not a king—then at the very least the warriors who serve his cause. One by one the young people drifted in. They sat down and ate a hearty breakfast, though no one wanted to overeat. Too full a stomach is worse than one that's too empty especially if there's fighting to be done. Still, they didn't have any idea about their next meal. After the table was cleared, Mr. Teagarden brought out the ordinance maps.

The Dragon and The Rose pub was built into a hillside. In fact, the hill rose so steeply that while there was a flight of steps from the street to get into the pub, the rocky hill formed part of the back wall of the establishment. There were other houses in the town of similar situation, Mr. Teagarden noted.

"And there's no telling how many of them have access to the caves as well," he added. "It's always been a possibility, but I've never known with certainty that it was so."

At last they stood, joined hands and prayed. The Welsh sounded so very melodic in Katie's ears, but she could make no sense of it until Mr. Teagarden switched to English: "And grant, oh Lord, as it is always your property to do, to have mercy on us standing before you. Give us singleness of purpose, strength to meet the task before us, and resolve to see it through...in Christ's Name, Amen."

"Amen" rang round the table.

Michael had assembled ropes, backpacks with supplies, and torches (known also as flashlights), in the front hall. Each of the party picked up something that came to hand. Brian chose a coil of rope in addition to the sword (which Michael had wrapped in oilcloth to avoid undue notice). They readied themselves in the hallway before Michael would consider opening the door; that way they would spend as little time on the streets as possible. It would be difficult not to draw attention, accoutered as they were, but they would not add to the distraction by shifting ropes and packs. So, they stood inside and positioned their loads as comfortably as possible.

"I believe it's nine o'clock," said Mr. Teagarden looking at his watch. Michael checked his as well and nodded. And then he gave his mother a quick hug and opened the door. They left the front door single file, but walked side by side as they moved up through the town to the pub. Two others joined their ranks, good young men Michael had recruited. They were Thomas and Andrew, and were familiar both from the day before driving away the thugs and fighting the fire at the New Century.

They drew up to the pub and halted. A lorry driver was wrestling with a keg of beer, trying to get it "just so" on the hand truck for its trip to the cellar. The door to the basement was let into the sidewall of the pub. The stair went down just inside the door. The driver was fiddling with the padlock. Aside from his attention to the lock, there was no other display of life about the place.

Mr. Teagarden noted that the windows could have done with a good cleaning, and the front stoop—the stairs—needed to be swept. Further along the street was a pool of vomit. Mr. Teagarden shuddered at the evident lack of care.

Without so much as a glance their way, the driver opened the double doors and wheeled his load inside and down the stairs.

The exploration party walked to the open cellar door and began to descend. Reme noticed several window curtains in houses fronting the pub twitch back. Someone was noting their presence.

The deliveryman had reached the bottom of the stairs and the door stood wide open. Mr. Teagarden approached first and began his descent. Following him, the party blocked off the daylight that illumined the driver's work. He turned from his barrels and stood to watch the approach of the group. His arms crossed over his chest, the squat man looked most like one of the barrels he was delivering. His nut-brown face was creased in consternation.

When at last they stood before him he growled: "What's this? What's this? Does the owner know you're about? Unh? What are you doin' down here? And with bairns, too?" He had noticed

Reme, Katie, and Brian. "You'd best turn around and get out of here before there's trouble."

"Oh, there'll be trouble all right," said Michael, stepping forward. "But it's nothing to do with you. I'd recommend that you finish your delivery here and leave." The other young men of the party—Thomas and Andrew—showed themselves by his side, and the lorry driver, realizing he was outnumbered, retreated up the cellar stairs with an oath. Michael sent his two peers to assure that the driver had indeed departed and, then, that the cellar doors were closed behind him and barred from the inside.

Thomas moved down the stairs again, away from the cellar doors, crossed the basement floor into the gloom to the far corner of the basement. There he put his left foot on the first tread of yet another stairway leading up—this one inside the pub. Katie felt buoyed by the remarkable similarity between her vision and the actuality. Yes, this was the same place, she realized with a shiver. She looked around once again, and by the time she'd completed her survey, Thomas had reached the top of the stairs. There, he turned his attention to the door leading into the main floor of the pub. He coerced an ancient, encrusted deadbolt into its socket. The sound of the bolt snapping into place echoed through the basement. They had now managed to seal all the entryways into the cellar, at least from above.

Then, starting in one corner, the men began canvassing the floor, searching for a loose flooring stone. They moved aside everything, including the full new barrel of beer that sloshed merrily when it was rim-wheeled to the far side of the room. Mr. Teagarden took his walking stick and bounced it on each of the flags to hear if it were loose or if it sounded especially hollow underneath. Flag by flag.

Almost three quarters of the way across the floor two things happened almost at once. The first was a rattling of the door at the top of the stairs. The second was a most definite "Thonk" where all the other tiles had sounded "Thack."

"Who's down there," roared a voice from above. "I'll have the law on you if you don't come up now."

Then came silence, until the cellar doors that led to the outside were rattled. Shortly after the last rattle, curse upon curse—some of them new even for Mr. Teagarden—assailed their ears. They were each and severally damned to Hell for all eternity. But the party had not been idle. Michael and Thomas had pried the hefty stone from its dusty bed and set it carefully to one side. Michael bent over the hole and shined a torch into the black.

"There's a built in ladder here and a sort of room below, but circular. Several doorways lead off in different dictions. And that's all I can see." He stood up and dropped his backpack down the hole. Then he descended, trying each metal rung (which was mortared into the wall below) before asking it to bear his full weight.

"It's fine," he said when he jumped from the last rung the three feet or so to the floor. "There's a layer of dust here. And no footprints. This has obviously not been used for a long, long time, probably centuries."

Katie was next down the ladder, followed by Reme, then Brian, carefully passing down the scabbard and sword before him. Doris was assisted by Mr. Teagarden, who followed her. That left Michael's friends. They repositioned the stone so that it would fall back into place, and together, both standing on the same rung, they carefully lowered it on top of themselves. It was a matter of no small skill. Reme watched their arm muscles quiver as the very last of the light from the cellar was snuffed out.

"Do you think they'll find it right away?" asked Doris.

"I shouldn't wonder that it would be quite noticeable," said Andrew. "All you'd have to do would be to check for the stone with no dirt worked into the cracks. But it'll give us a few more minutes before they get it up. Which, of course, is after they break down the doors. Or," he said laughing, "maybe they'll just wait to see if we come up again."

Below, in the caverns, Michael was busy consulting with Mr. Teagarden for the best direction. His lantern shone down the various passages.

"We've no clue which is the right way," Michael explained. "It's possible they all head to the same destination, but it's just as likely that they head in opposite directions."

Mr. Teagarden deferred to Katie: "You are, after all, the only one of us who has been here in any real sense."

Katie nodded and tried to recall. "It might be any one of them. All I remember is coming out and that's not exactly like going in.

Maybe if I could wander in a ways for each one and then turn around and run out, that might give me some idea."

Andrew appointed himself her guard as she walked through the first doorway and into the tunnel. He turned on his torch and let Katie lead the way. Her shadow eerily preceded them. Their light had vanished before Katie turned about and charging came out. Andrew followed at a more sedate pace, still carrying his lantern.

"I don't think so," said Katie. So, she and Andrew tried the next doorway. The same process was repeated with the difference in the report: "Maybe this one. But I'm not sure. I don't remember and I don't want to start remembering things that weren't so in the first place."

So they tried the third doorway. This time, after Katie came out she was shaking.

"This is not the tunnel," she said adamantly. Then she and the rest waited for Andrew to appear. There was no sign of him, no warm glow of the approaching lantern, and after a few more minutes Michael moved into the tunnel.

Mr. Teagarden halted his progress. "Michael, do not press on alone. I think all of us should go or none." Michael nodded and the party proceeded *en mass*. They followed each turning in the passage for a distance of perhaps four hundred yards. The dust that lay in the circular room was nowhere evident this far in the tunnel. There was no sign of Andrew. Nor were there any intersecting passages or holes in the floor into which he might have dropped. Andrew had simply vanished.

"This is farther than we came," said Katie. "If he's not here that means that he went further in. And, even though this isn't the passage—it feels all wrong—I think we should follow him."

Mr. Teagarden surveyed the faces that surrounded him. In the lantern light they appeared resolute. Katie's face was especially set, almost defiantly so.

"So, we push on, then?" he asked for confirmation. Michael turned and led the way. The bulk of the party followed after with Thomas bringing up the rear. The tunnel led down and then up, turning and twisting until any sense of direction had been long left behind. And when he pulled out a compass, Michael found it was useless; all points were North. Whenever they came to an intersection Mr. Teagarden and Michael would examine the floor with the lantern close by, seeking any sign. With a shrug, they would arise and choose a turning—either left or right. Over the unused path, they laid a length of string to indicate the true passage for their return.

Once, after stumbling about, they found themselves coming out over a string. "There's no way of telling how far back this is in our path," said Michael. This could be the last turning off. Or the first. We may have made any number of wrong turns in between."

Tom, who had been in charge of laying the string bent to examine it. "This is the last one," he said, standing with the string in his hands. "I took the liberty of tying as many knots in the string as we've had choices. There are thirteen knots. We've laid thirteen strings. So, we need to go lay this string in the path we've come out and try another direction. This was just a circle."

It took Reme a few minutes to think through the logic. "There's no guarantee that any given tunnel will go anywhere, is there?"

"No," Mr. Teagarden agreed, "no guarantee."

"That means that we might wander about down here forever. I think of the combinations, the mathematical possibilities. We've only dealt with thirteen so far, but on another turning there may be any number of branches. There are likely to be thousands of choices, and we have to find the right one."

"Well, we didn't this time," said Michael. "But I'd say we need to move on. I can't believe that Andrew would willingly wander away. To my mind that means someone or something forced him to leave us. And that means he's in trouble."

It was then that Doris thought of something: "You know, sometimes we can't see things because we don't have enough light. We were worried about that down here. What happens if we have too much light? Wasn't there a line about finding our way in the dark in the rhyme we heard?" She looked to Mr. Teagarden, who nodded and recited:

'Behold the maid—no spot or shade
Behind her is the gloaming.
She carried there beneath the stone

Her safe keeping now her dooming.
The Rose, the Dragon ever war
Their battle still a-raging.
While men above their toasts do raise
And set to with their waging.
  Follow them and follow down
  The path in darkness treading
  To swing the sword, the only blade
  That full foul Rose is dreading.'

Doris resumed: "We found our way under the stone and we've gone down and down and maybe we need to walk in darkness. There's no dust in these tunnels because it really couldn't fall from anywhere, not like when we climbed down the ladder. There may be other things that would mark a pathway, though. Aren't there molds and funguses that give off phosphorescence when they're crushed? Like where we've been walking or where somebody's been dragged? All we'd have to do would be to turn off our lights...and see."

The two electric lanterns were shut off at the same instant. Slowly, as their eyes acclimated to the dark, they noted something on the floor: faintly glowing green patches that perfectly matched their shoes.

"How many do you see?" asked Mr. Teagarden to Doris. "If there are seven, that accounts for those of us here...everyone except Andrew."

"Just seven," said Doris.

"Then," explained Brian, "we need to go back toward the beginning of the tunnel and see if there's a turning that we didn't make that somebody else did."

The lights came on again and they tracked back along the path. At each intersection they doused the lights and waited as their eyes adjusted to see if there were any other prints.

Finally, at the fifth intersection back, they found a glimmer, perhaps what they were looking for. Something nearly a foot wide had been dragged down the corridor. Tom, who had been picking up strings as they came along, repositioned one across the way they'd just come and they moved off down the trail that glowed before them.

"What could have made this?" Doris marveled. "It must be very, very smooth. Maybe something like a tire with a badly worn tread? But it must be a big tire."

Mr. Teagarden looked at Michael and minutely shook his head. No one answered. Brian had noticed the shaking of the head. His palm, which he carried on the hilt of the sword, grew wet with nervous sweat.

At each intersection they stopped to read the phosphorescent trail and, guided by that, turned left and right down an odd branching of corridors. Toward the end, they left the lanterns off all together until they found themselves in a space that sounded far larger than the corridor. The walls that had been at hand had fallen away. They could feel an openness before them, and they stopped as a body.

Katie sniffed. "This is it!" she whispered. "This is the room where the statue is. I can tell by the smell of it. It's funny: kind of bad and kind of...I don't know."

Now all of them were sniffing, but quietly.

Michael turned to Mr. Teagarden: "Do we turn on the lanterns?"

"No, not yet," said Mr. Teagarden. "If this is the cavern where my Lord Vrolich's bride waits, this will be the final battlefield. Our enemy will know soon enough that we're here. For now, let us tarry and listen."

They sat. All they heard was a susurration, a "shhhhhh"ing sound now and again from across the cavern—or at least where they though the cavern might extend. It never grew louder, never softer. After what seemed hours, Mr. Teagarden whispered to them: "I think it's time. Let's approach but without lights until I give the signal. Be careful: there may be holes in the floor. Test every step before you trust it."

As soon as they entered the chamber they spread out, just at arms' length. They touched the tips of their fingers. Again the noise came from in front of them, a dry rustling. They stopped in a line.

"We've come," said Mr. Teagarden addressing the void.

"Yessssssssssss?"

It came so softly across the floor that Reme could not be certain he'd actually heard it or imagined it.

"Where is Andrew?" Again Mr. Teagarden's voice boomed out.

"Heerrrrreeeee. Commmmmmme toooooo meeeeeee."

"Now!" Mr. Teagarden said as a signal to light the lanterns. Before them, perhaps a hundred feet away, rose a roiling column. The undulating surface gave back the light in a slick sheen. How tall was it? Thomas gauged that it might be man-high or a little better. Katie saw it was certainly taller than she, and much, much more stout. But what was it? They approached and Brian could finally discern thick coils of muscle, squeezing around and around.

Nearer they came: forty, thirty and, finally, twenty feet. And in the mass of coils, two venomous eyes opened and a head—a snake's head—reared from the mass of moving flesh and stared unblinking at them.

"Heeee issssssss heeerrrrrre.....ssss...sssss....ssss." Slowly the giant snake uncoiled. At the center was stone pillar, and smashed against it was what remained of Andrew. He had been pressed against the stone and rolled around it again and again. When the last coil released him, he fell lifeless to the floor. Michael and Thomas both started for the unmoving figure. All thirty or forty feet of the snake, meanwhile, moved off indifferently and waited. They reached Andrew together and dragged him back from the pillar.

Katie had never seen anyone who had died in a bad accident. His limp body showed bruising and rawness where he had been crushed against the stone. She studied Andrew's face for some clue of how much pain he had endured, but she found nothing there. His eyes were half open and his jaw hung slack.

The snake slithered in their direction and Brian kept glancing nervously between the beast and Mr. Teagarden, looking for a signal that it was time to withdraw the sword. Mr. Teagarden noticed his anxiety and motioned for him to keep the sword in its scabbard. The snake advanced and stopped.

In whispered and lisping speech it addressed them. "Do I know you?" it hissed. "Yeesssssss. You are the meddlerssss. Bothersssome. Behold your fate." He looked to the open doorway through which they had come. Katie, Brian, Reme, Thomas, Doris, Michael, and Mr. Teagarden turned at the sound of shuffling. In the light of torches held aloft by misshapen arms there could be seen a lurching and crawling ragtag force issuing one by one.

Llewellyn led the way. There were perhaps fifty men and more were joining them. And not only from that doorway; two other lines straggled in from other entrances to the cavern as well. A gathering mob, they surrounded their foes.

"Take them. Do what you will. Yessss."

Unhealthy arms reached out to grab them. Mr. Teagarden shouted at the snake: "You need these poor deluded souls to do your own work? What a poor magician you must be!" And to Katie's surprise, he laughed out loud.

The arms paused. The only sound was that of the great snake sliding among his men.

"Poor magic? I?"

Mr. Teagarden was still chuckling, even as the arms of the rag-tag army remained outstretched, straining toward him.

The snake reared above the crowd that surrounded Michael's party. Brian had trouble squaring the incongruity of the mammoth snake—whose body was perhaps as thick as that of a fat man—and his friend's laughter. For, far from quailing before the serpent, Mr. Teagarden was bent with laughter, struggling to catch his breath. And he was pointing now, too, at the snake as it swayed above him.

The snake grew more angry. He was venomous before in his malignancy, but now he was doubly dangerous. "You shall ssss-see my power and then feel my anger," it hissed with a hate that had been stored over centuries.

In a single hissing exhalation, he breathed on each of his men, and one by one they dropped. The issue was foul, but for Katie and the others it was merely that; they could bear it, covering their faces with their hands, tugging out shirttails to use to cover their noses and mouths.

The men of his army, though, were consumed. Left and right they were felled, their burning torches slipping from their suddenly powerless hands. The torches landed with dull clatter, but were still aflame. Compared to the torches, the men sank slowly to their knees—which were now unable to hold them. Some then pitched forward onto the faces; others rolled onto their sides and backs, writhing uncontrollably.

And as soon as the men collapsed, their flesh began to fall away from their bones and to bubble as it disintegrated. Thin bloody liquid ran out from under the piles of their garments, and their bodies seemed to deflate until there was nothing but greenish bones, rotting ichor, and sodden clothes. Llewellyn, the last to fall, glared balefully at Michael as he began to dissolve. His mouth moved as if to say something, but no sound came forth.

A stench arose from the floor, the same smell Brian had noted when he'd run into Llewellyn, but now overpoweringly strong. Katie bent at the waist and threw up into the mess at her feet.

"Now you sssssee. They were alive only for my pleasssssure, and I will deal myssssself."

"Oh, we see all right," said Mr. Teagarden, still laughing. "They were yours to start with." With infinite relief, Brian saw Mr. Teagarden turn to him and wink as he cast his arm in gesture over the remains of the fallen ruffians; he intended to anger the serpent. He turned back to the snake and smiled up at him. "How long ago did you suck the life out of them? Six months? A year? No wonder they couldn't get the better of us, of even a boy: they were already weakened with your power."

"My power? You will feel it. Sssstand!"

Michael felt as if his muscles had been replaced with wood. He couldn't move as much as a finger. He couldn't even feel himself breathe, but he could see and hear.

Only Reme had any ability to move. And that was limited to his neck and head. He was whimpering; it would have been a scream, Brian knew, if he could have taken in enough air. All the rest of them were frozen. Immobilized, they could only watch as the snake glided among them, sniffing with its flicking tongue.

"Yesssss...yessss...yesssss." Mr. Teagarden, his smile now seemingly permanently affixed, heard but did not feel the beast brush against his leg as the length of its sinuous body moved past. The snake slithered from one of them to the next, hissing and caressing.

At length, he coiled about Doris. She was begrimed with the unholy sludge from the floor but could make no motion to protect herself as the snake began to squeeze. Reme opened his mouth and tried to fill his lungs. What came out was squeaky and shrill: "Help! Help! Lord Vrolich, help!" His cry echoed feebly from the cavern walls.

"He will not hear you. Sssss...sssssss....ssss."

Another snake laugh.

To the last susurration was added a "chuff."

But it didn't come from the snake. From the far side of the cavern, an area deep in darkness, came a second "chuff" and then a third. To the foulness of the air came the smell of fire and sulfur, wafting across the room. Smoke drifted lazily toward them, tendrils exploring the reaches of the cavern roof.

Chapter 17

VENOM AND FIRE

"He issssss here? Here? My brother? My dear brother!"

With infinite slowness, the dragon crossed the floor until he crouched before the snake as it tightened around Doris. In the dim and flickering light he looked like a giant rock, having adopted the coloration of his surroundings.

"Will you sssssave her?"

"*Ita. Statim,*" growled the dragon.

Reme, freed momentarily from his panic, translated: "It means, 'Yes. Immediately.'"

The snake kept tightening his hold. Doris' face was turning an alarming red, moving to purple. Then, with great care the dragon stretched forth his long neck and, opening his jaws, bit into the snake's roiling flesh. Wounded and screeching, the snake spat venom and tried to return bite for bite, but a dragon's hide was tough, plated with great overlapping and interlocking scales.

The snake loosed his hold on Doris and thrashed back and forth, hissing, coiling and uncoiling his great body. The dragon, seeing Doris freed, bit down harder and dragged the snake away from the frozen retinue; a blow from the snake's tail would easily prove fatal to a child.

Smoke preceded fire as the dragon attempted to consume his enemy. At the first tongue of flame, a flash illuminated the cavern. And the snake was transformed first into a giant spider, only one of whose legs was held by the dragon. Then, in another flash, the spider vanished and in its place was a weasel-like creature, all teeth and flashing claws. The weasel, which was held only by the hair on his back, transmuted into something that looked to Brian like a foot-long bald-faced hornet, which flew out of the dragon's maw before he had time to close his jaws. The hornet buzzed angrily above the party and then veered out toward one of the walls of the cave.

There it changed yet again, this time to an ancient man, withered and sunken. He stood, only with the aid of his staff. His clothes, once fine robes, bejeweled, hung in tatters about him. With great effort he held his staff aloft and mumbled arcane words that fell far short of his audience. There grew about him a blue light that radiated ever outward. Its intensity overpowered the few remaining guttering torches that lay on the floor. Inch by inch it crept across the floor until it reached the dragon. After the first touch of it against his giant paw, he withdrew, step by step, until he was hard pressed against a wall of the cavern. The blue light pulsed toward him in unceasing waves.

The same light was washing over the children and adults. Still paralyzed, they could make no move to avoid it, but when at last it fell over them, there was no sense of further distress or discomfort. Instead, they were suddenly very sleepy and relaxed. If they could have lain down, even in the middle of the charnel-house mess, they would have done so and thought no more about it than when they lay down in their beds at home. They stood sleeping, except for Reme who was able by dint of sheer determination to keep a drowsy watch.

"*Mors tua, vita mea,*" said the ancient magician.

"'You must die so that I may live.'" Sleepy as he was, Reme heard the words and understood them.

The blue light washed over the dragon and his head was nodding.

Reme rallied as he saw through his barely open eyes that the dragon was in serious danger. His first attempt at calling out was a mumble. He cleared his throat and called out again. Although it was soft, his voice carried. Still the dragon nodded. His third call was more firm, and by that time he, too, was more awake: "Lord Vrolich, wake up! Don't sleep now. He'll kill you. And then he'll kill us."

The dragon snapped his head up at the cry. He focused most intently on Reme. The giant orbs grew brighter. He chuffed and snorted and finally sent a great blast of flame over the floor to the magician. The blue waves, beaten back, abruptly ceased as the old man wavered and staggered as if under a heavy load.

With the spell defeated, the others of the party began to revive. Mr. Teagarden yawned as he awakened.

"*Non placet*," said the ancient sorcerer at last when he regained his balance. Reme translated it as "It does not please me."

Again the magician waved his staff and the upright stone against which poor Andrew had been crushed began to change. What appeared as a rough but undistinguished surface began to flake off. A pile of white powder accumulated around the pillar and slowly there emerged the figure of a woman, kneeling and bound in chains. She appeared as a finely sculpted work of art, pale stone upon a pedestal. The magician feebly walked to her, tapped the stone with his staff and then stood with the pillar separating him from the dragon.

With the touch of the wand, the stone turned a rosier hue, the chains to a deep, blood rust. Reme observed that she breathed. Her lids, closed for centuries, opened with delicious slowness. Her eyes, a brilliant blue even in the dark of the cavern, looked out calmly at the dragon.

"Vrolich!" she said with joy, recognizing the dragon immediately. This, then, was the fair Triosha, the young queen.

Mr. Teagarden had to allow that the myths and legends had not led him false: she was as fair and lovely as ever any young woman had been. Her face was well formed with features that worked together to give her an expression of intelligence. Her skin—and all of it was exposed; anything that had been clothes had fallen away in dust—was pure and unspotted. Her form was womanly. And her steady gaze rested entirely on the dragon.

Lord Vrolich held in his breath for fear of singeing his bride. There sprang to his eyes and then clattered on the floor the diamond tears so highly prized by others. And the wizard, crouching behind the fair maiden, began his taunting.

"*Nihil obstat*," he crooned. The children, by some grace, began to understand what the ancient said: "Nothing stands in the way."

Truly, there was nothing between the dragon and his ladylove except ten or so feet of rough floor. But as he took his first step toward his wife, she cried out as if in pain. The dragon moved back and the look of excruciating torture passed from her face.

She shook her head to rid herself of the tears that had run down her cheeks. The chain that surrounded her bit more tightly into her delicate flesh. *"Non dolet,"* she said. "It doesn't hurt." Again the dragon approached but more carefully this time. And again pain creased Triosha's pale brow. The dragon withdrew.

"Non semper ea sunt quae videntur," whispered the Rose. "Things are not always what they appear to be." He spoke on so that all of them could understand him: "Her very life depends on my whim. Now it pleases me to let her feel pain—very great pain—when you approach. I doubt that will make her love you all the more."

The dragon chuffed in perplexity and frustration.

"But enough," said The Rose. "It is time for all this to be finished. Again I tell you, you must die that I might live. That is the sacrifice demanded. And you shall pay it to my great pleasure."

"Malo animo," growled the dragon. "With evil intent."

"Oh, yes, of course. Evil, if you will. *Damnant quod non intellegunt,"* said the Rose. "'They condemn what they do not understand.' Still, I would prefer that you have every opportunity to suffer before you die. That, after all, was the reason behind your punishment. And so it will also be the reason that you must watch what happens next. You wouldn't want to miss the death of your very own, true bride?"

Brian saw The Rose strike the ground with his staff and heard the mumble of enchantments. Smoke rose up from the stone floor and began to swirl around the magician. As the whirlwind picked up speed it began to emit a low rumbling. With the magician's attention and concentration elsewhere, Brian found he could begin to feel his hands and feet. Little by little, he could move them. Katie was flexing her right arm, bending it at the elbow.

"Quick, while he's busy," she shouted over the sound of the wind, and she moved to Brian. Reme found he was free, too. The adults, however, were having a harder time of it. Mr. Teagarden could move his jaw and speak; Michael could move his torso and arms, but not his legs. Doris had her arms pinned to her side, but could walk about. And Thomas had fallen over and was doggedly trying to stand, all the while muttering. Brian and Reme, rushed to his aid and helped him up. They had to hold him, for his balance was out of commission. Katie moved to him, her arms beginning to free.

"We need to stop yon wizard," Thomas shouted, stumbling uncontrollably toward the cloud.

"Grab him," shouted Katie. It was only by the fast intervention of the children that Thomas avoided falling into the maelstrom. As it was, the fierce outer winds tore off part of his shirt cuff. ...Except it wasn't torn: it was cut as if with a pair of very sharp shears.

The wind swirled about in a tight tornado, building intensity all the while.

"Our only hope now," said Brian, "is that he's too busy to pay attention to us. Maybe we can help the others and then be ready for whatever comes next."

It took some work before Michael, Doris, and Mr. Teagarden were limber enough to move freely under their own power. Whether it was that all the magician's strength was demanded for the ever-faster swirling vortex or that they were at last finding defenses against his powers they wouldn't be able to tell until their next encounter, if then.

The magician lifted aloft his staff and the wind shrieked even louder and began to move toward the chained woman.

Despite the confusion before him, the dragon nodded to his party and summoned one: "Kaaaaattttiiee," he breathed. Through the wind she heard his tender call. She—fully mobile now—detached herself from Thomas' side and ventured to Lord Vrolich. She stood looking into the glowing and glittering orbs. The dragon, staring steadily, took her in and all that whirled behind her. He lowered his head close to hers and spoke through his thoughts. It wasn't Latin, but the words of some lost poet: "'Hell hath no power over true virginity.' The next part is for you and you alone."

Katie nodded once. What was demanded? That she advance.

She turned so that the dragon was behind her, and she walked resolutely to the vortex. The storm had progressed mere inches from the queen. The woman displayed no fear but calmly looked instead at the girl who was walking toward her.

Katie tore her eyes away from the woman, took and held a breath, and, flinching slightly as the outer veil of the storm brushed her hand, walked inside the fury.

As though jamming a stout stick in the middle of a rapidly spinning wheel, the howling terror stopped in mid shriek. The debris of the storm settled to the cavern floor and Katie stepped closer. The magician still held his staff above his head, his eyes rolled back so that only the whites showed. He, too, was stopped like the wheel, if only briefly. In the interim, Brian moved behind him.

Soundlessly, he had withdrawn the sword — the blade that The Rose feared — from its scabbard. The blade, which felt alive in his hand, was raised above the clearly evident skull of the wizard. Tiny sparks flew from the steel. It would have been a simple matter to send the shattering blow down upon his head. But Brian waited, looking from the old man to the dragon. But he would not attack an enemy unaware, even a remorseless and relentless enemy like The Rose, unless Lord Vrolich ordered it.

The magus, hearing the crackle from the singing blade, turned about with his staff still above his head. A look of dread passed across his face, instantly replaced by a controlled fury.

"What would you do, young puppy?" he quizzed, glancing rapidly between the sword and the boy's face. He raised his staff in one hand and using it deftly moved the blade aside. He said a few short words and Brian found his arm numb. Satisfied, the wizard edged away from the sword but closer to Brian's face.

"Have you strength greater than all mortal men combined? That's what it would take. For each life I have claimed, each year I have lived has given me strength over my enemies. Or, is it that you lack courage now that you have met me? Would you strike me dead if only I weren't looking? Shall I turn around again? Hah!"

"N..nn...no," said Brian at last with some confusion. "It's better when I can see you face to face."

"And what face would you like me to wear?" To Brian's eyes there was a subtle reforming over the ancient visage of the wizard. New flesh was added to the cheeks, the lips. The skin glowed a healthy color. The hair grew thick, dark, and healthy. Brian found himself looking into his father's face. If he looked away he would miss seeing his father for one last time. He felt only love. Brian took in his breath with a sob.

And his father's voice. Brian heard him again, fully as vibrantly as ever in life: "Oh, my son, I have longed for you from beyond the grave. Have you missed me, too?" Brian nodded. "I have come back to help you. There are those here who would work your destruction if we let them. I will help you. And you will help me."

The sword arm came down all the way, slowly, helplessly, to the boy's side. Brian's face wore an expression of pained delight.

No one else in the party was deceived for each could see only the old man as he truly appeared. But they could hear what the evil sorcerer said in his cracked cackle. And they could sense some witchcraft, some trickery directed at Brian alone.

"Brian," shouted Katie. "He's lying. Look at him: he's not our father. Look at his hands and feet. Look at how short he is."

But Brian only had eyes for the wizard, who was crooning to the boy in an odd singsong.

"You must help me now to finally and utterly destroy my enemies. Otherwise, I'll have to go back to the land of the dead. If you help me I will be with you always. Will you help me?"

Brian again nodded.

"The sword," began the magician. Mechanically, Brian brought it forward. The Rose drew back with aversion. "No, not to me."

"All you have to do," he began. "...All you have to do is point your sword at that man." The sorcerer gestured with his staff toward Mr. Teagarden. "Take your sword and just tickle his throat. I'll do the rest. He wants to harm us, to hurt you and send me away forever."

Brian turned and advanced on Mr. Teagarden, who had the good sense to stand very still.

"Bring up your sword, now," said the wizard from behind him. "Draw a line under his chin. Right across his neck." Brian slowly raised the sword and just scratched the fair skin just under Mr. Teagarden's chin. No one else in the cave moved.

"Now, relax," said the wizard. "And I'll help you."

But Brian had stuck at the first command. His sword point, on the surface of the skin, merely a half inch away from the artery that ran up the left side of the neck, was stopped, and poised stone still. Brian looked at Mr. Teagarden, taking in the face of his old friend, and then he looked at the end of his blade. A trickle of bright blood, starting at the sword point, ran down Mr. Teagarden's neck and under the collar of his shirt. Brian stood mesmerized watching the thin scarlet line and the rapid throb of artery just under the skin. Then, his eyes followed the line of the blade back to his own arm. With a dawning awareness of what he was about, his mouth opened in revulsion.

And he felt the pull of the blade as if it wanted to go deeper. All he had to do was follow it, to allow it, to hold on to the sword and let his arm to be drawn in with the weapon. He tightened his arm muscles, beginning to pull back.

At just that instant the wizard moved toward him from behind and shouted: "Kill him, kill him, kill him!" The last command rang in the air as Brian struggled to pull back. Every sinew was taut, every joint stretched to its full. With all the force he could muster, he jerked the sword away from Mr. Teagarden's neck. It was as if something had held the blade and then suddenly let it go. He lost his footing and, trying to regain his balance, spun around with the blade outstretched. Brian whirled the sword just as The Rose leapt to meet him.

The weapon sailed right through what seemed his father's neck and cleanly severed the head from the body.

The head rolled next to Katie and lodged against her shoe.

The eyes blinked up at her in vast surprise and the mouth worked spells, but to no avail. At last the face stopped twitching.

Brian rushed to her side and saw it was no longer the face of his father but a malignant thing, sinking in on itself, rotten with corruption and stink. He looked back toward Mr. Teagarden, who was busy with a handkerchief, blotting up the leakage from his own neck. At his feet the body of the wizard lay not quite still. There was motion beneath the robe. And the robe was slowly sinking to the level of the floor. At length, great fat white worms crawled out from beneath the cloth and moved in slimy trails toward the dark corners of the cavern. Left behind was nothing but bones.

Sword still in hand, Brian rushed to Mr. Teagarden and tearfully embraced him.

"I almost killed you," he sobbed. "I was going to kill you and I would have."

"But you didn't, you know. I stand here quite alive, just with a shaving nick. But I can't say that old wizard was any too fortunate. You might have a care where you point that thing."

Brian looked down to see that the sword and his arm were roving about as if it had a will of its own. Carefully, he brought the sword low and asked Mr. Teagarden for the loan of his handkerchief. "There's no grass, and I haven't any other good cloth."

Mr. Teagarden, gave him the white linen and then hugged him with one arm and stroked his fair hair with the other hand.

"You've done well. I'm proud of you and your real father would be proud of you, too."

"My real father," said Brian as he bent to work cleaning the blade. "He looked like my father, he sounded like my father. But he wasn't."

"We could see that but you couldn't," Mr. Teagarden said. "And how did you determine it wasn't your father?"

"I wanted to believe. I miss him so much. But I'd seen what he was before. And then he wanted me to kill you. Only it wasn't really you then. But my father—my real father—never wanted to kill anything. Never. And then I looked again, and I saw it was you and that the sword was at your neck, and I was holding it. It was like waking up from a bad dream and realizing it wasn't a dream."

"But you woke up in time. For which I am most grateful," said Mr. Teagarden fingering the nick on his neck.

"Why didn't you move?" asked Brian. "Why didn't you get out of the way?"

"There are some risks worth taking. You are one such risk. I did not truly believe I was in any danger. I know you, Brian, and I know your heart. It is your father's heart.

"We often talked, your father and I. He loved you and Katie so much, and he was a very brave man.

"And you know that only a coward would ask you to do something he would not do himself. The Rose intended to use you to do his bidding. And that use was both cowardly and dastardly.

"And there was the sword itself; it could not be put to an evil use. The Rose could never have touched the blade. To do so would be death for him. That sword—and The Dragon—were likely the only physical entities that could have harmed him. Why else do you think the sword was buried? It could never serve him. You can be sure that the man who held the sword was forced into his grave at the order of The Rose, but by hands other than his."

Brian looked at the sword, now cleaned and polished. And with a start he realized that there was still much going on in the cavern.

Chapter 18

YET, ALL MUST DIE

With The Rose dispatched, the enchantment of Triosha was put to an end…all of it. She still was chained to a pillar, and she still was flesh and blood. But she looked out from an older face, a rapidly aging face.

The dragon approached; his form was still fixed as a monster.

Brian looked at Mr. Teagarden for an explanation.

"The enchantment has failed all together for the queen. She is dying as the forestalled years now accumulate. But my Lord Vrolich, even as an unnatural dragon will live a dragon's life span…almost eternity," he said. "Only when he dies will he come to himself again."

The dragon nuzzled his bride, his tears bouncing off the floor. Her tears ran down her wrinkling checks.

She aged even as Katie studied at her. Her hair became brittle white, her skin lined parchment. .

Haltingly, she choked out: "*Vale. Farewell. Nemo liber est qui corpori servit.*" No one is free who is a slave to his body. "*Et non est vivere sed valere vita est.*" And life is more than just being alive. And, finally, looking longingly at the dragon she whispered: "*Amo te.*" I love you. Her eyes, dimming, held her husband in focus. Here eyelids closed and a sigh escaped her lips.

"*Consummatum est,*" said the dragon. It is finished.

He drew in a shallow and ragged breath and then exhaled a sob, and the Queen's desiccated flesh crumbled from her bones. Her dry bones fell in disorder.

Brian turned around and looked at Katie. There was evidence of tears that had coursed down her cheeks. Still, she managed a brave smile. Brian nodded at her and turned to the dragon.

With a puff of smoke the beast cleared his throat.

"*Die gratia,*" said the dragon. Mr. Teagarden picked up the translation and added to it: "By the grace of God we are delivered. ...By the grace of God and your bravery."

The dragon looked entirely bereft.

Brian handed the sword to Mr. Teagarden and walked until he stood just beneath the great beast.

"What happened to your brother? I mean I know I killed him, but what really happened to him?"

"*Nemo malus felix,*" began the Dragon by speaking and then by directing his thoughts to Brian: "There is no peace unto the wicked. And his wickedness was what he chose. Again and again."

Brian looked down at his feet. "I'm sorry about your wife. I believe she loved you very much."

"*Ita.* Yes. *Dabit deus his quoque finem.* God will grant an end even to these troubles," rumbled the dragon in speech and thought. "It is time, indeed, that He does just that." The dragon paused, as if collecting his thoughts. Perhaps he was searching for the right way to address the youth who stood before him. "Heretofore I have asked and you have obeyed. ...In small and large. You have followed me here. You have trusted my guardian," and he nodded to Mr. Teagarden. "You have worked bravely and tirelessly. You have vanquished my foes.

"Obedience is the path of maturation, a habit of willingness," thought the dragon with a far-away look in his giant eyes. "You are on the verge of manhood; no longer a boy. That which I ask you to do next will be the most difficult. You have already been faithful in much, but there is yet one more thing I ask, and it is a man's task."

What more could be required? Brian looked from the dragon to their friends. They stood still in a mess of bones and gore. What more was there to do? And how could it be harder than what had gone before?

"Come," thought the dragon. "Let us reason together." The beast set off with his lumbering gait, the young man—so lately a boy—at his side. They crossed under the highest spot of the cavern dome and walked to the far edge of the room. The dragon stopped and looked intently at Brian.

"You must release me from this horrible spell, from this loath-some and hideous shape of a monster. The only way from this prison is death. So, you must, in short, slay me."

"Why? How?" responded Brian with alarm.

"I am as old as my bride and my evil brother. I belong entirely to another age, an age that should be only a dim memory in the minds of men. But here I live, burning until the socket, like a candle burning below the rim of the candle holder: past my time, past the time of all that I knew. And you, of the long line of dragon slayers, have one more dragon to kill. I am he. And I come to you in supplication: I beg you."

"I can't do it!" said Brian adamantly. He folded his arms across his chest and glared at the beast. "There has to be another way."

"There is no other way. It must be you, it must be here, it must be with my own sword—you know there's enchantment in the blade—you've seen it. And, it must be now."

"Can't we even say goodbye?"

"Of course, but consider: every moment I linger is an eternity I am separated from my queen, the Lady Triosha. Even so, I will wait here. Go and tell the others. If they wish to speak to me I will see them."

With his head hung in dejection, Brian crossed the cavern to his friends.

"It's not fair!" was the first thing he told them. "He says that it's time for him to die. Why does he have to? That means that he'll be gone from us forever."

Mr. Teagarden advanced and took both of Brian's shoulders in his hands. "Brian, just think of all he's been through. He's lived for nearly a millennium as a hated beast, a curse upon the land. For my Lord Vrolich, that will continue unless he is killed. And he has completed his work. His bride, his queen, is now beyond any evil or punishment anyone can mete out. And his brother, the evil Rose, is dispatched to the Hell he had always sought and served. *Dei gratia*—by the grace of God—The Dragon's work is done. And we must understand that."

"But he says I must be the one to kill him; that it's the work my family did."

"It is, indeed, the calling of your family, and you are the one who must do it. And you alone."

Brian reached out his arms to pull Mr. Teagarden close. His sobs were muffled in the older man's coat. Mr. Teagarden clasped him tightly. At last the storm of tears abated, and Brian told Mr. Teagarden of the dragon's willingness to speak with each of them.

Before setting off across the room, Mr. Teagarden ruffled Brian's hair. His brisk walk halted as he fell to his knees before the dragon. The children saw man and beast deep in animated conversation. Mr. Teagarden frequently shook his head in agreement. At the last, the man stood and hugged the dragon about the neck. The beast sent up a chuff of smoke. Katie set off as soon as Mr. Teagarden turned to rejoin the party.

As she stood before the dragon there passed between them a silent communication, one heart to another. She sensed all the love that she would ever need deep within the golden eyes, and she drank her fill. She, too, hugged the dragon, and headed back with tears in her eyes.

Next was Reme, who talked long and carefully with the dragon. "Your mother will need your help when you return. She is now very fragile. But with your understanding, she will again be strong. She will learn that even in our worst moments—the times of Hell on earth—there is nothing to fear. Your father already knows this and with your help the two of you will teach her to again be strong and hopeful. You have proven yourself a brave man, a scholar, and a true friend. Wherever you go you will be welcome."

There was another hug for the dragon.

Next came Michael and then Thomas. Both bowed in obeisance. Both were blessed. And then knighted with the dragon's foreclaw. They then went and returned with Andrew's body. The dragon sniffed carefully, shook his head slowly, but posthumously knighted their companion. They carried his body away.

Doris was the last to converse. With a smile she walked to the beast.

"My Lord Vrolich…do you know how wonderful it is to call you 'my Lord?'" The dragon snorted. "You have given me my own life, a gift I cherish. I am sorry for all the evil things I have done, all the thoughtlessness, all the cruelties. But I intend to lead a new life, and it is thanks to you. May I also hug you?" The dragon nodded. Doris not only hugged him, but took his massive head between her hands and stared into his eyes.

"I will miss you," she said. "But I will never forget you. And will I see you again at my life's end?" The dragon nodded.

"Then," she said. "That is more than enough for me."

Brian marveled at her radiant smile as she returned. It was his chore now, to cross the room once more carrying the sword that would spell a dragon's doom. Brian approached and knelt.

"Rise up, Master Eames," thought the dragon. "I will tell you what you must do. Here, come closer."

Brian walked forward until he and the dragon—that held his head low—were eye to eye.

"There is only one spot where a dragon is vulnerable: just beneath the breastplate. A dragon has five hearts, so it's not an easy matter to put a stop to him. But here is where all the nerves come together. And it's here you need to plunge the sword. You'll have only one chance because if I am only wounded I shall be as dangerous as any natural dragon. I will seek to slay you and all the others. And, even so, I may fall directly on top of you, or thrash you with my tail or scorch you. You must both do the job and look to your own survival. Come, let us begin and then make an end."

The dragon stood as high off the ground as he could. Crouching over, Brian could just squeeze beneath him. It was, he imagined, like crawling beneath a snorting steam engine; anything could happen.

The dragon twisted his head to see when Brian was standing. "Just there," he indicated when the sword point reached the edge of the large plate on his breast. "The sword must go straight up. And the faster you can thrust, the less pain I will feel."

"It will hurt, then?"

"Most assuredly. It will hurt as much as any dying. I fear it, but less than I might. You, after all, are a dragon slayer. That bodes well."

"But I've only read the book. I've never done it before," said Brian in some panic.

"There has to be a first time...a first dragon. And I am he. I trust you will do your best. That's all I can ask.

"Now, let's be about our business. I pray you success, young Brian. Remember, if your father were here, he would do this for me. You are to serve in his stead."

Brian positioned the sword, and the dragon turned his gaze away from the young man.

"Goodbye," said Brian, and with all his might he pushed up the sword against the thin spot in the dragon's carapace. At first there was resistance, but suddenly it gave way. Brian kneeled down to better push the sword through the rent in the dragon's armor. It felt like shoving a stick through a tree. But the sword moved. Brian re-exerted himself, watching the blade bite deeper and deeper in. At length...really a few seconds, but what seemed like hours...the sword had traveled the full length of the blade up to the hilt and the great beast quivered for an instant. Then it leapt in a last spasm, snorted fire and blood, and fell to its side, unmoving.

Brian, at the first sign of the quivering of the beast, had ducked out from under and run far enough away to avoid being crushed. Now he stood twenty feet away and watched the still form. There were charges of lightning running up and down the length of the carcass. And with each flash there was a changing. The dragon was sublimating into a rising mist. In its place was the body of a man. Brian cautiously approached. The sword lay to one side, but the wound it had left in his chest was fearsome. There could be no doubt that it was fatal. Still, his lips moved. Brian bent over the man. Here, then, was the real Dragon, the mighty Lord Vrolich. His eyes opened and locked onto Brian's face.

"*Deo gratias* — Thanks be to God," he thought to Brian, smiling. "*Non omnis moriar* — I shall not wholly die. You will find me again and again. As often as you seek I shall be found."

Mr. Teagarden and the others had crossed the cavern floor on a dead run. They arrived in time to see the king breathe his last. "*Paaaaxxxxx.*" Peace. And he was still.

Soon the transformation of the ages reduced him, too, to dust and ashes. The only things left behind were a few teeth, two gold rings, a wristband of gold, and the sword. Brian retrieved the latter and marveled that the blade was both unbroken and unmarred. And there was no need to clean the blade: there was no gore anywhere.

Mr. Teagarden bent down to pick up the rings and bracelet. "These may find another use," he said, looking about him at the children.

"My Lord Vrolich has no need of earthly baubles. And these things," he glanced down at the jewelry in his palm. "...These things have a power and life of their own. They were important in the past and may be so again."

He gave one of the rings to Reme, another to Brian, and the circlet of gold to Katie. She looked up at him: "What about you? Don't you want any of this? Surely these must be valuable treasures."

"Oh, they're incredibly valuable all right, but worth far more than money. They may be good at need in some time in the future."

Brian moved to offer the sword to Mr. Teagarden. "No," said the white-haired gentleman. "It is not mine and I have no claim to it. You do. When we get home, set it aside to store it, but keep it near you always...in the back of a closet, on a top shelf. Make sure it's within easy reach."

"But doesn't it belong in a museum?" asked Brian.

"It does...and it doesn't," said Mr. Teagarden. "There's no doubt that any museum director would give his or her eye teeth for such a sword with such a history. But there is a copy on display — at least we know it's a copy; the museum thinks it's the original. That should suit most antiquaries. And, it's possible that this sword is not yet ready to be put away. I know you will take care of it. The fact of the matter is this: The man from whom you took this sword..."

"The man buried alive at the old castle?" piped in Katie.

"The very same," said Mr. Teagarden. "He is your long removed but direct ancestor. If he had lived he would have passed the sword along to his son, who would have passed it to his son, or daughter, and so on down the line. This would have come to you along with the book from your grandfather. Instead, you got it from the most recent of your family who made use of it. He held it to defend his lord and master; and my Lord Vrolich no longer has use for such earthly paraphernalia. But he also held it in trust for you, so, by rights, it should go to you."

Each of the children marveled at the adornments and then tucked them safely into pockets. Brian resheathed his sword. Then, as a group they walked toward the tunnel from which they entered the cave.

At the entrance they turned to look back. The scene was one of carnage, death, and destruction. The rotting bones of the thugs lay in pools on the floor. The miasmal stench of cadaverine still assailed them.

"Mud, blood, and crud," said Katie.

Thomas nudged Michael and pointed across the way. The battered body of Andrew lay where they'd placed him, stretched out upon one of the few clean spots on the floor. They hurried to retrieve him. Thomas alone picked up his remains and carried him as one might a child, Andrew's head lolling gently against Thomas' chest. There were tears in Thomas' eyes.

Mr. Teagarden put his hand on Andrew's crushed skull and bowed his in prayer. The others stood silently. At length, Mr. Teagarden dropped his hand and turned again to the wasteland of the cavern.

"Let the dead bury the dead," said Mr. Teagarden in condemnation. Michael and Thomas answered with a deep "Amen."

Chapter 19

TOWARD THE LIGHT

The outward trip, back to the world of light, seemed to take forever. The wanderers never mistook their way; the string guides kept them on the right path. But they were encumbered with grief and exhaustion. Then, too, the smell of the charnel house followed them. And Doris was fouled with it. Michael occasionally called a halt to rest. Thomas, who carried Andrew, asked for neither pause nor rest.

After hours of slow going they found themselves standing at the base of the runged ladder, standing in deepening gloom. The last working torch was fading as the batteries drained; the others had been discarded as they failed. There still remained the flagstone overhead. With a weariness evident to all the rest of the party, Michael climbed the embedded rungs and pushed against the stone. Nothing. The flag might as well have been cemented in. Perhaps the publican had moved one of the heavy barrels of ale or stout over their entry to this netherworld. Or, perhaps some other force kept it pressed down.

Thomas unburdened himself of Andrew, carefully placing the body at some distance away from the others. He straightened and walked back to stand below Michael. "Do you want me to try?"

"You're welcome to," said Michael. "But I fear that the outcome will be the same. And there's not room enough up here for both of us to push."

"If we just had something to tap against it, maybe a walking stick," said Katie hopefully. No, there was the sword, but that would never do. Michael asked Thomas for the torch he was carrying. It would soon be otherwise useless unless as a tool to make sound.

"Maybe I can signal for help by banging this against the stone," he said, and switched it off. The little light it had shed was gone. Michael proceeded to tap out a signal, not Morse code, but far too regular to be accidental.

By Mr. Teagarden's reckoning, Michael stood at the top of the ladder, banging with all his might for a full hour, maybe longer. When at last he gave up and climbed down again Reme brushed up against him. He was drenched with sweat. Doris worried aloud that he might take a chill in the cool air of the tunnels. His voice carried his discouragement: "Nobody's coming. I can't believe that nobody'd hear us. That means that the pub owner intends for us to stay down here."

"What about taking another path?" said Brian.

"After all," said Reme, "the dragon got in some way. And we don't know that all the thugs all came this way; seems unlikely."

"That's true," said Mr. Teagarden, "But I'm fairly certain some of them did. When we arrived here I looked at the floor. Surely we didn't leave all those tracks in the dust here. And there were plenty of places along the path that showed a fair number of people had been along the passage: odd bits of cloth snagged on the tunnel walls, signs that something moist and running had been that way; wet hand prints against the sides. I think most of them came in this way and it's possible the publican wanted to make sure that none of that lot would ever come out. He certainly wouldn't expect—after seeing them go in—that we ever would. Even if he heard us, it would be worth his life to lift up that stone to see just who was down here. He may not be the best of men, but I can't blame him for not wanting to meet up with the likes of Llewellyn and his crew again.

"As for finding another way out, we've gone in circles down here once already. We might be able to find our way again to the cavern if the phosphorescence will still lead us. But once we're there what will we do without a light? Frankly, getting out any other way would be unlikely.

"No, I think we must stay here."

They all sat with their backs to the walls, glumly considering their collective fate. They were perhaps two or three inches away from freedom, and that thickness might spell their end. Of them all, Reme was most agitated, squirming first one way and then the other.

At last Michael turned to him: "Are you frightened, then?"

Reme stilled his movement. "Well, sure, but probably not any more so than anybody else here. I was thinking, though. There has to be a way, even with everything Mr. Teagarden has said. I agree that we'd be foolish to try the tunnels again, but I can't believe we'd get this far and no further." He turned to Brian. "What exactly did the dragon tell you? What were his exact words?"

"His exact words? About what?" asked Brian.

"About if we ever needed help."

"Oh. OOOOHHHH. Well, these aren't his exact words—at least I don't think so—but he said that we could call on him. I think he meant any time."

"Does this classify as any time to you?" said Reme with a quick smile to himself. "It seems like it might be a good idea."

"Okay, but how? How am I supposed to call for him? I don't know any spells or incantations? And I wouldn't want them; that was The Rose's way."

"No," said Mr. Teagarden. "I don't think you'll need any of that; and it can't be all that hard. Start by putting on the rings and the bracelet." The children did as he asked. "Then, take the sword and make the sign of the cross on the floor and pray for his intercessory help. At least, that's the way I'd do it."

In the total dark, Brian traced the mark of the cross. Then he knelt, and he heard others do the same. His head was bowed, but his eyes were open and slowly, infinitesimally he could sense a brightening in the cavern, a lightening in the pitch darkness. When Brian raised his eyes he saw something that radiated light in the shape of a man. Brighter and brighter until his features were recognizable. Could this be the late king?

"Arise, Brian, son of Raymond. I promised that I would come at need." It was Lord Vrolich, but different. Brian stood and looked straight into the blue eyes.

"We're trapped. In the tunnels. The pub owner must have covered the opening with something heavy. And he's not about to open the way for us to get out. We might be able to take some other route, but we're likely to lose our way. Will you help us?"

"I will. But it may take some time. People are slow to answer when a spirit calls. But call I shall until someone pays heed. Do not dismay. You will not perish, even if you have to wait for some days. First I need to find someone in prayer; that's when souls are most receptive."

"My mother," said Michael. "You could reach her any hour without waiting more than fifteen minutes!" It had often been a point of jest between mother and son. Now it was serious.

Lord Vrolich laughed. It didn't sound like the laugh of someone who had recently died a painful death.

Emboldened, Reme stood: "Are you a ghost?"

"You might understand me best as that. I am spirit and no longer bound to earth. And I have already been here an eternity with eternity before me."

"What about Triosha?" It was Katie who piped in.

"We are whole now, and together. Our bitter separation, though it lasted for hundreds of years, is nothing but a dim memory."

"And my father?" asked Brian. "Is he there, too?"

"Most certainly. And while he cannot come to you now, in time—a long time by your standards—you will walk to him. His love for you will still be here, as fresh as ever it was. That love surrounds you now, and has since his death.

"Now, unless you desire to tarry longer in the darkness, I had best be about your business. I take my leave, but I leave my thanks, thanks for your service and your love. A dragon can be a poor companion, yet you were willing to carry part of my load. I thank you again. With all my heart."

Lord Vrolich vanished with a "pop." And the darkness returned.

At last, Michael got off his knees and stood. "I guess if Lord Vrolich is going to send a rescue party, I'd better give off some more noise so they can find us." He again climbed the rungs and resumed his tapping with the otherwise useless torch, less frantic than before, but still strong and regular.

So the hours passed, tapping every few seconds. Occasionally, Michael would pause and put his ear against the stone. At intervals, Thomas spelled him, but the bulk of the banging fell to Michael.

During one of Thomas' stints of banging against the stone he paused and they all heard, faintly, the sound of something being dragged across the floor above. Thomas put his ear to the stone: "Hurrah!" he shouted, and began banging furiously. Within seconds came an answering tap from directly above. Thomas stood stock still. None of the others moved as much as a muscle.

From above, attenuated, came shouts, perhaps screams. "We'll get you out." "Just gotta get something to move this stone." And, then: "Are you all right?" Thomas banged three short replies.

Next came the sound of an iron bar being dragged across the stones. The screeching of the metal against stone and the subsequent sound of stone against stone were nearly deafening to those below. Involuntarily, they covered their ears. At long last they saw a sliver of light, intensely bright after the darkness. Michael remembered how dimly lit the basement had been. He knew it would take their eyes some moments to adjust before they'd be able to go outside.

The great stone above them was manhandled back from the brink, and a round face poked over the edge, shining a flashlight directly into their faces. Thomas nearly lost his hold on the ladder while he tried to shield his eyes. The holder of the light saw the effect of the beams and redirected it to illumine his own face. It was the village constable, Thomas noted, a phlegmatic man who rarely bestirred himself. But he was excited now.

"Michael...Michael Owen...I can see it's you...and Thomas," he said. "Now, where are the others, not that I really care for the most of them, but almost all the young men in the village are gone and there are stories they all went with you. And, who else do you have here," he said, noting the presence of the youngsters, Doris, and Mr. Teagarden. "Well, let's get you up here. It took a fair piece of work to gain admittance to this basement. The proprietor says we've no business here. And, in truth, by law we haven't. But I reminded him of the time or two when I've looked the other way at late closings and he became somewhat more reasonable. Then, too, we've a contingent of all the town's mothers and they want their sons. They will NOT be denied. So, after all that, are you coming up or not?"

Michael helped Katie out first, then Doris, then Reme, then Brian. Mr. Teagarden pulled himself out of the hole, followed by

Michael who turned midway up to help Thomas move Andrew's body along. At the first sign of his inert form a murmur went around the room. His mother rushed forward and crumpled as her legs gave way. She saw her son was not moving and broke into sobs, even as her hands went out to hold him. Michael laid him out on the cold floor, and Thomas finished climbing out of the dark pit.

Andrew's mother could not fathom that her son, her lovely son, was dead. There had to be some mistake; perhaps he was only unconscious.

The other women, one of whom was Mrs. Owen, gathered around her and helped her to her feet. In a somber procession, with Thomas again sustaining his burden, they climbed the stairs to the out of doors and then marched to the church.

The door of that building was held open by the parish priest, who, once Thomas had entered carrying Andrew, rushed to the altar and swept everything aside—cross, candlesticks, chalice. All clattered to the floor. Thomas again gently laid down Andrew and then dropped to his knees before the altar. His sobs could be heard throughout the church.

Andrew's mother, with the women of the parish, flocked to the altar and looked beseechingly at Thomas and Michael.

"What of the others?" Mrs. Owen turned to ask her son.

Michael shook his head. "They were forfeit to a higher and worse power. Their bodies—or what little is left of them—are rotting in a cavern that runs beneath the mountain. They have inherited death. Surely you knew they were no longer masters of themselves." He addressed the mothers, including Llewellyn's. "Your sons had sold their souls and, came the time to collect, the evil one did just that. Andrew alone perished who was not a willing subject. We also would be fodder for the evil one if it had not been for the Grace of God and these young ones." Here he indicated Katie, Brian, and Reme.

The mothers had known that their sons had gone to the bad, but even such intuition did not assuage their loss. Michael moved from his position near the altar and came down to his mother. She reached out her arms and pulled him to her. The women had taken up a wailing chant, a sort of eerie cry. Andrew's mother had gone to stand over her dead—but not lost—son.

"What happens now?" Reme asked Mr. Teagarden.

"Oh, the women will bathe Andrew and prepare his body for burial tomorrow. But, before then, we've work to do." With Mr. Teagarden at their elbow, the youngsters walked out of the church. Once outside, they turned to watch Michael, his mother, and Doris leave, too. At the foot of the church stairs Mrs. Owen agreed with Mr. Teagarden that hot meals and hot baths were in order.

Mrs. Owen preceded them down the street to the house with the low red door. She twisted the key in the lock and entered. Without waiting, she sent Doris to bathe and gave her some clothing that would do. She made her way to the kitchen to set out a meal that was largely ready. She had been busy, she said, trying to take her mind off possible dangers that her son and the others might have been facing. The more she was concerned, the more she baked. The result was before them.

Seated at table, and with the grace said, Mrs. Owen said she needed to hear everything.

Mr. Teagarden started the telling, even though much of it wasn't dinnertime fare. About halfway through the meal, Doris slid into her seat at the table, her hair still wet.

When they had finished both the meal and the tale Michael asked his mother: "What led to our rescue?"

"It was as you surmised," she said with a twinkling smile. "I was at prayer, and there came to me the thought that you needed help. I had to keep asking myself what I was to do, and the only answer that came was the image — in my mind — of the pub. So, I took myself off to The Dragon and The Rose. Along the way I met the others and the constable, who had been hounded into coming. Each of us got the same message: we were needed. The publican first tried to stop us. In fact, he warned us that all the powers of Hell would be let loose if we so much as touched a stone of his floor. It took some time to convince him to cooperate, but in the end, he led us to the right stone; he'd seen Llewellyn follow you. He didn't help him, mind, but he did replace the stone. And then he moved a barrel over it. The rest you know."

By the time they cleared the table the sun had set. Mr. Teagarden urged Katie and Brian and Reme to join him on a stroll. "We have an unfinished piece of business," he explained.

That unfinished business led them outside the door where Mr. Teagarden pulled out his cell phone. In minutes Brian and Katie were talking with their mother. They assured her that they were fine. When it came time for Reme to talk with his mother, Mr. Teagarden intervened to explain to her the purpose of the unexpected trip. Then Reme closed the call by assuring his mother that he and Katie and Brian would be back in a few days.

Mr. Teagarden made a final call, this one to his wife. All was finished: "I have lived to see a miracle that was the stuff of legends. Tomorrow we have a funeral for one of the lads who helped us, Andrew. Then home."

After the calls, they walked through the silent village. Silent, but the spirit of the place was lighter. They walked past the charred ruin of the New Century Inn and then back to the Owen household.

That night they slept soundly, without so much as a disturbing dream to awaken any one of them.

Chapter 20

ANDREW'S LAST RITE AND
HOW THE STORY GETS OUT

By the time they reached the church at midmorning it was more than three-quarters full. Andrew's body had been prepared for burial and placed in a plain wooden casket. The casket was then laid on a bier before the altar. It presented a stark reality as the children moved into the church.

The service was like nothing else in which the youngsters had ever participated. There was a singing quality to the scripture and, since most of it was delivered in Welsh, there was precious little for them to understand. Mr. Teagarden translated as much as he could on the fly, but the continuity was still missing. Still, they understood when the minister, the priest, read in English: "Greater love hath no man than this, that a man lay down his life for his friends." Tears sprang to Brian's eyes and he wiped them away.

At the close of the service, the mourners followed the casket as it was conveyed on an ancient two-wheeled barrow. The wheels rose as high as the shoulders of the six men, among whom were Thomas and Michael, who steadied the box holding Andrew's mortal remains. With care they pushed up the village street that led to the cemetery just outside of town. Along the way they would pass the pub.

Along the walk, the street was dotted with those few souls who were not in the procession. Among their number was the publican of The Dragon and The Rose. He stood scowling in his dirty apron, arms crossed over his ample gut.

Reme drew even with the front door of the pub before he felt what was to come. First beneath one foot and then the other there came a tremor and trembling of the street. The funeral procession stopped, the men struggling valiantly to keep the casket from crashing to the cobblestones. Reme saw the ground open just at the street's edge and the level of the pub rose up and then slid down. The publican jumped off his entryway and ran across the street. He turned in time to watch his pub plunge below the level of the ground.

In the silence that followed, dust rose upward in an exhalation of the earth. The earth had breathed out the stench of decay and putrescence. It was, Mr. Teagarden, guessed, a subsidence of the cavern and the tunnels, perhaps sealed for all time.

As the dust began to settle, the publican crept carefully across the road and looked into the hole where his business had stood.

"I need a drink," he croaked.

Only the children and Mr. Teagarden were near enough to hear his assertion. Mr. Teagarden turned to them and said: "I guess now there's only one Dragon and The Rose." He winked.

The rest of the mourners prepared to start out again. Miraculously, the casket was still balanced.

After the graveside ceremony, there was a luncheon meal and attendant gathering planned at the church hall.

The afternoon slipped by in a relative blur of eating and conversation. By the time all was finished, it was early evening. It had been a long day and Katie, Brian, and Reme were ready for some quiet. Mrs. Owen gave them her key, and by themselves they walked through the village streets and wordlessly made their way back to the warm house. By the time the adults returned the children were asleep.

The next day Katie, Brian, Reme, Doris, and Mr. Teagarden would begin their journey home by traveling to London.

Michael arranged for cars to come and collect them for the ride to the nearest rail station. Mrs. Owen sent them off with food and her best wishes, although in saying her goodbye to Mr. Teagarden she expressed a concern.

"How will those children board a plane? And Doris? They have no passports. And assuming you have one, you'll have no entry stamp."

"I don't know what we'll do. Just go forward. And if I wind up in gaol, send me a file in a cake."

With hugs and tears the visitors took leave of Mrs. Owen and were whisked off. As they were driving out of town they passed a television news truck heading the other way.

"Just in time," said Mr. Teagarden.

In half an hour they reached the rail station and had only to wait a few minutes for the train to Worcester, where they'd change for London. Once aboard the London-bound train they discussed their best options to leave the country. They decided that they should consult with the American Embassy but arrived too late to schedule an appointment. They next day Mr. Teagarden called and convinced a skeptical secretary that he and the others really did need to meet with someone that afternoon who could help them secure the proper documents to leave.

The meeting began badly. The undersecretary doubted their story from its inception. Oh, yes, he confirmed that they could well be who they said they were…a little basic research revealed that there were people who lived in Misty Haven with their names. But the adults and the children seated before him could be imposters with who-knows-what intentions. They didn't look like terrorists, but then again….

Yes, he'd heard about the tragic subsidence of the caves in Hay on Wye and ill-fated group of young men who had been exploring there. What had Mr. Teagarden and the others to do with it? In desperation Brian brought out his ring—he'd left the sword back in the hotel—Reme held out his ring, and Katie took the arm circlet from her pocket. Together they laid them on the desk and the undersecretary reached to pick them up. As soon as he touched the first he stopped motionless. In less than a minute he raised his eyes from the artifacts.

"Yes, I see," he said. "In fact, I saw it, all of it. And it wouldn't do to have this spread abroad, would it? There would be no end to difficulties."

He waited while he thought, and then: "I think there is something I can do to arrange matters."

Within the hour those arrangements were complete: temporary diplomatic passports with prior authorization from British emigration to board an aircraft. There were no problems, not even with a long case that enclosed a sword.

Chapter 21

HOME AGAIN, HOME AGAIN

After landing in Grand Rapids, a large regional facility some forty miles from Misty Haven, they were met by a crowd of friends and family.

Reme was the first through the gate. When he saw his mother, he took off at a full run and wrapped his arms about her. Katie and Brian found their mother with silent tears coursing down her cheeks.

After being hugged for the twentieth time, Brian stepped back to see a tall figure behind his mother. The man, who had been standing in the shadow, advanced. It was Detective Grosskopf. He offered Brian his hand. The young boy took it and looked up at the near giant. "In addition to being very worried, your mother is very proud. As are your grandparents."

"Are they here?"

"No, but your mother has been calling them each day for the week and more that you've been gone."

"Has it been a week? I guess we've lost track of time."

"Actually," said Detective Grosskopf, "A week and a day — eight days in all."

Dr. Cavanaugh worked his way to Mr. Teagarden. They two shook hands and then embraced. "*Gdo wi ges...*Well done, Amos. Well done," said the scientist.

There was no one on hand to meet Doris, but at the signal from Mr. Teagarden, she fell in with him. They'd gone a few steps when Mr. Teagarden was met by his wife, at once anxious and overjoyed. She wanted to know everything about the adventure. Mr. Teagarden finally got a word in edgewise: "Let's all go back to The Dragon and The Rose," he said raising his voice. "And we can tell the story once and for all."

It took nearly an hour before they were reassembled at the pub. First came appropriate drinks all around. Mr. Teagarden raised his glass in toast: "To the Dragon...and other absent friends." Then the story unfolded at length. Finally, only Mr. Teagarden and Doris were relating the tale. Their charges were sound asleep.

"They were brave," explained Mr. Teagarden. "I know you might very well hold me responsible for all this. And in a way I am. But the adventure was more than solely of our own doing."

Reme's mother by this time was white. "You had no right," she stammered. "He could have been killed and it would have been your fault."

"You're correct," said Mr. Teagarden. "They were my responsibility. Their safety was second only to our calling."

"Second for you, perhaps," she responded. "But not to me. How could you?"

"With great fear and trembling. But we could not have done this without Reme; he was essential to the success of this venture."

Reme's mother stood resting her hands on the sleeping form of her son. "I am very angry and I'm upset and it may be a long while before I want to speak with you again. But I am also grateful to have my son returned." With that she and her husband left the pub, her husband carrying the small sleeping form of their son.

Mrs. Eames turned to Mr. Teagarden. "I know how she feels, sort of. But mostly I am relieved. I know you would never put Katie and Brian in danger unless it was unavoidable. And The Dragon chose them; you didn't. I have a lot to think about. But you don't need to worry about me not speaking with you. In fact, I'm sure I'll have questions. Now, who will help me get these two sleepyheads home?"

Both Doris and the detective volunteered and they left the pub. Dr. Cavanaugh took his leave with a promise to stop in on the morrow for lunch and a chat.

Only Mr. and Mrs. Teagarden remained. "Oh, Amos! You all could have died. But I'm so happy everything is done."

"Well, done for now. These children will soon be grown. I wonder how many legends will be left for the rising generation. It would be terrible if we ran out of dragons and enchanted queens."

"I'm sure there'll always be more, but let's allow some other old man to lead the quest, eh?"

Mr. Teagarden agreed as he switched off the lights and turned to the way home.